*"You have a lover who
doesn't make love to you?
And he thinks he can hold you?
You, Hester!"*

He gripped her wrist. "Whoever he is, he'll never come between you and me. Let me tell you something I've never told anyone in the world. I killed a man once because he came between me and what I wanted. It was not as difficult as I thought it would be."

His voice turned suddenly thin, boylike. "Stay here with me, Hester. For a little while. You've come to me because you had to. Because I'm the one man you're never going to forget. Hester, I want you!"

Hester

THE
ROUNDTREE WOMEN

Book III

Margaret Lewerth

A DELL BOOK

Published by
Dell Publishing Co., Inc.
1 Dag Hammarskjold Plaza
New York, New York 10017

Dell ® TM 681510, Dell Publishing Co., Inc.

ISBN: 0-440-14884-7

Printed in the United States of America

First printing—October 1979

A savage place! As holy and enchanted
As e'er beneath a waning moon was haunted
By woman wailing for her demon lover!

SAMUEL TAYLOR COLERIDGE

Part One

Thatcher, 1894

Chapter One

The land lay gripped in winter. The leafless trees snapped with frost. Sere leaves skipped across frozen, stark lawns. The road, its autumn mud congealed into rock-hard ruts, torturing man and horse, stretched into emptiness.

Still no snow fell.

Waiting, Henrietta Roundtree told herself as she stood at her bedroom window. The land was waiting. As she was. No one knew better than Henrietta that waiting was an art she had never mastered.

Tout vient à point qui peut attendre. She could still hear the low, warm voice of her beautiful New Orleans mother. "Patience, *ma chère*. You must learn it or you cannot govern yourself." But in all her forty years Henrietta had never found that anything came to one who waited. If you did not go out to meet it, you would never have it. As for patience, it was like the laced corset her slight figure did not need. The tighter you drew it, the less you could breathe. And if she had not learned to govern herself, would she now be standing behind Brussels net curtains looking out on West Street for husband and son? Logic faltered with a final inconsistency.

But no matter. The dimple in her left cheek flashed, her face still young despite repeated childbearings, lit with an impish smile. No matter at all. Her ruby silk dress from Paris hung straight and glowing against the wardrobe door. Her living room boasted the newest of tufted and overstuffed chairs and sofas. Striped satin draped the windows to the floor. And her great delight, a new small room created by an added cupola, was filled with ferns and the fashionable Moorish hangings.

In little more than three hours the rambling, old house in its refurbished splendor would be crowded with people and heady with voices and excitement. For they would come, all of them; she was sure of that. They would come despite all the gossip and whispering, because they could not stay away.

Mr. and Mrs. Isaac Roundtree at Home, New Year's Day. Three O'clock. West Street, Thatcher.

A clatter of hoofs and a whinny brought her again to the window. It was not Isaac. Isaac would have better sense than to ride a horse full-tilt up that road, to rein him up, open-jawed, at the gate. She watched Simon, her second surviving son, throw the reins to the stableboy. Simon, black-haired, not quite as tall as his father but as strong, saturnine of face, and enigmatic of soul. Simon, whose upbringing Isaac had taken entirely in hand, charging her with coddling him.

She opened the window to the cold. "Simon . . . !"

He looked up, unsmiling. Like Isaac. In Thatcher, ladies did not call from upstairs windows. How little they knew. How often her mother had called and waved to her from the grilled balcony of their New Orleans home. So filled with sunlight. So long ago.

"Simon, go around the back way. Everything's ready in the front rooms."

He nodded and held up a saddlebag. She could see the long arch of pheasant feathers protruding from it.

"Seven," he called. "And two buck. I left them at the farm to hang."

Simon never missed a target.

She closed the window. Welcome as she knew the birds and venison would be before winter was out, she loathed the hunting. She would not go out to the farm until the deer were dressed. She had come as a bride when she saw her first kill, the lovely neck limp, the wide, soft eyes surprised in death. Later she learned for herself how to strip a game bird. But a deer, never.

She heard Simon's step in the hall, drew her robe close, and opened the door.

He was wiping his mouth with the back of his hand. "You've got enough out there to feed an army."

She laughed. "If this were New York City, I'd have nine kinds of meats instead of six. And in Washington Mrs. Cleveland served eleven sweets and ices. I'm only serving eight."

His face broke into a smile, and for an instant his resemblance to his father was gone.

"Pretty rich going for Thatcher!"

His brief smile had restored her. "They'll devour it." She touched his cheek. "Simon, you're frozen! Go downstairs. Sadie is keeping the washboiler filled with hot water."

"I'll do as I am, maman." Maman. The childish derivative of madam with which Simon always addressed her. She had grown used to it. It had a French sound that was not without endearment.

"You'd better change, dear. Your father will be home soon."

"Not for a while. He went to the jailhouse for his New Year's Day clemency call. The Jeffrey boy is in for stealing again."

"Oh, no!" Pity quickened into her dark eyes.

"A sack of pipe tobacco. They caught him down at Juno's Landing trying to sell it to the ferryman. But Father will have him released."

"They'd do better to keep him where he is!"

"Oh, he'll get another beating for sure when he gets home. Father knows that. But a broken Commandment deserves the rod, Father says."

Justice untempered by mercy. Righteousness before pity.

She sighed. Of all her children, Simon was nearest Isaac, bred into this stubborn, rock-strewn land, its forest silence, its chilling distances. She would never know this son, as she had never truly known her husband.

"I won't be needed this afternoon, will I? I'd like to go out and dress those deer."

"But I do need you, Simon. I want you here."

He hesitated, then nodded. He was not a recalcitrant youth. She watched him walk down the hall, solemn of tread, secret of mind. But she had spoken the truth. She did need him, as she needed all her children against the inner solitude of her life.

But Henrietta would not let any mood linger too long. Everything had gone well. Everything would go well. The hall was icy. The fire in her bedroom was dying. She shook the grate vigorously, added coal from the scuttle. She would dress now. She would not wait for Isaac. Her underthings, of sheerest French flannel ordered from London, lay on the bed like a new self. She stepped from her robe and slipped into the cream-white shift, exulting in the softness against her body. She turned to the new pier glass with its marble step and lifted her arms. Then on one of those impulses that Henrietta had all her life found ungovernable, she began to turn, spinning faster until she was caught up in dance as secret and lonely as a night bird's call.

Isaac Roundtree walked slowly up Main Street from the old brick jailhouse. Muffled against the cold in black overcoat and tall black hat befitting Thatcher's chief magistrate and first citizen, he bowed solemnly to one passerby and another. He had done his duty and that was what Thatcher trusted him to do. But it was an unsmiling matter, the dispensing of justice. The forgiveness of misdoings should be left to God. But men's weaknesses were such that someone had to serve as surrogate. Isaac carried the conviction that self-discipline and an infallible sense of right and wrong alone justified success. Had not twenty years of back-breaking labor on the land and as many of solitary night study lifted him from miller's boy to his present prominence? That and astute investing in something called Boston Shares in the new steamship trade. Though he was not apt to speak of that. In Thatcher a man lived by the labor of his hands and head. Anything else smacked of speculation and the Devil.

At fifty Isaac Roundtree was a satisfied man. As satisfied as any man could be who had begotten ten children and whose wife and home were warm and waiting. He bowed to another passerby and filled his lungs with a deep draft of the still and icy air. It blanketed for the moment the torment that lay molten as brimstone within him.

An approaching train shrilled from the bridge. Isaac probed beneath his overcoat for his heavy gold watch. The only northbound train today, it was on time to the minute. Isaac took pride in that. It would be different when the snows came. He paused and watched it thunder into the small station, a monster of iron, steam, and smoke, evoking a boyhood delight. In another instant nostalgia vanished.

Out of the clouds of vapor a single passenger emerged. A youngish, graceful man, enveloped in plaid cape, soft hat, and muffler. He carried a leather traveling bag and walked purposefully across the street toward a gray verandaed house that bore the sign LODGING. His path, like destiny, carried him directly to Isaac.

The same thin, ascetic face, Isaac noted. The same gray eyes, mournful as a sick hound's, though women thought differently. Colin Thatcher was a man Isaac had hoped never to see again, a man he hated with an intensity he could share with no one.

He lifted his tall black hat. "Good day, Mister Thatcher."

The younger man bowed with that damnable ease that never failed to remind Isaac of his own origins, of his mother who had long ago worked as scullery maid in Nathaniel Thatcher's fine home. He, Isaac, was

master of that home now but there were times when it
served more as a shell than an anchor.

"Good day to you, Mister Roundtree. May it begin
a good year." The smile was quick and warm, too
quick, too warm ever to have suited Isaac.

"You come at a cold season, sir."

"I'm on my way to Boston. This is only a stopover
to pick up the last of my great-aunt's papers."

"There was nothing left in the house when I bought
it, as you well know."

Colin Thatcher smiled pleasantly. "True. Whatever
my aunt may have left will be in the public recorder's
safe. I would like to have it. Matter of sentiment, you
know." He looked steadily at Isaac. "I do not expect to
return to Thatcher again, Mister Roundtree. Good
day, sir."

It was then that Isaac Roundtree said something for
which he knew he must someday answer before God.
It was rooted not in the goodwill in which he had
basked since leaving the jailhouse but in shadows too
deep for probing.

"Mister Thatcher. . . ."

The sandy-haired man turned.

"Mister Thatcher, the Recorder's Office will be
closed all day. If you are at loss with your time, Mrs.
Roundtree and myself would consider it an honor if
you would call on us. We are at home after three."

In the silence the train keened into the distance.

The eyes of the two men met.

Colin Thatcher straightened his shoulders and
seemed to grow taller. "It would be a pleasure, Mister
Roundtree."

That was all. Nothing had happened, except the
simple courtesy to a man who had been gone—was it
five years now? Four years and ten months. Isaac remembered years like scars. Nothing had happened, except the sky had grown bleaker, the light paler. The
church bells began to toll noon. Isaac pulled his tall
hat closer on his ears and quickened his step.

The new year was already as leaden as his spirits. He longed for the snow, the quiet, healing snow.

Isaac found his wife not as he imagined, seated at her dressing table, her small quick hands fluttering among combs and ointments, her black hair falling to her bare shoulders and the still youthful curves of her white, white breasts that were never far from his thoughts. Nor their counterimage, another man's hands. Even as he opened the door, the first scent of violet water stirred his demons. He had already paid their price in God's judgment with the loss of his first- and fourth-born sons. This ostentation, this surfeit of richness too, would be a stench in God's nostrils. But let her have this day. It might yet serve its purpose.

Henrietta, seated in a low chair before a bright-burning fire, was cradling a sleeping child, their last born. Dark-haired, blue veined, fragile as a moth wing, little Susannah at eighteen months was still too delicate for human arms, or even a bed's mattress. She was carried on a pillow, her large eyes silently, blankly searching her small world. Survival seemed beyond the tiny frame. To Isaac this was the latest of God's curses.

Henrietta looked up with a smile, exquisite in its tenderness.

"She took all the beef blood. And a tablespoon of port wine. Isaac, if she can get through the second summer—"

"Should you be holding her?"

Henrietta dropped her eyes to the child and tightened her arms around the pillow. "Who else, my darling, who else?"

Isaac turned into his own room. In a little while she would be laughing and jesting, her head high, her eyes shining, a cynosure for the gossip of women and the desire of men. As he closed the door he heard her begin the Creole lullaby he had always considered heathenish. He had seen the shimmering red gown splashed across a chair. And on her dressing table the

brooch of diamonds, pearls, and jet that had come to
him long ago through the Devil's hand. He would not
tell her of Colin Thatcher's appearance. Let what
might, happen.

On the other side of the door Henrietta rose with
her burden and pushed a buzzer. A broad-faced
woman entered.

"She's sleeping now, Sadie. And smiling, isn't she?
Oh, isn't she beautiful?"

The old woman held out her arms.

"Oh, Sadie, whatever would I do without you!"

"God willing, you won't have to, ma'am."

She kissed the wrinkled cheek. They were loyal to
her belowstairs. She loved them for it.

She drew her robe close and walked to her husband's closed door. She lifted her hand to knock and
changed her mind. She had married this man for better
or worse. She had married this harsh, brooding Yankee
because on that July night so long ago, she had wanted
him as she had never and would never want another
man.

If her baby were taken, the last fragment of her
heart would go. But there would not be another child.
She would make sure of that. Not for nothing had she
carried the secrets of wild-limbed Rosalee and Le
Vieux Carré with her all these years. Not for nothing
did she order the finest of flannel from abroad. Sinful
as it once seemed, Henrietta no longer troubled her
mind about good and evil. They had become frozen
abstractions in this hard country, unbending, unyielding, inhuman. Like love.

The connecting door opened. Isaac in his dressing
gown stood looking at her.

"I thought you might need help with your dress."

"No, thank you. It's quite simple. And Sadie is
down the hall to hook me up."

He closed the door behind him and entered the

room. She glanced at the clock. Less than two hours until her guests would arrive. She shivered as her husband approached.

Colin Thatcher hung up his traveling cloak, shivered, and wrapped himself into it again. Then he stretched on the bed and contemplated fate. He did not believe in it but he realized that, for those who did, it brought comfort against life's bitter incongruities. His meeting with Isaac Roundtree was one of them.

He intended seeing her. Intended? It was the sole and long considered purpose of this trip. He remembered Thatcher during his five-year exile through prisms of summer and autumn light. Now he was appalled by the dismal grayness of the little town, as if time had tossed it like a pebble out of the stream of life.

How well she would suit the city, a house on the square, a box at the opera, her own carriage in the park. He could afford these things now. And London. The man who does not love London does not love humanity, Dr. Johnson had said, or something nearly like it. Colin rolled over on the hard bed. He had lived with her extraordinary face all these years. He loved her with the single passion of a man starved for bread. Yet he loved her enough to have worked and waited.

In another two hours he would see her. Had he been foolish to accept so quickly Isaac Roundtree's invitation? The man hated him, not without justice. Yet the meeting had happened. Fate. The least that could be said now was that it removed the agony of indecision.

A knock at the door brought him to his feet. The girl outside could not have been more than sixteen, full of figure, glowing of cheek. The harsh climate bred a hardy kind of beauty. And withered it just as fast.

"Mister Thatcher, sir, there's a gentleman down in the parlor to see you."

And he had barely arrived! He hesitated and she giggled.

"You don't remember me, do you?"

"My apology. . . ."

"Bessie Haskell. Remember now? My father's orchard. I was only eleven when you and Mrs. Roundtree used to ride out for peaches. I never forgot." She giggled again. "The day your horse took a start and dumped you in the drainage ditch and Mrs. Roundtree said you'd better take hers. It was quieter."

The girl meant well, and her giggle was disarming.

"Of course I remember, Bessie." He laughed. "You've grown up."

"And going to Teacher's School in Bollington next year. Mrs. Roundtree's arranging it with her own daughter."

"Splendid."

"If you want anything, you'll have to ring for the other girl. I'm going off now."

"I shan't want anything. Except. . . ." He grinned at her, and she thought again he was the handsomest man she had ever seen. ". . . you might tell me who is waiting downstairs to see me."

"Oh, it's Mister Appleby. Didn't I say? Amn't I the dumb one? But I'm all a stir-up, going to Mrs. Roundtree's to help serve this afternoon."

"I'm sure you are," said Colin with his kindly smile.

It was encircling him already, this small throttling town. He had not planned it this way. But he would see her, thrust the note he had already written into her hand, and tomorrow. . . . Damn Hanson Appleby!

"Heard you were in town, Colin. Took my constitutional to the station and Fred in the freight office told me you'd gotten off the train. Glad to see you. This town needs its Thatchers back once in a while. Remember where it started. But you're not to stay in a lodging house. Elsie says you're to put up with us for as long as you're here and she doesn't take kindly to no."

"I'll only be here tomorrow, Mister Appleby."

The older man gave him a closer look. "Mighty short visit?"

"I'm picking up any family papers my late aunt might have left, then I'm on to Boston."

Hanson Appleby knew only too well that that shrewd old lady Ada Thatcher never in her life left papers around. Everything she had ever owned had been neatly disposed of five years ago.

"But please convey my most respectful regards and warmest thanks to Mrs. Appleby. Perhaps I shall see you both at the Roundtree at-home this afternoon."

That'll skim the cream, thought Colin. He saw surprise, then something like relief in the sharp eyes. But it still called for explanation. "I met Mister Roundtree on the way from the station. He very kindly invited me."

"Good. Very good indeed. Delighted." Hanson Appleby had been a newspaper man far too long to be wearing his thoughts on his sleeve. He picked up his hat. "Devilish cold. We'll get snow if the temperature rises. And it will be a big one. Good to see you, Colin, and looking so well."

Colin Thatcher knew he meant it.

He dressed slowly, shaved in cold water, and would have liked a brisk walk to take train travel out of his legs and lungs. But already half the town seemed to know of his arrival. He toyed with the idea of not going to the Roundtree reception, then gave it up. He could no more resist it than he had resisted this journey. London was his destination. The idea of Henrietta possessed then obsessed him against all reason.

She was, after all, two years his senior. A woman of forty could settle into drab skirts and close bonnets at the flick of a year. But surely not Henrietta. He began to think of the day young Bessie had unfortunately not forgotten and found himself shaving twice.

It was the late summer then, with the sheen of autumn in the glow of goldenrod and purple aster, in the deeper blue of the sky. They were riding out to the ravine on the far side of the Ridge. It had almost seemed that Isaac had thrust her company on him.

"You like to sketch, Colin? Let Henrietta show you the view from the Ridge. And the great oak tree. More than two centuries old. My grandfather used to say it was here before the white man. A man of God, sir. Taught God's might and hell's fire under the open sky."

Colin had found it easy to forget almost immediately Grandfather Roundtree's hellfire. And even Isaac himself. So he and Henrietta followed a footpath up the Ridge, letting the horses pick their way. They sat on a sun-warmed ledge, above the dark depths of the ravine, a tangle of fallen rocks and clinging pine, juniper bushes and head-tall catbrier. In spring and autumn raging torrents swept it; in winter snow erased its dangerous drop.

Behind them a cave gave evidence of a vast and ancient earthly upheaval. Overgrown, no footpath led to it.

"No one goes in there," said Henrietta solemnly, her eyes bright. "It drops away in the back to nothing. There's supposed to be a fault that runs from the top of the Ridge to the river. I don't know why they call it a fault. Just because it's different and dangerous. I think it's exciting. Would you like to see it?"

He had followed her through the curtaining vines and into an eerie dimness that faded almost at once to total blackness. She stepped forward, and he pulled her back.

"Afraid?" she taunted.

"Only for you."

In the sudden silence an awareness took shape, filling the cave like a presence. She broke it.

"We have a long ride home, Colin."

"We haven't finished the peaches."

"We'll leave them for the birds."

"And the pits?" He wanted to keep her talking, to hold this moment spun of light and glass between them.

"Maybe a peach tree will grow." She laughed nervously. "For a souvenir."

"Or a beginning?"

Then she was in his arms and he was covering her face, her lips, her eyes, her throat with kisses, and she was clinging to him. But only for a moment. With a strength that surprised him she broke free.

"Oh, my God!"

"Afraid!" He heard his own voice thin as an echo.

"Yes. No. No! Of course not. We're sensible people! We—"

He caught her again. Her hair had tumbled from its net; she looked wild and free as a gypsy and as lovely as night.

"I love you, Henrietta. I'm mad about you. You've known it—"

"No . . . !" She flung herself away from him and ran from the cave. He caught up with her as she stood on the ledge, her hands in her hair.

"Should I apologize?"

"Not unless you want to."

"Then I shan't. You might be angry but you can't be surprised. You're too much woman not to know how I've felt about you since the first day I set foot in your house."

She did not answer. The deliberation with which she finished netting her hair piqued him.

"If you didn't want this to happen, why the devil did you come out riding with me every afternoon?"

"You wanted to find places to sketch." But her voice trembled.

"My God, what a glory of illogic is the female mind!" He picked up a peach, flung it into the ravine.

Its fall was soundless. "What are we going to do about it?"

"Nothing at all, Colin. I'm a married woman. I have six children. I—I love my husband."

"How many times a day do you tell yourself that?"

"But I do. In a curious way. He's a man imprisoned within himself. Someday perhaps I shall know why."

"You can even talk about him after what's happened!"

"Nothing has happened."

He went to her.

"At least let's be honest. Everything has happened. I've never met a woman who wanted, needed love more. I offer you a lifetime of it. But I'll wait . . . as long as it takes to make you see the truth."

They rode home in silence. At the road she lifted her horse into a canter, he beside her. The rush of wind, the pounding motion was flame to their awareness.

At the gate on West Street she did not offer her hand.

"Good-bye, Colin."

"You don't believe that?"

She ran quickly into the house. But he had been right. Their good-bye was as hollow as the unused cave.

Chapter Two

"By God, sir, I'll never have the thing in my house! Leave yourself open to every Tom, Dick, and Harry to interrupt a man's privacy anytime he pleases!" The judge's voice boomed over the room.

"Fillmore got so angry at the sight of that—what do they call it?—telephone that the only thing that cooled him off was watching Little Egypt do the—what was it, dear?"

"My God, Amelia, don't you remember anything? Hootchy-kootchy!"

"Now there, your Honor, is something you wouldn't mind having around the house."

A burst of laughter. The reception was going splendidly. Even Judge Townley and his little brown wren of a wife had come, all the way from Bollington. Henrietta moved toward the group. The judge bowed.

"Ahhh, here you are, Mrs. Roundtree! You're a woman of the world and a damn fine one. You settle the question. . . ."

"Dear Mrs. Roundtree! Such a lovely reception! Such elegance. Everything so *comme il faut!*" The judge's wife bubbled. "We were just discussing the exposition out in Chicago last summer. Such a dreary little town. But the exposition! So marvelous! I do hope that you and Mister Roundtree saw it."

"I'm sorry we couldn't. Mister Roundtree was so busy."

"Sensible man."

"Fillmore, you adored it. We went out by Pullman.

Cut glass and roses on every table in the dining car!
And the sights at the exposition. . . ." The little
woman sighed. "There was a whole building about
women. Gorgeous as an Italian castle. The architect
was a woman. Every painting, mural, and statue in it
was done by a woman!"

"You tell me what a woman can paint or sculpt
that's better than what she can create out of flesh and
blood and I'll tell you she's less than a woman!"

Henrietta gave him a ravishing smile. "I couldn't
agree with you less, Judge Townley."

The judge looked at her admiringly. "Ah, but you,
madame. . . ."

His childless wife managed a smile. "Dear Fillmore.
He's so used to things the way he wants them. If he
took off his blinders, he'd bolt like our old Ned at the
train whistle."

Henrietta touched the thin hand compassionately.
"If any man ever took off his blinders, Mrs. Townley,
he'd learn a lot that was good for him."

A ripple of laughter. Henrietta moved on. It was a
bold thing to say but she had learned long ago that
only boldness could bring this thin-souled town to its
knees. And she was succeeding. Her living room was
crowded; appreciative voices flowed from the dining
room. More guests were arriving.

Her small head high, her piled hair glistening like
the fashionably cut ruby silk of her dress, her figure
young as a girl's, she moved with a grace as supple as
flame. If she was aware of men's glances, she gave no
sign. Her smile went as quickly to women as to men.

As she returned to her receiving post at the far end
of the living room, she caught sight of Isaac. He was
coming toward her. She had not forgiven him for the
hour before the reception. It was increasingly hard to
forgive him. But there lay her strength, her invulnera-
bility. She would not be humbled.

His voice was harsh in her ear.

"Did you give Amos permission to sit at the top of the stairs and watch?"

"Isaac, let him be. He loves it."

"I asked you if you gave him permission?"

"No—but—"

"I don't want the boy in sight. If you—"

"I'll go to him right away. Let me talk to him. . . . Dear Mrs. Fleming. We're delighted you and Mister Fleming could come. Aren't we, Isaac?" Only a very close observer might have heard the tremor in her voice.

There were other guests to greet. To her relief she saw Isaac being waylaid by the judge. She would go to Amos as soon as she could. She would talk to him, put a bonbon in his hand, lead him gently back to his room. It was not Isaac's way. But then there was no part of Isaac in him. Blond of hair, gray-green of eyes, sensitive, and too imaginative, he was in an odd way so like her own father, that princely failure of a man who in the end had found life too ugly for his own visions and put a bullet through his head in the quiet of a New Orleans night. So long ago. But the blood was there. And the gifts. And the capacity to suffer. She would do her best to protect this darling four-year-old child from the malevolence already shadowing him.

"Mrs. Higgins! Doctor Higgins! How nice of you to come. . . . Reverend Loveland, delighted. . . ."

It was a triumph, but now her thoughts went anxiously to the little boy on the stairs. She caught a glimpse of Isaac and the judge edging toward the study.

"*I, Henrietta, take thee, Isaac. . . . Forsaking all others . . . keep only unto you. . . . To obey . . . till death us do part. . . .*"

In the last four years the broken phrases had drifted, like flotsam on a subterranean stream of her mind, surfacing when she least expected. She had broken that vow once, only once, and the beauty of those hours haunted her as much as their betrayal.

She had longed often for the kindly darkness of the confessional she had learned to trust in New Orleans, the warmth of Father Benoit's rich voice. "Go thou, my daughter, and sin no more."

For that is what she had done.

But here, in the blanched silence of Puritan unforgiveness that was Thatcher, sin was a lance you carried in your heart through eternity. Sin. When was real love ever sin?

"Dear Mrs. Roundtree . . . so charming . . ."

Henrietta came back to the present.

"Lovely of you to come, Mrs. Gage. How is Professor Gage?"

"Doing well, thank you."

Colin Thatcher handed his plaid traveling cape to a maid and declined to drop his card on the silver salver. There was no reason to leave any reminder of this call. He already regretted his decision to come. The living room was filled with people, and another throng crowded the dining room, many of whom he would know. He had an impulse to turn and leave, but at this moment destiny seemed more powerful than common sense.

He did not see Henrietta but then he would not expect to over so many heads and hats. She would be standing somewhere, slight as summer wind. He would choose his moment as soon as he could stop the pounding within him. Meanwhile he would move to the dining room for a steadying drink.

"Eeeee . . . !"

He glanced up. High on the staircase a small blond boy perched like a curious bird, peering down through the banister.

"Well, hel-*lo!*" Colin moved nearer to the staircase. "Who are you?"

"I'm the watchman of the castle. Who are you?"

Colin laid a finger to his lips. "I am Keeper of the Queen's Beasts."

"What are they?"

"A griffin, a unicorn, a tiglon, a dodo bird, a liger . . ."

"Do they bite?"

"No."

"Why not?"

Colin lowered his voice mysteriously. "Because the instant you look at them, they turn to stone."

The little boy's laugh pealed out.

"Will you get me a bonbon?"

"Where are they?"

The boy thrust a small fist through the railing toward the dining room. "In there."

"Just wait."

"Then will you tell me more? About the—" But he did not finish. Instead he scrambled to his feet and fled up the remaining stairs.

"Good afternoon, Mister Thatcher."

Colin turned. Isaac Roundtree, standing before him, held out his hand. Colin took it reluctantly.

"Very good of you to come."

"Thank you, Mister Roundtree." Colin knew now with a dreadful certainty that he had made a mistake. Isaac Roundtree had an air of authority that fitted him as well as his black frock coat. He was in command of his world, master of this house, and he had God on his side. It was all evident in the brief, wintry smile, the scarcely veiled hostility in the dark, brooding eyes, the total joylessness. Did any human being on earth know Isaac Roundtree? Colin wondered. Had he ever inspired love in anyone? Colin surprised himself with a twinge of pity. He had wronged this man. He intended to wrong him further. Yet right and wrong seemed no part of this moment in his life. It was nearer a matter of life and nonlife. He would stay in this house only until he had seen her.

"Sorry the boy disturbed you."

"Not at all."

"He's Amos. Our four-year-old. Somewhat too willful for his own good. We had the baby too since you were here. But come along. You've had a bitter-cold walk. A hot rum punch might do very well."

He permitted Isaac to usher him toward the dining room. He had not thought of her having any more children. The boy indeed disturbed him.

"Colin! Colin Thatcher! Why, it *is* you! You're back!" The voice pierced like a darning needle. He was aware of faces turning toward him. A gaunt woman in puce stripes pushed her way through the throng around the long dining table. "Colin, how lovely! You don't remember me, do you? But why should you? My, you look handsome and prosperous!" She pecked his cheek and he caught a strong and long forgotten scent of lemon verbena sachet.

"Miss Eggleston. . . ."

"You do remember! Oh, I know you and your brother called me Eggy behind my back and I'll never forget that summer you were visiting your dear Aunt Ada. I taught you catechism and Latin verbs, and you were quite naughty. . . ."

Her voice was carrying now into near-silence. He heard his name whispered back and forth like a shuttlecock, and he marveled even now at his own foolishness in coming. What was done was done. Henrietta was not in the dining room. He would somehow have to push his way out, find her, and push the note in his pocket into her hand. And then. . . .

". . . a delightful at-home, isn't it, Colin? We haven't had such elegance in Thatcher since. . . . You must try the woodcock in aspic—and a bit of the jugged hare. . . ."

Colin found himself pushed against the long table. It glittered with the splendor of two lofty silver candelabra, a pair of fruit-bearing silver pheasants, the finest of lace tableclothes, and an array of dishes such as Colin had never seen.

"Look," Miss Eggleston's minty breath was close on his face, "Capon *en gelée*, cold trout, smoked wild turkey, fresh lobster, Scotch salmon, potted quail with truffles . . . I've been here an hour learning the names of all these dishes. I have no idea how dear Henrietta did it but. . . ."

Somewhere a single violin began to play a somewhat uncertain Tosti.

"Farewell forever," breathed Miss Eggleston. "Don't you adore it? Now come and see the sweets . . . there's a swan made entirely of sugar and fruits glacés. . . ."

He escaped. In the doorway he passed Hanson Appleby.

"Good to see you here, Colin. This town needs to be reminded of the family that founded it. But it was naughty of you not to come to us."

If there was more, Colin did not hear it. Henrietta was alone in the hall, looking up the stairs. Her exquisite head caught in a half light, her throat and breast a symmetry of line and loveliness, her incredible beauty richer than he had even remembered in the long, lonely years when he had tried to recapture it on canvas. He would paint her someday in that dress. He wondered whether the pounding in his chest could be heard throughout the house.

She started up the stairs, turned her head, and saw him. Her face flamed, went white. Her hand reached for the railing. He thought for an instant she would faint, but Henrietta was not a woman to faint. Instead she met his eyes, her own wide with surprise, with wonder, and with something so beseeching, so sad, that it caught his breath.

"Henrietta. . . ."

She shook her head and ran up the stairs.

Then he understood. She had not been told he was coming. Isaac had planned this as subtly and cruelly as a moletrap. The pounding within him ceased, replaced by anger, then something deeper than either, a kind of singing. She had not changed. No woman ever revealed more clearly and silently her feelings.

He would wait to see her if it took the rest of the day and night. He crossed the hall into the living room and heard his name in a living whisper from group to group.

"Colin Thatcher!"

"There's Colin Thatcher!"

It was Miss Eggleston who summoned him. "Do join us, Colin. Mrs. Bishop was just telling us this is the coldest she remembers since she went to General Grant's second inaugural ball. Zero in Washington! Nobody could take off their cloaks or even their carriage boots!"

"One lady did, Mister Thatcher, to show off her gown. And died the next week!"

He looked around the room and saw Henrietta's Moorish alcove filled with ferns and hangings. And quiet. Slowly, courteously, Colin made his way toward it.

The tide of chatter rose, the violinist found a livelier schottische, and in the scullery young Bessie Haskell, scraping plates, felt her eyes fill with tears.

It was not at all as she had planned it. Hadn't she practiced for a week the proper way to wear the stiff lace cap Mrs. Roundtree had sent all the way to Boston for; that is, the best way to show off Bessie's own bright, darting eyes. Hadn't she taken in the new black dress here and there where it counted most? She had a good figure. She had had little enough chance to display it to the gentry.

Instead Cook had brought her own horsefaced sister to serve and had put Bessie to work out back, with the door closed. She could see nothing. Meanwhile plain, scrawny Aggie, wearing the lace cap like a helmet, stumbled around in the front of the house on her big, flat feet. Oh, Bessie understood it, all right. It was the only way Cook could get the table leftovers home to Aggie's brood in Pinesville. Hadn't Aggie arrived with a basket big enough to carry a sow?

Bessie's small soul struggled vengefully with the injustice of the world. A plate slid through her hands and smashed on the stone floor. At the same time she heard faint horses' hooves approaching. That did it! In no time at all the guests would be leaving and she would not have seen anything, even Mrs. Roundtree in her Paris dress. She left the plate lying in pieces, snatched her cloak, and slipped out. It was nearly dark, the air brisked with cold. Snow by morning maybe. It seemed to Bessie she stood on the brink of finality.

The house blazed like a great ship above her, she a swimmer in the dusk helplessly reaching for it. The drapes were not yet drawn. From a side window unobstructed by the veranda she stared directly into the living room and sideways into a red-draped alcove, the essence of luxury in its heaped pillows, its scimitar and brass and its concealing ferns. Someone was standing there alone—

At that instant, without warning, she felt herself spun around, toppled over, and a man's hand against her mouth.

"Spying, are you?"

"Master Simon!" But her cry was muffled.

"Seems you need a lesson!"

"No!" His hand muffled her mouth, his weight pressed on her while the other hand pulled up her skirts. She kicked savagely but she was no match for young Simon Roundtree's strength. His face was hot against hers, his breath fetid.

"You'll like it, Bessie!"

She could not cry out, she could hardly breathe. But Bessie Haskell knew who she was, a decent girl brought up God-fearing. As his hand touched her thigh she sank her teeth into the fleshy palm across her mouth. With a yelp he jumped back.

"You slut!" With the warm blood trickling down his wrist he struck her.

Bessie Haskell hardly felt it. She was on her feet, all the pent-up fury of the day bursting from her.

"You think you can play the fancy with me, Simon Roundtree! Let me tell you something. I'm a good girl. I've always done right. Not like some I could name, what with the dressing up and flaunting jewels and. . . ." She knew she should stop but she was incapable of damming the torrent of words. She could hold back nothing, not even the deepest secret she had sworn would never pass her lips, the secret Aggie had whispered to her and her own Aunt Sadie had slapped her for telling.

"If it's bastard doings you want, I should think you'd have enough under your own roof!"

Simon caught her wrist. "What are you saying?"

"Ask *him* in there! Just ask him. Why he's come back here! Then you'll find out what Christian decency means!"

He pushed her aside.

Bessie stumbled into the night, the darkening cold enveloping her like a world in ruins. She looked back once to see Simon standing motionless outside the window watching Colin Thatcher.

Henrietta came slowly down the stairs, her smile ready but not yet fixed. She had given Amos his bonbons, left him soothed and happy drawing something he called Beasts. She had heard the baby's thin cry and Sadie's low comforting. But she had not gone into the room. That good woman would read her distress as quickly as the baby's.

The afternoon had peaked. Guests would soon begin to leave. The salver was piled satisfactorily high with calling cards. By every standard her reception was a victory Thatcher would not forget, its very lavishment her security.

But none of that steadied the spinning in her mind, the nameless fire and chill that alternated within her. *Isaac knew Colin Thatcher was coming.* Colin would not have dared come otherwise. Yet Isaac had not told her. Instead he had come home, seen her and. . . .

She had learned to live with the torment of her husband's behavior. But this she saw as an abyss, terrifying as it was unknown. Why? Why? She had not even been able to sort out her own feelings. All that she was aware of was that a door that she had firmly closed had suddenly been flung open. The man, who for a few brief weeks one long-ago summer had held all the giddy young happiness she would ever know, had come back; he was here under her roof. She would have to meet him with others around them. She would have to keep her voice steady and her talk light. She would have to—

Through the open door of Isaac's study, she could hear men's voices, heavy, serious, normal. At least Isaac was occupied. Henrietta stood for a moment listening as she gathered strength.

"We want you in on this, Mister Roundtree. There isn't another man in the county who carries more weight."

"The country's coming out of its slump. Expansion is the word. Progress, Isaac, progress. No limit to where this nation is going."

"Why, out in Chicago they had a generator lighting the whole damned exposition. Electricity! The new power. No limit to it!"

"And we've got this power right here in Thatcher." The quieter voice of Hanson Appleby prevailed. "You saw my editorial this morning. We have one factory down at Juno's Landing now. In another ten years we could have six. The South's ready to sell us all the cotton we can use. We can turn out a cloth as fine as anything England can send us. We've got the means right now to open up this part of the state to such prosperity that Thatcher will become the new industrial center of the East, the gateway to the Middle West. Progress, Isaac! All we need is some farsighted investment by the leading citizens of this town."

"Gentlemen, please!" Henrietta heard her husband's voice thin with protest.

"Listen to them, Mister Roundtree!" It was Judge Townley's familiar bellow. "This project needs moral

stamina and vision as well as money. You're a respected leader," the judge was interrupted by a burst
of assenting voices, then a curious silence.

"Isaac," Hanson Appleby was speaking again quietly.
"I think we'd better meet the question head-on. If it's
the talk that's in your mind. . . ."

"Gentlemen, I will not—"

"Oh, sit down, Roundtree!" the judge roared. Then
he lowered his voice. Henrietta pressed closer to the
wall. "Gossip is woman's stuff. Old towns, like old
women, feed on it. Nothing else to do with what minds
God gave them. Any woman as pretty as your wife is
going to be the butt of it. Damned handsome woman.
Could grace a king's court if she had a mind to it."

"I will not permit this discussion!"

"You will, sir!" The judge could be heard to the
river. In the hall Henrietta's face burned, her feet were
leaden.

"Isaac, it would be better if you heard us out." Another instant of silence. Appleby's calm voice continued. "You took a wise, high-minded step in asking
Colin Thatcher to your home today. I don't know why
the Devil he came back but he has every right to. His
family—"

"This doesn't concern me, Appleby."

"It concerns all of us. You showed good judgment,
Isaac. No right-thinking man in this town would be-
lieve that scurrilous talk now. And I assure you, Mrs.
Round—"

"Leave her name out of it." Isaac must have moved
to the door of the study. His words came pinched but
clear.

"I offered you my hospitality, gentlemen. But not
the license to discuss my private affairs. The matter is
closed."

Henrietta was hardly aware of returning to the living room. She slipped among her guests, nodding,
smiling, chatting as mechanically as if she were outside

her own body. That they would openly discuss her! Excuse her, subtly hinting she needed vindication! If they had said "We want you with us, Isaac, in spite of your wife," they could not have done worse. If they wished the truth, why hadn't they come directly to her? Why hadn't Isaac? She would have told them! Their chill, narrow town could blight a woman's soul. Faces and minds as winter-bound as the hills around them. She who had been born to sun and flowering. Deeper still in her mind words fluttered to a long-forgotten flame, her father swinging her high, "I am that merry wanderer of the night, I jest to Oberon, and make him smile. . . ." A spill of laughter, shrieks of delight, her soul a kitten scampering across the secure paving of the hot courtyard, Jubilee's trumpet voice in pursuit. "Henriett' child, you stay where you belong!"

Aeons of silence ago. For silence was Isaac's way and theirs. Silence, until time encrusted them in self-righteousness.

"A stunning woman. . . ." A man's whisper in her wake.

"More than old Isaac could manage."

She was wrong. The silence was not total. It was a veneer. Like this whole reception. Like all her efforts. One crack and she would sink again into the fetid tangle of whispers and malice.

"A charming afternoon, Mrs. Roundtree."

She nodded brightly at the stout woman. "My guests make it so, Mrs. Bishop."

At last she reached the momentary solitude she craved, the haven of her little alcove where she could cool her face. And her humiliation.

"It's taken you long enough."

He was standing half hidden by the greenery, his voice as rich as she remembered, his eyes as warm, in his face an intensity she hardly knew.

"Colin!"

"My darling!"

"No . . . no!" She steeled herself. More than anything else she wanted the sanctuary of those arms. "I had no idea. No one told me. When I saw you walk in. . . . When did you . . . ?"

"Let's not waste time. I've been waiting here too damn long as it is."

"But I might never—"

"Oh, yes, you would. Haven't you heard of mental telepathy? Well, believe in it. Or call it fate. You knew I'd come back." He looked at her, and she felt her strength dissolving. She would not give way. All that was behind her.

"No, Colin, that's—that's—I am glad to see you. I'm sorry with so many people that I—I—"

"Stop it, Henrietta."

Deliberately, gently, he turned her from the room, shielding her with the breadth of his back, and kissed her. So deeply, with such longing, that all the might-have-been glowed as if it had never left her.

"You see. Nothing has changed. Except that I can at last take care of you. I can offer you what you should have—happiness."

"Colin. . . ."

"Hear me out! There wasn't a night, Henrietta, in these four years when I didn't see you in my room, hold you. There wasn't a day when I didn't work for this hour. I've had some success. I have a reputation, I've been offered a fine post in London with a chromolithography firm in Queen Anne's Gate, with plenty of time for my own etching. And for travel." He spoke more rapidly. "You are coming with me—"

"Colin!"

"Don't interrupt! I have every detail planned. I've been planning for four years. What's happened in between doesn't matter. We'll be together."

She turned from him.

"Don't answer me, Henrietta. Don't say anything. You've already told me all I want to know. I'll be here in Thatcher for another day. I'll leave early the following morning from Bollington for Boston. I'll stay at the Parker House and wait. You will come as soon as you can, within the week. You will stay at the Victoria. The following Wednesday we sail together on the *Western Star* for London.

"I—I. . . . It's—"

"No! Not now! You have a week to make your own plans. If you don't come—but you will. You know it's right. For both of us. Isn't twenty years of servitude enough?" He held out an envelope. "Your train ticket, my darling. And your hotel reservation."

She took the envelope dizzily and thrust it into the folds of ruby silk above her breast, staring at a vision she dared not grasp and dared not let go.

"I love you, my darling."

The vibrancy of his words might have swept her into his arms again. But a burst of voices from the hall told her that guests were beginning to leave.

He nodded. "I know. Just a little longer." He lifted his head abruptly, his voice bright and casual. ". . . so I thought if the snow held off, I'd go up to the Ridge in the morning as far as the ravine and make some sketches. Marvelous strength of line and mass at this time of year."

She turned toward the living room. Framed in the arch of the alcove, through the green growth, she saw Simon. Behind him, similarly darkened of face, stood Isaac.

Henrietta had never surrendered to fear.

"You'll enjoy that, Colin," she said lightly. "Have a nice visit. Isaac, I believe our guests are beginning to leave. Will you join me?"

She passed Simon and met for the first and last time the hard, accusing eyes of the stranger who was her son.

As she moved toward her guests only the sharp edge of the envelope folded between her breasts reminded Henrietta that her world, with its true and its false, had exploded forever around her.

Chapter Three

The long winter night was beginning to pale when Simon strode toward the barn. Behind him the house lay silent. Lamps showed in the kitchen, but only one window was lit upstairs. His father's dressing room. Not the window beside it, his mother's. He preferred not to think about that.

The stableman's breath blew white on the air. Inside the barn a horse whinnied.

"Get the horses ready for my father and me, Jed."

"You're early this morning, Master Simon."

"We've got to get out to the farm before the snow comes."

"It's coming, sure as apples. I can smell it. And the wind's swung northeast." The man held up a wetted finger. "Yep. North or a little east of north. Be here before dusk."

"Start tacking up the horses, will you, Jed?"

"Should have told me last evening, young master. Much as one man can do. No warning. No warning at all." The man went mumbling into the barn.

Simon glanced up at the house. A second, adjoining window was lighted now. The sky was graying rapidly. He too could smell the coming snow, as any country man could. It had only to hold off a few hours. The ride out to the valley was never easy at this time of year. If snow came—but they'd be back well before that was likely.

He went into the stable, dimly lit now by a hanging

lantern that made grotesque shadows of the stooping groom and the restless horses.

"You take care of Father's horse, Jed. I'll saddle Danny."

He felt better with the big warm body of the horse beside him. A man's horse was his only reliance in a dirty world. Never asked questions. Gave the best he could. Took the bit and bridle of servitude willingly. Simon slung the saddle over the bay gelding's back and rubbed his hand along the thick winter coat. Sound. That's what he liked. Soundness. Things as they should be. In order. His father had taught him that. He cinched up the girth and wondered how soon his father would join him. Or if he had changed his mind.

Henrietta stirred in the depths of the double bed. She had been alone all night and grateful for it. Once in the darkness she had risen and tried the door to the dressing room. It was locked. Isaac fighting himself. Relieved, she had returned to her bed and toward morning fallen into fitful sleep.

Now as the graying day slid through the curtains, she was aware of sounds on the other side of the door. Isaac was moving around. She caught a heavy tread. He was booted. Riding out so early? For what? She remembered the coming snow. But they had all predicted last evening that it would hold off another day. Too cold still.

Fully awake, she remembered something else, so sharply that it sent her scrambling across the bed. Colin! He had come back. He was here, only a few blocks away perhaps. And he had turned her world, everything she had settled to, upside down. The tickets. She had taken them from him numbly. She had kept them close to her body, until at last undressing alone, she had slipped the envelope between the pages of the small suede-bound book on her bedside table,

one of her father's set of Shakespeare. Isaac never
opened those books. Not the comedies at any rate. Not
As You Like it.

The book was gone.

For an instant her mind went blank. He had not
come into the bedroom last night. Or had he? No. She
must have hidden the little volume somewhere. She
would remember in a minute. She could not have left
it lying beside her bed. She stood, unaware of the
piercing cold on her bare feet, through her thin gown,
while the envelope ballooned into a monstrous guilt in
her mind. She had been swept away impulsively, in
ecstasy, once long ago, and the glow of those hours
would remain with her all her life. But this, this was a
deliberate, planned betrayal, as cold as the elements.
For an instant, in her panic, Henrietta hated Colin for
returning.

Then she remembered. She had slid the suede-
covered book with its burden among the lavender
sachets of her underthings. She ran to the bureau,
pulled at the drawer. The door of the dressing room
opened. Isaac, in a thick hunting coat, stood looking
at her.

"What are you doing?"

"I heard you up, Isaac. I'm going to get dressed."

"It's nearly zero. Go back to bed until the girl comes
in to light the fire."

"Aren't you going to your office this morning?"

"Simon has two deer to butcher and salt down before the snow comes. I'm riding out to help him."

She was shivering now, not so much from cold as
from the emotions that had swept through her. She
was glad enough to return to the warm depths of the
bed, if only to escape his eyes. They were fixed and
they were knowing. Dimly she heard the morning
sounds, the cranking of the coffee grinder, the rattle of
the milk can, the baby's hungry cry, small threads of
reality to which she could cling. He came to the bedside.

"When will you be back, Isaac?"

"When I have finished my business. I must also ride up the Ridge."

"The Ridge! With the snow coming?"

"Your concern touches me. I could wish it had governed your extravagances yesterday. Filling my house with gossips and snoopers who now think I have so much money that I would be willing to pour it into Birch River for their favor. That's what you've brought me to, madam. But that's not the business of the morning."

She lay silent, waiting for him to leave. His voice, so grating of late, bored like a chisel. She longed for silence. She had her own spinning thoughts to set in order.

"No. My business this morning is very simple, if you are interested."

"I'm always interested, Isaac."

"I intend to meet Colin Thatcher."

She stared at him, then she remembered. Isaac in the entrance of the alcove last evening, Colin filling the sudden emptiness with idle talk. Sketching up at the ravine. But surely Colin would not go up to the Ridge on a morning like this. He was a city man, a civilized man. He might already be getting ready to leave Thatcher. She was aware that her husband's eyes had not shifted from her face.

"You are smiling?"

"No, Isaac. But when you had so much time to talk with him yesterday. . . ." She would keep her voice steady, she would speak of Colin as casually as of another. Yet deep within her lay a nameless uncertainty, a small uncoiling fear.

"Yesterday, madam, my plans were not complete."

"What plans?"

"To learn from Colin Thatcher whether he intends to take my wife from me."

"Isaac!"

"I was not born a fool, Henrietta, though once you took me for one. If I had known nothing else of you, one glimpse of your face yesterday when you were with Thatcher told me everything. A mare at the teasing pole, a bitch in heat!"

So it was out at last. Vile as he made it, it was almost with relief that she could shatter the long, stubborn silence between them.

"There's no need to debase us both, Isaac. And there's no need to go up to the Ridge to ask Colin anything. I'll tell you whatever you want to know!"

"I ask you nothing!"

"But you will listen, Isaac. For once in our life together you will listen to me!" She flung herself from the bed as if with the lightness of her body she could force her desperation on him and shield the small secret brightness of the past.

"I am not ashamed of what I tell you, Isaac. Once Colin Thatcher loved me. And I loved him. For just a little while I loved him for something I had never known. I took nothing from you. This was a love you never wanted from me, or gave to me. Sweet. Kind. Kind, Isaac! Kind! And complete. Like a summer day. When you had turned all of my life into winter. Then it was over. I did not think I would ever see Colin again. I did not want to. Can you understand that? I did not want to!"

Had he heard? He was looking past her, at something he alone saw. He had not moved a muscle. She had spent herself, yet she could not guess his thoughts. She pulled a robe around her, her feet still bare.

"Isaac, if you knew all that, why did you ask Colin to this house?"

He turned toward her. She saw his forehead gleaming with sweat, the veins standing out, his skin the color of wet clay and his eyes blazing. Not with anger, but with triumph. Suddenly she grasped his chilling vision. He had wanted this to happen. He found what he had long sought. He could be his own god. He would punish her, not for her betrayal of him, but for the seduction of his own marriage to her. It was the triumph of a man in the ecstasy of immolation, the inner madness she had seen and felt before, that only she could invoke.

The fear that had begun as doubt rose to her throat. But it was not for herself that she was afraid. He wiped the moisture from his brow; still he made no move toward her. Instead he spoke as if to himself.

"And the whore shall clothe herself in fine raiment that all men shall look upon her and lust." The words shook from him, heavy with judgment. "But the Lord shall smite down the harlot. And the man who has lain with her He shall crush. And banish forever the seed of evil from the house of the godly."

He went to the door. But he was not finished. For the first time he seemed to see her. His next words fell as dry and emotionless as pebbles.

"I've noticed the boy, Amos, is not doing well. He looks pale and he is too high-strung. I have decided he must be moved to a less inclement climate. I shall tell you what arrangements I have made at the end of the week."

"Arrangements! Arrangements for what?"

"This house is no place for him!"

"Isaac, what are you saying? He's only a little boy! He can't be sent away now. Why, he's your own son!"

He looked at her long and hard. Then she understood.

The door closed. She listened to the booted steps, solid on the stairs, more solid on the living tissue of her being. The great clock in the lower hall began to chime. Automatically she counted. Seven—seven thirty. Suddenly the wildness that never lay far beneath Henrietta's thoughts broke through her numbness. She must find Colin! She must warn him! She had no idea where he was staying, but she would find

him somewhere. She would do this, her last testament
to him.

Before she could open her wardrobe, she heard a
light, nervous knocking. Nora, the young upstairs
maid, stood outside with frightened eyes.

"It's the little boy, ma'am. He's crying and he won't
stop."

"I'll go."

"Mister Roundtree said"—the girl's voice trailed her
down the hall—"Amos was to stay in his room all day
for being on the stairs last night. But it's too cold for
him."

"Light the grate in my bedroom, Nora. And bring
hot milk."

Quietly, inevitably, Henrietta sat in her low rocking
chair, cradling the sleeping child. The hidden snare
she had not seen. At last the gasping sobs ceased, color
returned to the small pinched face. Timelessness filled
the room. In the even breathing so close to her own
heart, in the pulsing of life between them, Henrietta
sensed the truth of her own destiny. A truth transcen-
ding all passion, all defeat. This was her child, her
flesh, conceived in loneliness as all her children had
been, so the more completely hers. Let Isaac think
what he would, do what he would; this was hers.

She carried the sleeping child at last to her bed and
knew in the grayness of full morning that it was too
late. Too late to find Colin, too late to change anything. It had always been too late. She went to the
bureau, pulled open the drawer, and found the little
suede book, intact with Colin's envelope and tickets
within it. In mockery on the page beneath lay familiar
words, make-believe words she had once tossed like
bright coins in the sunlight of summer. "I had rather
have a fool to make me merry than experience to
make me sad!—Come woo me, woo me . . . !" He
had swept her into his arms.

She shut the book, went to the grate, and dropped

the envelope with its contents on the live coals. It flared with stabbing brilliance and crumpled to ash.

She had need of words of her own now. But how did one pray? . . . Pray for the snow, the deep snow, that would keep him from the Ridge, safe.

Chapter Four

"Your Aunt Ada never left a loose end in her life, Colin. All records proper, no papers unaccounted for. Tied up everything neat as knitting when she sold the house to Isaac Roundtree."

Colin Thatcher shifted impatiently. He knew all this as well as Mr. Artemus Fitch. But he would see this charade of the records out before he walked up to Baxter's Livery Stable to hire a horse to carry him up to the Ridge. It was bad judgment last evening when he had looked over Henrietta's head into Isaac's face and said the first thing that came into his mind. Even a city man would know better than to ride up to the Ridge under this sky.

He would take the noon train from Thatcher back to Hartford, then to Boston and wait there for her. Yet, in the dirty dawn after a sleepless night, he saw as he had in so many dawns her incredible face, eager, tremulous, her eyes dark with banked fires. She would have taken his words as intent. Even now she might be waiting only for Isaac to leave for his office to be on her way to the Ridge, indifferent to risk, indifferent to talk. Perhaps to tell him she would go with him this very day. The thought became hope, the hope reality.

"I'm much obliged, Mister Fitch."

But Artemus Fitch was in no hurry. He spent his days among dead documents. Rarely did he have a chance to savor immediacy. His dried, curved fingers tapped the open record book.

". . . and in my opinion the only mistake Ada

Thatcher ever made in her ninety-one years was to let
that house go to Isaac Roundtree. That was Thatcher
property, same as the valley was. Sixteen forty-three by
royal grant to one William White Thatcher, right here
in the records. Oh, I know, I know. Young Isaac took
money for going to fight the southern rebels in place
of old Nathaniel's son. But that don't change history.
Abe Lincoln paid a man three hundred dollars to take
his place in the militia. But that didn't change history
either."

"That's a long time ago, Mister Fitch."

"You think so, Colin. You think there's nothing for
you to do but drop into town by one of those rattlers
they call the cars, drop out again quick as you please,
and brush the dust of it all off your feet. Bing, bang!"
The clawed hands struck each other. "That's the
world today! No sense of duty, no sense of belonging!
But let me tell you something, young sir, if you want
to do the right thing with your life, you'll come back
here to Thatcher, settle down, and stand for what the
Thatchers have always stood for, before Isaac Roundtree spread his name all over this valley. Upstarts!
That's what they are!"

Colin edged toward the door. He did not like the
turn of the conversation. The whitened bones of this
town were no part of his life.

"Upstarts!" snapped Artemus Fitch again. "Old Solomon Roundtree, Isaac's father, ran the grist mill.
Never gave a right measure in his life. Too much or
too little! Couldn't measure a proper bushel and
didn't care. Too busy nights up there on Preacher
Hill, hollering hellfire and damnation! Oh, I saw him
often enough when I was a tyke, the flames blazing on
his face and him yelling 'Wash away your sins, broth-
ers and sisters! Wash 'em in the blood of the Lamb!
Pray for salvation! You're standing at the gates of hell,
all sinners in the eyes of the Lord!' And everybody
would be throwing themselves on the ground. I tell
you, used to scare us young ones to death!"

"I'd think that sort of thing is best forgotten, Mister Fitch."

"Forgotten, you say!" The little man slapped a cloud of dust from the record book and flipped it open. "It's all down here, black and white. Solomon Roundtree fined for disturbing . . . and here, Bunty Stiles. Know who she was? Solomon's mother. Isaac's grandmother. Bonded as housemaid to the Thatchers. Ran away, she did. Caught hiding in that cave up above the ravine. Record's right here. Bunty Stiles, indentured domestic, found, returned to Timothy Thatcher, Esquire. Upstarts! That's what all them Roundtrees are!"

Colin knotted his muffler. "Upstarts built this country, Mister Fitch. I do thank you for your time."

Mr. Fitch dropped the cover of the heavy volume. "Guess you don't take much stock in all that. No reason you should. But sitting here at this same desk, year after year, I don't look at what I'm doing as putting down names and numbers on a page. I figure it's flesh and blood and in the end it's all anybody will know of any of 'em."

He thrust the book into the ancient black safe. "Reckon I'm nearing my dotage to think a fine gentleman like you would come back to Thatcher." He sidled up to Colin. "But if you did—oh, I know the talk—if you did, you could have her too. The lady. Town would get used to that. It's gotten used to most things in the past two and a quarter centuries."

The sky seemed to lighten as the horse picked his way along the Ridge. The tingling cold that filled Colin's lungs also cooled his anger. On every side bared hills rolled to meet the heavy overcast. Below, the land stretched desolate and empty as far as he could see. Not even a thread of smoke lifted from the single brown farmhouse braced for winter on the valley floor. He had met no one on his ride out; he saw no sign of life anywhere.

He was grateful for the solitude, if only to rid himself of the crabbed thoughts and fingers of Artemus Fitch. He would take her away, so far that no words written or spoken in that town could touch her again.

He looped the horse's reins over a broken branch and on foot climbed the backbone of the Ridge to the ledge overlooking the ravine. Behind him lay the cave Henrietta had shown him on their first ride so long ago, its entrance now a tangle of dead vines and briar. It had not witnessed their love. They had found shelter for that lower down on the ridge, in the dry midsummer scents of sweet grass and hay-smelling fern.

There passion had possessed them, so complete, so mutual that nothing on earth could ever again match it for either of them. Finally she had lain in his arms, sunlight dappling her body, her face suffused in a peace to which there could be no other answer. A few rare hours in the long span of a lifetime. They had both thought of it as passing until the day before he had left.

"You know I will come back."

"No, Colin. Never. My life is here. My husband. My children."

"Is that enough?"

"What is enough?" Her voice had a dreamlike remoteness. What she saw lay far beyond them. "A woman takes what life brings her. She has choices, but in the end her choices mold her until she becomes what she must. I must be what I am, Colin, or I will be nothing." She stirred against him, and he saw tears in her eyes. "But if once, just once, I have found such wonder—"

"I love you!"

She yielded again, giving herself in a final frenzy of desire, taking all he could bring to her in the desperation of parting.

When the last wild embrace was spent, a wordless and impossible promise lay between them.

Now he had kept it.

* * *

On the ledge of rock, overlooking the ravine, Colin tried to regrasp the headiness of those summer hours. Despite the walling bleakness of the town, despite the stifling domesticity in which he had found her yesterday, their love was alive. Surely they had a right to it, at last. They would make it right by the perfection of their new life together. But she had not ridden to the Ridge to meet him in the frenzy he had imagined. It was as well. They would have to move more circumspectly now.

He brushed a snowflake from his sleeve and tasted another on his lips. He heard a rustling in the underbrush, perhaps a homing rabbit or a shelter-bound deer. Farther down on the Ridge his horse whinnied. It was time to go. He stood for another moment, a solitary figure against the lonely sky, willing, eager to leave this isolation forever. As he turned the shot rang out. For an instant in the numbing cold he felt nothing. Then in the surprise of pain he felt the warmth of blood streaming down his back. Slowly Colin Thatcher twisted, flung out his arms, and toppled backward into the matted growth at the entrance of the cave, marked now by an ever spreading stain.

The snow thickened. The wilderness claimed its silence. Overhead a wintering hawk coasted. Somewhere a freed horse whinnied piercingly again and wheeled toward town.

There was no one to see the tall, solitary figure who made his way up from the underbrush to the ledge. He looked around, stooped once over the still form, then quickly dragged it, leaving a long trail of bright red, through the brambles to the interior of the cave. At the rear, through some ancient glacial whim, the slides of rock had parted, leaving a split no wider than would allow a man's body to drop into the black bowel of the Ridge itself.

The snow was coming in stinging swirls. In another

hour there would be no trace of life or death on the Ridge.

Henrietta, watching the deepening snow, heard her husband's return, his steps on the stairs, and the bedroom door opened.

"Go downstairs, Henrietta. I want the room to myself."

"Did you go to the Ridge?"

He did not answer.

She left him. There would be such silences forever between them now, for the unasked question had no answer. Yet she knew, as surely as if she had heard the shot that the silence itself held finality.

She went downstairs. There were extra chores ahead, scuttles to be filled, water stored, wood brought in, the path kept cleared to the barn, the house made tight against the storm. Mechanically, as she would do all things now, she gave the orders and set herself to laying the table for dinner.

The snow fell for three days and four nights, the heaviest in a half century. It smothered the town, closed the valley, blanketed the Ridge. When Thatcher at last dug itself out, few people took time to remember Colin Thatcher. Some had it that he had caught the last train out. Others that he had been lost in the blizzard.

In February young Simon Roundtree left to make his own way in California. A fine thing, Thatcher declared; the boy had spirit.

Isaac Roundtree declined any part in plans for a greater Thatcher, but in March he announced his gift of a new wing to Thatcher's struggling library. At its opening a grateful citizenry hung a painting of their benefactor with his wife Henrietta at his side, her hair properly netted, her eyes at last properly grave.

Part Two

Thatcher, 1973

Chapter Five

Hester Brady knew that men looked at her twice. Often she looked back with bold eyes and a shrug of her handsome shoulders. Sometimes they took that look as an invitation, other times they turned cautious. It did not matter to Hester. She had long ago made up her mind that most men were put into her world to be managed, to be useful, or to be ignored. And the Devil take the rest of them.

It had not always been so. But Hester preferred to lock away the days of her innocence when all that filled her giddy young mind was Michael Roundtree and his proud talk, until one painful night Michael left town for good or bad. Martin Roundtree had blamed her and neither forgiven nor forgotten.

Well, let him. Let them all. She wanted no part of the Roundtrees, now or ever.

She gave the polished bar in Brady's Pub a last irritable swipe and turned her back on the tall young man seated at the end of it. She would have thought John Roundtree, a congressman now, would have the decency to drink his one evening beer in some other place in town. There were better places for the Roundtrees, with their name all over the county and on the biggest monument in Thatcher's cemetery.

"The top of the evenin' to you, John, my boy." Tom Brady, once the bantam-weight pride of Galway, took one look at the set of his daughter's head and marched to the end of the bar. It was not that he was a peace-loving man by nature, but as any man knew, a woman could savage a man out of his mind when she put her will to it, and Hester had more than her share of the talent.

"Evening, Bantam." John's craggy face lit up. He was not a handsome man, not like the glib-talking Michael, but he was a sensible man and he was a Roundtree. Besides which he was a customer if you could call it that. Tom cast an expert eye on the half-emptied glass.

"And how is it in the seats of the mighty, Congressman?"

"About the same as it is anywhere else." John finished his beer in one draft, which surprised Bantam. "Join me for another?"

"Why, I don't mind. Don't mind at all. The nights are settlin' chillier into the bones." The little man drew two more glasses and hunched cozily over the bar. It was what he liked best in life. Good talk—and a friend buying the drinks. "Sure and I know them politicians. Same the world over. Blathering to wake the dead and promising a man his soul back on Judgment Day. If there was a pebble of truth in the one of them, he'd swallow it for another vote."

"Not swallow it, Bantam. Maybe spit it out for somebody else to find."

"You'll do it, John. If any man will. Though much good the truth will do a man if his hands aren't big enough to hold on to it. As my da used to say. . . ." Bantam's metaphors mixed happily with the subsiding foam.

John glanced down the bar. Hester was lifting clean glasses to a shelf. She had white, molded arms and a full figure that made John think of a ship's prow, or one of the mist-ridden Irish queens who with spear and shield taunted her followers into battle. Yet she was as pliant as a willow. *Deirdre of the Sorrows.* The name sometimes drifted into his mind, then he checked himself with a smile. He had no clear idea who Deirdre was but Hester Brady would not have thanked him.

Any more than she would look down the long, polished bar at him now. He came here when he was in town only out of a sense of responsibility. As he had done most things since the night of the raging quarrel between his brother, Michael, and their father, when Michael had stormed out of the house, never to return. John and his mother had found Martin crumpled and ashen in his black leather chair. That night had altered young John's life forever.

Eight years ago. He glanced at Hester. She still had the wild-auburn-haired witchery that could bring any male in town to her side. But she had tossed her heart over the fence to Michael, and when he went, she had left Thatcher too. When she returned, she carried a shield of bravado and a spear of contempt. It was a pity she had come back at all. But John knew the reason and he could guess her rebellion. Yet on his plane flights to and from Washington, he had sometimes looked deeper than the dreary reports he studied and admitted to himself he was not sorry Hester was where she was.

Bantam Brady drained his glass and set it on the bar. He had caught John's glance.

"And what in the name of glory am I wastin' the night like this for? When I've got that Divil of a bill collector breathing black fire down me spine again! Hester!"

Hester did not look up.

"Don't be shinin' them glasses through. There's men wantin' to drink out of them, not be lookin' at themselves in 'em. Take care of yer customer now, will you, girl?"

Hester bent her attention to the glasses.

So the bar might have held them in silence had not the door opened. John saw Hester lift her head, her hand go to the rich mass of her hair she kept tied back. He saw a look of interest in her eyes. She tossed the wet dish towel under the counter and smoothed the front of her blouse, already sleekly drawn over her full breasts. It was maddening. That he felt protective was a further irritant. Michael's girl. Once. She never let him forget it. As if he could.

"Hester," he called down the bar. "How about a refill?" He held up his glass.

She took her time. He did not want another beer, and she knew it. She slid the glass to him without mopping up the foam.

"Thanks."

"You're welcome." Her eyes were on the stranger.

He was of medium height, and everything about him was neat. His thin blond hair, neatly cut, his mustache neatly trimmed, his careful gray slacks neatly coordinated with a tweed jacket, in which he obviously felt comfortable, and tasseled moccasins. Neat, thought John. Too damned neat. Even his muscles moved neatly on the balls of his feet, like an athlete. His face had a young-old alertness John could not define. He guessed women would find him attractive.

The man seated himself at a small side table. He intended Hester to come to him.

"Friend of yours, Hes?" John could not resist a grin.

"Maybe." She slapped his check on the bar and moved toward the stranger.

The man glanced up at her. John saw his eyes travel and realized what was odd about his face. His eyes did not blink. Rather they compelled. John had seen a look like that in a copperhead he had surprised on a warm rock in the valley. And suddenly the look was gone.

"Do you have a good brandy in this place?"

"Everything we have in this place is good."

The stranger smiled, revealing neat, white teeth.

"I can quite believe that. What's your name?"

"Hester. What's yours?" It was bold, and John knew she was acting for his benefit. He had already stayed too long. To his surprise the man answered.

"Alexander Bookman. Doctor Alexander Bookman, though I don't use the title."

"Oh, but you should, Doctor—I mean—Mister Bookman." The quick ease of his answer had rattled her.

"Alex will do. So will Three Star if you have it."

This time Alex Bookman did not smile. He was showing Hester a studied deference.

John Roundtree dropped three bills on the counter and walked out into the night. He was returning to Washington the next afternoon. He would not be back for several weeks. What Hester Brady did with her time did not matter to him. Yet as he turned up his collar against the cold October drizzle, he knew, as he had known for so long, that until the day his brother, Michael, came home, if ever, it would matter.

Women, thought Edythe Roundtree, are the primal movers, no matter how little or how much fuss they make about it. She glanced over her needlepoint at her husband's empty chair. Primal movers. Not because they brought life out of their own bodies. That was biological. But because they brought sound out of silence, movement out of stillness, and spirit out of space. That was their uniqueness, born of their inescapable destiny—dealing with small things, alone.

She rolled up her somewhat dizzying pattern of freestyle violets. Edythe liked secret little flings and sat a moment longer listening to the great clock in the hall. The ticking seemed to get louder (or was it more insistent) every year, making time an intruder in the house. Edythe did battle by determinedly ignoring the swiftness of the days. But it was a losing battle. No shouts, no bursts of excitement, no quarrels, no cries of outrage, no yells of exuberance. The children were gone. The old house had soaked up their uproar like parched land onto which rainwater had spilled and vanished.

Instead adults came and went, near-strangers with the lingering faces of her children. Adults she wanted to hug close to her but found it best to deal with as friends. It had not been easy to substitute a show of liking for a show of love. But one learned. That at least was a gift of time.

And she was grateful. John's astonishing election to Congress, which had not astonished her.

"I didn't win it. Just a lot of people around here who knew the name and believed in some things I believed in." Edythe knew better but she would not argue with John's modesty.

There was Lowell, her clothes smart, her hair fashionably cut, weekending from her New York life.

"I'm just a secretary, I guess you'd say, but I like it. And I'm all right. Honestly."

Lowell came home surprisingly frequently now, with a new tranquility in her eyes and the quick smile Edythe had not seen since Lowell abruptly canceled her wedding the day before she was to marry the Reverend Duncan Phelps.

Past, all past now. Who would have guessed that young Claude, made of quicksilver and light, would be the first one married?

"I am not too young. I love Hutch and he loves me, and the best thing is to get it done and over right here in this room. Dunkie can do it. I don't want a lot of fuss."

Claude had made it sound like a tonsilectomy, but her face was radiant, her dress was apricot, and she had looked at Davison L. Hutchins as if only through him was there any future in life. Edythe hoped it was so.

"He seems sound enough, but ten years is a big difference." Martin had been put out by Claude's refusal to be given away.

"Dad, he doesn't want me as a gift. We just want to walk out of here together and this seems the easiest way. For everybody. Don't you understand?"

That left little Kim still at home. Sometimes. A teenager now, baby fat stretched to new height, brown hair straight to the waist, gray eyes steady behind steel-rimmed glasses. Kim kept her own counsel, except once.

"I don't see anything funny about wanting to be a veterinarian."

"Dirty work, Kim." Martin liked women to be fastidious.

"So what? Look, if I was going to Bollington to watch a human person x-rayed, you'd say okay. But because it's Maybelle, Mister Fletcher's cow who's got double bloat—"

Martin was now, fortunately, too busy. Since John's election he had put aside his cane, brought briefcases of papers home, and crowned it all by moving into a new modern office. John had done all that. By some easy gentleness of his own, John had managed to lift the invisible, ever-present shadow of Michael's defection. Bit by bit the open wound of Martin's anger had changed to stolid unforgiveness and at last acceptance. Wherever Michael was, he had made his own way or lost it. That too was a gift of time.

The clock's quarter hour brought Edythe to her feet. She would fix Martin his hot cocoa. He had been closeted in his study long enough. Instead she saw her husband standing in the doorway.

"Where's John?"

"My goodness, Martin, how do I know?"

"Not home yet?"

He glanced at his watch, the heavy pocket watch she had given him years ago to hang on his father's watch chain. Martin had not yet adjusted, perhaps never would, to his grown children, she told herself. He stood straight but he looked gray and his hair was noticeably thinner. Sixty. Sixty and working like a man of forty. Well, why not, she asked herself fiercely. He still had the best, most conscientious legal mind in Thatcher. *Use yourself. Use time. What do we save it for?* She shivered.

Martin went to the fireplace. "Cold in this house. We're going to have an early winter. I'd better check on our fuel tomorrow. I'll rebuild that fire."

He lifted a heavy log from the iron basket.

"Martin. . . ."

"Edythe, for heaven's sake!" She saw she had hurt him. "Edythe, once and for all. I'm a well man now. This afternoon when Sam was taking in the shoulders on that brown worsted suit, he said I had the straightest back in Thatcher. 'They don't make men like you anymore, Mister Roundtree,' he said." Martin lifted a second log. She turned blindly to pick up her needlework.

"There we are. Now when John comes in, we'll have a drink. Lowell home?"

"She will be." She saw his expression and gave a little laugh. "Martin dear, they are grown up. Let's be thankful—"

She was saved by the opening of the front door, saved from a thoughtless reminder to Martin of the son who had never come home. He needed no reminders. He would still wake abruptly in the night, toss and turn in his struggle for forgetfulness. She had coped at last by installing double beds in place of the old creaky four-poster. Martin understood. Or tried to. Their eldest son, Michael, had branded their marriage with an invisible failure. He still walked the house.

John sat back, twisted his glass, and wondered why he was no longer comfortable when his father talked. Lowell, so changed, so distant, sat hugging her knees on the ottoman, not even the firelight penetrated her careful composure. His mother's head was bent in studied serenity over her needlework. Despite the patina of affection in the old room, the generation gap was alive and well. It did not narrow. It could never. It was made, he realized, not by years but by secrets. Each his own.

"You see, John," his father's face was lively with interest. "You must ally yourself now not merely with local issues. Heaven knows we need a new bridge over the river. I'm taking it up now with the State Senate through Jim Stewart. In your name, of course. But your job is to concentrate on national issues. Nuclear power, for instance. Ben Orlini's been buying up land around Juno's Landing. He's taken a few nibbles toward the old factory down there. Of course we'll never let him get it until he states precisely what he intends to do with it. If it's nuclear, it's out. The people don't want that nuclear thing around. They don't like it and they don't trust it. Of course Orlini doesn't give a damn about Thatcher. Excuse me, Edythe."

"Then why would he buy up land?" Lowell asked, rather unexpectedly.

"Make-work for that sick son of his. If you ask me, he'd do better to put the boy—I guess Nick's no boy. Thirty now. Nearer thirty-five. His mind no better, I hear, than when he drove his car over the Ridge three years ago. But I'm wandering from my point. My point, John, is that nuclear energy is the coming problem. It's already splitting the country down the middle. Between big-money interests and the people who want to keep this land sweet. Come out strong against it, John, and you'll have a fight that will take you right into the center of the arena. That's where a man makes his mark. I can get a lot of support for you on that up here."

Suddenly John knew why he was uncomfortable. He had dutifully come home after Michael's defection, studied law instead of his beloved forestry, taken Michael's anticipated place in his father's law firm, and unexpectedly won an election against old-time political corruption. But Harlan Phelps was dead now. Young, dedicated men were coming along. John was not sure he had the stomach or the wish for the kind of fighting he'd found in politics. Yet he knew as surely as he listened to Martin's animated talk, that his career had somehow become his father's lifeline.

For an instant he saw Hester Brady's face. How she would mock him for avoiding a fight. Yet the mockery itself warmed him.

Lowell jumped to her feet. "When are you going back to Washington, John?"

"Tomorrow evening."

"Too late for me. I'm going down in the morning. Mister Carruthers told me he'd give me banker's hours but not politician's."

They seemed already half-gone from the house. John turned to his father. The question had vacillated in his mind all evening. Now, obstinately, he wanted his father to know where he'd been.

"New boy on the block, Dad. Ever meet a man around here named Alexander Bookman? Doctor, I believe."

He was aware Lowell had stopped near him.

"Why, yes. As a matter of fact, I have. I met him last week at the Lions benefit. He made a nice contribution, I understand."

"He gets around. Who is he, Dad?"

"Some sort of specialist Orlini has hired for his son. A psychotherapist, I think he calls himself. I don't hold much with these fancy titles. If a man's sick, he needs a doctor. That ought to be good enough for any man. This man seems to be more of a male nurse or companion."

"You mean he lives up at the Orlini place?"

"Full time. It must cost Orlini a pretty penny."

"What would that matter if it helps his poor son?" Edythe bit her thread. "Where did you meet Mister Bookman, John?"

"I didn't meet him. I saw him out at Tom Brady's pub tonight and heard his name."

Martin's mouth tightened, as John knew it would.

"I didn't know that was one of your stopping places."

"Bantam's got the best draft beer in Thatcher and the best corned beef in the county. Right, Lowell?" But Lowell was walking slowly from the room, a flush of color on her cheekbones.

Secrets. The room suddenly pulsed with them, and Michael's unspoken name leaped to life in his father's expression. John stooped to kiss his mother.

"I've got some reading to do."

He was not sorry the talk had come around to Brady. He had wanted them to know how it was since he had first begun dropping into Bantam's pub. He would see Hester Brady when he wished. He wanted nothing furtive about it.

Yet John was not easy as he mounted the stairs. He remembered Alexander Bookman's neat confident presence, Hester's all too available smile. He knew that he would meet the man in Brady's bar again.

Chapter Six

Hester Brady stretched herself on the ledge of rock above the ravine and let the false warmth of Indian summer bathe her.

She was not given to the indulgence of self-pity, nor to looking back. What was done was done, past was past. She rarely came to the ledge now. What drove her here this empty day she could not name. For it had been their secret place, hers and Michael's. They had made wild, young love on its unyielding surface. On gray days they had gone into the cave behind her, a dark, depthless shelter that Michael had cleared out and where she had brought a faded green-and-red quilt from the forgotten clutter of her mother's attic. She could still see the endlessly flowing pattern of those red-and-green circles that Michael would copy with his fingers on her body.

"No end, Hes. See, you're mine. Wherever I want you."

Madness. It had been a kind of madness. She had lived through the dragging duties of each day until she could escape to meet him. Sometimes at noon, sometimes at sunset, sometimes morning, she would climb the back road of the Ridge and come upon him sitting on the ledge, waiting. If she were there first, a small knot of panic would twist inside her until she heard his steps, crackling the underbrush.

They would scarcely wait to greet each other. Lips, bodies together, hands groping, clothes dropped. Passions, so near the surface in them both, fused until they lay spent and triumphant.

It would never end, this palpitating world of senses, summer, and light. It was the only reality of their youth. As the days grew cooler they made more use of the cave. Then she sensed a restlessness in him. He would dress quickly and she would find him sitting on the ledge, his eyes on the horizon, his face settled into new, heavier lines and turned from her.

"What is it, Michael?" She had left her blouse open because he liked to look at her after their lovemaking. Now she buttoned it quickly.

"I'm not going back to law school, Hes."

She was hardly surprised. It did not seem to matter up here. It was one of the many interferences of the world below them, which she put as far from her mind as possible.

"All right." She would tease him in return for his moodiness. "But what's your father going to say?"

"My father does not run my life."

"Doesn't he?" She tossed her head and laughed. "That isn't the way I heard it."

"Don't be a bitch!"

At another time he might have pushed her on her back, making love again until they were both swept into the frenzy of delirium. Without end. Without end. Like the entwined circles. Instead he sat staring across the empty sweep of the hills.

"Maybe we'd better go, Michael."

"Yeah." But he made no move. Instead he began to talk, more to himself than to her. "There's nothing in Thatcher. Nothing but a dead end. Law school. My father's office. Getting married. I might even work up to being a director of the bank and a trustee of the library. Thatcher's best. Hell, that's not what I want, Hes."

He turned to her almost savagely. "I had a great-uncle once, or maybe he was a third cousin. I don't know. I don't pay much attention to that ancestor business. His name was Simon. Simon Roundtree. They said he shot a man once. Right up here on the ledge."

"Michael, for the love of heaven!"

"Oh, nobody found the body. But if Simon did, I guess he had a reason. I can see how you could kill a man if you hated him enough. Anyhow Simon cleared out. He was young too, just about my age. He went west. It was all new out there then. A man could make money. He made it. Did he make it, Hes! When old Simon died he left a fortune big enough to buy the state of California."

She was listening with interest now. It was a sudden, blinding dimension to Michael. His eyes searched the distance again. "But my father wouldn't wipe his hands on Simon Roundtree."

"Why not?"

"Because of the way he made it. He didn't strike gold in the Yukon or work on the railroads or anything respectable like that. Simon headed for the old Barbary Coast in San Francisco. They say he hated women but he made his pile in the brothels out there. And the gambling joints. He had the whores and the crooks working for him. And he took care of them. Big man in politics too. When the city burned down in the earthquake, Simon made another fortune building it up again."

"How do you know all this?"

"I've been reading. There are a lot of records in this town if you know where to look. That's about all it has got. I couldn't spend all my summer playing house, now could I, Hes?" He reached for her breasts but she moved from him. "What's wrong?"

"I don't know, Michael."

He shrugged, and the smile that lit his dark face, faded. "Well, so now you've got the picture. That's what I want. Money. Big money. And I don't care how I get it."

The day, the sky, the world had changed. "What are you going to do?"

"Head out. Like old Simon. Make it my way."

"Take me with you."

"Well, now. . . ." he paused. "That wouldn't be too bad. Would you come?"

"Anywhere, Michael. To the ends of the earth."

He reached for her. The touch brought her into his arms.

"Take me with you!"

"If you're a good girl."

His hands began to move.

A timeless interlude, and then they both heard the steps, quietly through the underbrush, nearing, nearing like the tomorrow she suddenly feared.

So Michael had gone. More than that, he had vanished. He had not come for her that black night, he had not called, he had not written. There had been the quarrel with his father, and the silence. Then the raging hatred of all Roundtrees settling like lead at the core of her, until she had made her peace and found her opiate in the uses of her body. No man possessed her now nor ever would again. She would take but she would not give.

And a fool she was to come up to this place at all. Let the past bury the past; what was done was done. Let John Roundtree come to the pub as often as he liked. He was a Roundtree. She could take him to bed, she had no doubt of that. There would be the sweetness of revenge to laugh in his face and walk out.

Then Hester Brady sat up abruptly and addressed that other self who knew too much about her.

"You'll do no such thing, Hester. You've learned your lesson of taking without loving. You'll flirt and you'll laugh and you'll use your little tricks, but you'll do no more. You've got a body aching for love and you've got the soul of a repentant nun!"

She jumped to her feet. She would not come to the

ledge again. It was hers no more. Not since the Orlinis had built their great house of glass and granite further down the Ridge. Now a path led neatly as a walk on Thatcher Green from the house to this high point. The next thing, she would be caught up here and sent on her way like a cheap intruder.

She half ran, half slid down the wooded side of the Ridge to the abandoned farm tracks that led to the dirt road and her parked car. At the edge of a stand of tulip trees and beeches she stopped. A green sports car stood gleaming in the vestiges of the wagon tracks. In it sat two people. One, a pallid, black-haired man, whom Hester recognized as the gray echo of the once flamboyant Nick Orlini. Beside him at the wheel, sat a girl.

Hester backed slowly into the grove. Not for anything did she want to bear witness to the luminous look on Lowell Roundtree's face.

Chapter Seven

Thatcher's citizens took pride in the sameness of their days, in the familiarity of old streets and old names, in the notion that if a man sold you an honest pound of meat thirty years ago, he was likely to do it today. In a restless, rootless world they saw themselves holding firm to principles and pride within their bastion of hills.

But in one bright week every October their defenses fell. At dawn the county roads were clogged with farm trucks and machinery; raucous with bellowing cattle, protesting sheep, indignant fowl, excited children, and the shouts of sharp, good-natured, Yankee rivalry. By nine o'clock the state highway into Thatcher, once the old wagon-rutted turnpike west, carried a stream of cars and motorcycles homing in like a swarm of bees on the brilliant lures of posters leading to Racetrack Meadows.

Thatcher's annual rite of autumn, the County Fair, had begun.

Racetrack was a misnomer, a relic of the days when Victorian Thatcher had indulged a brief, well-bred taste for trotting horses. Now for fifty-one weeks of the year the old track slumbered. On the fifty-second, harvest magic touched it.

Its surface weeded and scraped, its fences painted, stables shored up, sulky sheds converted to exhibition halls, the track awakened to a new world. In blue jeans and nylon jackets, carrying soft-drink cans and blaring radios, trundling sleepy babies and candy-faced children, they came, among them keen-eyed men who waited through the parades of high school bands and self-conscious dignitaries for just one thing. To see good horseflesh.

For Bantam Brady it was a time of agonizing appraisal. At no other time of the year would so many excited, weary, hungry (and thirsty) people pass Brady's Pub. On the other hand at no other time could Bantam attend, so near at hand, earth's noblest spectacle, a fast-moving horse.

As usual his agony did not last very long, not any longer than it took him to take a seedy, hand-lettered card from a kitchen drawer and hang it on the pub door. CLOSED UNTIL SIX.

Now in gorgeous freedom, the day still young, Bantam moved happily through the crowds. It was all as he remembered and expected, a flawless sky (if it ever rained at Fair time, Thatcher promptly forgot it), a vibrancy of balloons and flags, the glitter of game stalls, the smells of hot dog stands and pizza-grinder counters, the clatter of rides, the squealing thrills of the Ferris wheel, and the ever present mayhem of rock 'n' roll.

He avoided, with practiced care, the displays of Thatcher's own citizens, the skills of earlier survival, the quilts and the wool weaving, the homemade breads and cheeses, the handcrafted iron and leather. He stopped once to admire a bird-life exhibit by teenagers. He liked the young released from their parents. He hesitated before the unsurpassed fried chicken and hot-buttered corn, courtesy of the Ladies' Auxiliary of the Thatcher Fire Department. But sampling the spread meant facing the ladies.

He moved on through the purpled temptations of the midway. Once he cast an appreciative eye on an ageless young lady undulating in tinsel and veils before a tent door.

"Step right in, folks! Ten gorgeous girls, nine gorgeous costumes!"

The crowd loved it. But to Bantan no woman born of man could equal the flowing splendor of a Thoroughbred horse. A woman was a necessity of life. A horse was its glory.

At last he reached the lodestar of his day. His cap pulled low, a straw between his teeth, he leaned his slight frame against the railing of the show ring where horses were displayed before racing or selling. His murmur was barely audible. "Poor spavined swayback of a critter." Or "Roman nose and two knock-knees." Or "breathing like a wind tunnel." A show of spirit or bloodline brightened his eye. His coterie of followers, gathered around him, brightened too. They would know where to place their money. As usual Bantam whirled on them.

"Now don't you be mindin' me there! It's a twitch in me eye since me mother was scratched by a one-eyed cat and she carrying me, in the County Mayo, God help us.

"Now you there! Did I say a word? It's a droop in me eye from when Bull-Ears Reilly brushed a mitt across me cheek. That was just before I knocked old Bull-Ears clean out of Galway town."

Finished at the showing ring, Bantam edged his way back through the crowds. The next event at the track was the steeplechase. He could have told them how to set a better brush jump but there comes a time when a man get tired of informing the ignorant.

He had an hour to wait. He wondered where Hester was. Somewhere near a horse if she had a drop of Brady blood in her veins. She had a good deal more than that, with her mother's beauty of face and his own stubborn pride. He had brushed off the talk that reached him about Hester and Michael Roundtree. She had too much spirit to go where she wasn't wanted. And Michael had a sideways look about him that she'd have early seen.

It was no life for her at the pub. Not what he and Mary had planned. But bad times came like hailstones, when and where a man least expected. Bantam Brady turned his mind to the day at hand.

He would watch the horse-draw as he had promised Mary. Not that the huge farm horses, digging in their great shaggy hoofs to pull a sledge of stone weights, interested him. Give him a Galway Thoroughbred, all clean bone and silken coat. But Mary loved the enormous beasts. He never failed to marvel at the delicate little woman who was his wife glowing at the sight of the massive heads, with their jangling brass-bright harnesses and their wide, gentle eyes. This year, for the first time, Mary had not come.

"But you'll write down everything for me, Tom!" She lifted a paper-thin hand from her lap. "If Bess and Sam are drawing this year and how much they pull. If they're in it, they're sure to win. And give my respects to Mister Hodges and be sure to ask about his daughter. She's just had darling twins. And don't forget to bring me home two jars of Edna Cotter's green tomato relish. Now, don't let Edna give them to you. It's for her church and it won't hurt your soul, Tom, to put something in a Protestant plate!"

She lay back in her chair. The effort had tired her. He had gone out with heaviness in his chest.

"The winner! Len Hodges's team, Bess and Sam. Final draw. Weight: twenty-two thousand pounds. Take 'em around the ring, Len!" As the massive pair of matched bay Percherons jangled past, Bantam dutifully moistened the stub of a pencil and wrote on the back of the race sheet. Winners: Bess and Sam. Weight: 22,000 pounds. That would please her. The figures blurred as he pocketed the paper. Mary herself weighed no more than ninety now.

He looked around for Hester and was relieved not to see her. No woman alive could understand how a man could raise such a mighty thirst at two in the afternoon. Twenty minutes until the first race. He started for the beer stand.

"Good afternoon, Tom."

There was only one man in Thatcher who could address a fellow like that and make him feel like a gentleman. Bantam doffed his cap with a wide gesture.

"And the top of the day to you, Will."

Willard Roundtree was, in Bantam's estimation, the best of the breed. In his seventies, lean as an arrow, Willard farmed ten acres of the Roundtree valley holdings. His only help was a native Indian, Charlie Redwing, given to silence and heathen ways. Bantam had never made up his mind about Charlie Redwing. What could you know about a man who looked past you instead of at you when he spoke, if he spoke at all? It was no use Will explaining that an Indian considered it a discourtesy to look a man directly in the eye.

"I'm showing my new hybrid corn, Tom. Seems to do well in this soil and resists mildew better than anything I've grown yet. Want to see it?"

"Sure, sure, Will." Bantam coughed dryly.

"I couldn't get Charlie to come. He says it offends the gods for a man to display his wealth. Well, maybe. We'll see whether the hybrid is our wealth."

They had passed the beer stand. It seemed to Bantam that Will was doing a lot more talking than usual. The old man kept a lot in his head but he wasn't one to carry on talk unless you asked him. Willard's voice suddenly trailed.

"Good day, Mister Roundtree."

"Good day to you, sir."

Bantam was aware that Willard's old-fashioned courtesy had slid into formality.

"Splendid weather."

"Yes, indeed. Tom, do you know Mister Alexander Bookman? Mister Bookman, my friend and colleague, Mister Tom Brady."

"Oh, yes. Hello, Brady."

Tom touched his cap. Will maneuvered people the way he played pinochle. You never knew what cards he held. But then, thought Tom, that was what had once made Willard Roundtree the most feared trial lawyer in the state.

Alexander Bookman, neat in suede jacket and knotted foulard scarf, nodded. There was an odd unevenness in his speech, a word clipped here, a syllable there.

"Marvelous spectacle, the New England County Fair, don't you agree, Mister Roundtree? A microcosm of life gone by."

Willard glanced toward the display of gleaming farm juggernauts.

"We think we're rather modern here in Thatcher."

"Oh, quite. Matter of fact I was just looking at your new hybrid corn. Red Gold, I think you call it. But I would say that mildew resistance was due less to gene structure than to an alteration in the pH factor. I'd like to discuss it with you sometime."

"At your service, sir. But if you read to the end of my paper in the exhibition, you will find the point covered."

Alexander Bookman moved away like a man who was less than sure of his purpose.

"Now, Will, what in the name of the saints was all that blather? Not a word did I understand."

"Very sensible of you. Mister Bookman is a knowledgeable man. He wants us to know it. So you've already met him."

"Not what you might call meeting. He comes to the pub every evening regular as you could set your clock by it. Drinks one brandy. The best, mind you, and leaves. A real fancy Dan, I'd say, for these parts but he makes no trouble and his money is as good as any. I'd like to see my girl less easy with him, but then Hester's got a mind of her own." Tom sighed.

The older man looked through the shining day. Then he asked the question that lived deepest with him. "How is Mary?"

The little Irishman seemed to squint. "Middlin'.

Middlin' to poor. I can't fool you, Will. Middlin' to real poor some days."

Dancing motes of light and dust filled the pause. Willard dropped a hand on the Irishman's skinny shoulder.

"Would you believe, Tom, that we've walked right past a beer stand?"

"Did we, now? I didn't know. Not at all. I barely noticed."

"As I remember, I have a small debt to you. A pair of jacks that beat me Tuesday night."

"Well now, I'd clean forgotten, Will."

They turned, Willard still talking. Not again would he mention Alexander Bookman to the beset little man. But he would not forget either his glimpse of Hester tossing her head and smiling at Bookman at the edge of the fairgrounds. In a way no man could understand, Hester was his concern too, a girl who'd hurt herself before she'd hurt anyone else.

Will did not really want the beer. When they finished, he would look for John, politicking reluctantly, Willard Roundtree guessed, in the noise and the brilliance and the thickening crowds.

"How you doing, Hes?"

"Okay, Gus. And you?"

"Can't complain."

Gus Berger ran the gas station, a rough guy but dependable. If any guy could be, she thought wryly.

"Hello, Hester."

"Hi, Mister Higgins. Taking the day off?"

"I try to, whenever Larry comes home from med school and tends store."

Big Ed Higgins, third generation of Higgins's pharmacy, with a widower's pride in his only son.

Hester walked on through the crowd, answering the smiles of men with a quick impersonal nod. A tall, gaunt woman with tight gray curls and a broad felt hat gave her a wintry stare. Hester answered with a lively smile. Hannah Poole, dressmaker. Anything Mrs. Poole could observe would be all over town tomorrow. Hester was used to it!

She was also used to the loneliness of a crowd. It was not the first time. Today she wanted it that way. The fair achingly recalled Michael to her mind. He had brought her here that autumn long ago. Sated and close in the invisible silver of their love, they had walked hand in hand through the spangled darkness, star visitors watching the silliness of lesser earthlings. They had sat beneath paper lanterns in the mock beer garden, knees touching, his hand finding her thigh. A week later he had told her he was leaving.

Not long afterward she had fled Thatcher herself, for good, she had vowed, until an incomprehensible fate had decreed her return.

"Hit the guy in the gut, lady, and win a teddy bear!"

The hawker, a coarse-faced man with an appreciative eye, held out the weapon.

"Five knives for a quarter. If you ring the bell, you get a prize!"

Another in the shoddy games of chance lining the narrow lane. The target was a life-size cardboard figure with a silly face and a simpleton's grin. A circle lay over the heart area. The weapons, six-inch knives, looked deadly, until she realized they were rubber.

"Come on, girlie! Take a chance! There must be some guy you'd like to knife!"

A laugh went up from the bystanders.

"I dare you, Hes!"

She whirled around, eyes blazing. Then she laughed. It was Pete Ryder, tawny-haired and scraggly-bearded owner of Pete's Rock, the shabby disco down at Juno's Landing, two miles below Thatcher. Whenever Hester wanted to defy Thatcher respectability she went down there alone, and each time Pete had seen her safely home. Once he had kissed her, open-mouthed. She had answered with a quick slap. "You're not so much of a hell-raiser, Hes. You just want people to think so."

"What I do is my business," she had snapped.

They had become friends. Now he stood grinning at her in the dusty light of the fair.

"Take a chance, Hes! If you ring the bell, I'll buy you a candied apple."

She picked up a rubber knife. It was weighted and well balanced. Much as the game repelled her, Hester could never refuse a dare. She hurled the knife. It fell wide against the canvas backing. A good-natured laugh went up. So did Hester's Irish blood.

"Try again, girlie."

Her eyes narrowed. She remembered mumbletypeg. She should have held the knife by the tip not the handle. The hawker had not told her that. She grasped the knife's tip and saw the hawker's face harden. The second knife struck the figure's head.

"Pretty good, Hes. Go to it!"

She picked up the third knife, holding it a little deeper on its point, took aim, and heard the hush behind her. It flew from her hand. A bell rang. A cheer went up.

The hawker pushed an azalea-pink teddy bear into her hand, half the size of the one on display. Pete was elbowing her through the crowd.

"I'd hate to meet you on a dark night, Hes!"

She shrugged. She had not enjoyed it.

"Love, I have ten minutes before the boys and me are due in the arena. Is it a candied apple or a beer?"

"Thanks, Pete. But I want to find Bantam."

"Sure. See you, Hes."

"See you, Pete." She gave him her warmest smile. She could do that with Pete.

But she made no effort to find Bantam. She knew him too well for that. Instead she let the tide of people carry her on and to her own surprise found herself thinking about Mr. Alexander Bookman. She thought about him because she had made herself conspicuous again. Just as she had laughed a little too readily when she had met him earlier. He had smiled but not with his eyes. Cold as two marbles, she decided. A hard man to figure, if she ever bothered. But she knew she would bother because whatever else he was, Aléc Bookman had what Bantam would call class. The word grated on Hester, but there it was, that indefinable sureness that made other people step back.

She would not laugh that way with him again, not even with the protection of the long mahogany bar of the pub, her secret barrier against bold talk and bolder glances. She would be quite cool. She would let Bantam serve him. She would. . . .

The crowd had carried her to the end of the midway, and now she found herself beyond the fair and at the rise of a field that sloped down to a stone wall. She shaded her eyes. Over the wall at the bottom a rider was jumping a horse, three times, four times. She stood watching. He jumped without much skill but got the horse over. Again and again he put the mare at the wall, laying his crop on the gray hindquarters. Hester began to walk toward him.

Suddenly she saw the horse refuse the jump. The rider raised his crop savagely. Hester broke into a run, the teddy bear falling to the ground unheeded. As she approached she saw the rider, a lanky, pimpled youth in an ill-fitting coat and a soiled hunting cap, rein the gray mare hard on her mouth, her flanks heaving, her small fine ears laid back flat. She was bleeding on the bit.

"In the name of God's mother, what do you think you're doing with that mare?"

"Mind your own business!" The youth's face was flushed and heavy with anger.

"A dozen times you've whipped her over that wall. It's no wonder she's refused now!"

"She'll not refuse again. There's four hundred dollars in the steeplechase. She's going to win it if I have to kill her!"

Hester reached for the bridle, but the youth was too quick. He lashed the mare. She plunged forward, jumped, stumbled on the far side of the wall, and went down. She lay there while the youth scrambled to his feet and with his crop struck her savagely across the head. Hester was on him. She caught him off balance, snatched the crop from his hand, stood with it athwart her, between the youth and the floundering, fallen mare.

"Touch her and I'll lay this on you so you'll not put a mirror to your face in a month."

The youth backed away, picked up his dust-stained velvet cap. Distantly came the bright notes of a horn. The races were about to start. The youth stepped toward the mare, thought better of it.

"I'll get the cops."

"Go and do!" yelled Hester. "And get the mayor and the governor. You'll not put a finger on this mare again today."

The mare struggled to her feet. Hester stooped and expertly ran her hands over the gray sweating body.

"Sweet Mary, she's in foal."

She wiped the open cut on the mare's off shoulder with her handkerchief. Then, because she was Hester, she dropped her head for an instant on the dappled neck and let the tears flow. "The wickedness! The mortal wickedness!" Gentled, the mare stood quiet now. Hester dried her eyes.

"You've got heart, girl. You pay for heart in this world. But if you've got it, they can't ever defeat you!"

She stroked the drooping neck.

"Now let's see you move a bit. Just a few steps. There you go. It looks all right but it'll take someone who knows more than I do. Now we'll stand here, the two of us, until you've caught your breath, and then if you're up to it we'll find a good vet to look you over."

The wail of a siren caught her ear. A police car was bumping across the field toward them. She had known Trooper Eddie Bixler in high school and beaten him two years running in the javelin throw.

"Hi, Eddie."

"What's up, Hester? What are you doing with this guy's horse?"

"Stopping him from racing her."

"See what I mean?" The youth lunged for the bridle. Hester raised the crop. He backed. "It's none of her business. If she keeps me out of that steeplechase, I'll sue her for the four hundred dollars!"

"Now, Hester. . . ." Trooper Bixler eyed the mare uneasily. On the highway with a ticket book in his hand, he embodied confident authority. But the horse, he decided, had a skittish look.

Hester wheeled. "Don't you 'now, Hester' me, Eddie Bixler! If you knew the difference between a horse and a flatbed truck, you'd see the poor thing isn't fit. This—this mealy-headed lout has nearly killed her already." She drew a long breath. "Okay. If it's four hundred dollars you want, I'll get it for you. But I keep the mare. Right?"

"For cash," snapped the youth.

Hester thrust the reins into Trooper Bixler's hapless hand and handed him the crop. "Now just stay here, Eddie. Don't be nervous. She's not going anywhere and she's not going to do anything. But if that idiot there takes one step toward her, let him have it!"

She was gone, up the field and into the crowds.

Alexander Bookman, about to start a dark green sports car in the parking lot, saw her. He turned off the ignition and opened the car door.

Hester had no clear idea of what she would do. Not for the first time had a flaring temper and overheated emotions swept her beyond common sense. She slackened her pace, hesitated at the edge of the stream of strangers, and considered her problem.

There was her small savings account in the Bollington Bank from the days when she worked there, before Bantam needed her. No matter that $400 would nearly empty it and with it her small sense of independence. But this was Saturday. She could not draw it out until Monday. She had not even asked the scraggly youth's name. Without the money he would take the mare and ride her to death. Bantam was somewhere on the grounds, but the less he knew about this the better. Bantam, she knew, had only one way of coping with shock, even if it meant opening the pub two hours early.

She pushed her way among the faces and caught sight of Willard Roundtree. Another time she would have avoided him. He was a Roundtree and his kindness disconcerted her. But beggars could only be beggars and surely a loan until Monday was not an overwhelming request. Strictly business.

She wheeled toward his disappearing figure, tripped on a child's pull toy, and crashed against a shoulder. An arm went around her, stopping her fall. She heard a laugh.

"Sometimes I'm lucky!"

She straightened. The arm had remained a little longer than necessary. She looked up into John Roundtree's amused face.

"I'm sorry," she said stiffly.

"Not at all. You might have had a nasty spill. Once in a while it seems I am where I should be."

She searched the passersby. She had lost old man Willard. She saw no one else she knew. The next thing Bantam would find her and the whole matter would go down in a tidal wave of argument. She drew a long breath.

"John. . . ."

He looked down at her, with amusement still glinting in his eyes. That was what she hated. He was so— so superior, as if he knew something she didn't. Besides that, he was her enemy. Now and forever. Hadn't it been John, so long ago, who had come up the ledge

path and found her with Michael? Who else could
have told Martin Roundtree and smashed her happiness? She came back to the present. It was business. It
was yes or no. It was now.

"John, would you do me a favor?"

"You know I would."

Maybe. Maybe not. But there was no time for by-
your-leaves.

"Will you lend me four hundred dollars? Until
Monday?"

Hester had long been a source of the unexpected.
But this was different. Her face was damp with perspiration, her cheekbones red, her eyes overbright as if
she had been crying. John led her out of the path of
strollers.

"What's happened, Hester?"

"Nothing's happened. Yet. But if I stand explaining,
I won't need it. I have to buy a horse."

He looked down at her. She was not as tall, nor as
commanding as she seemed behind Bantam Brady's
bar. She looked lonely, and he realized that something
outside herself had brought her to this unwilling confrontation. It was his nature to weigh, to measure, to
advise. But this was Hester. He would like to have put
a consoling arm around her again.

"Will a check do?"

"He said cash," she began. Then she did what was so
achingly familiar. She saw herself in perspective. Her
confident vision faded. She was Hester Brady, bargirl
for funny, feisty Bantam, who was her father. And she
was asking a favor, because that's what it was, of a
Roundtree.

Her chin came up. "As if anybody would be walking
around with four hundred dollars burning their
pocket and nothing better to do with it than—"

"Now just wait a minute."

She shook her head, fighting back tears of self-anger
and helplessness. "It's no matter."

He seized her arm and surprised her with this strength. "I happen to think it is. Where is the man who wants to sell the horse?"

"He doesn't want to. It's me. I've got to buy the poor thing. He's abused her—" She was hardly aware of pointing.

From the edge of the field he saw the small tableau. A crowd, mostly boys, had gathered around Trooper Bixler and the gray mare. The youth in the ill-fitting riding clothes was nowhere to be seen.

"He's there, all right," she said. "That devil with his whip. When he sees you, he'll double the price."

"I'm more of a man than you think, Hester." But John said it so quietly that she only half heard. For coming toward them out of the group of onlookers was Alexander Bookman, walking lightly, neatly. He smiled but with an authority, a familiarity that was new.

"Ah, here you are. How are you, Mister Roundtree? I had a pleasant chat with your uncle awhile ago. Miss Brady, Officer Bixler and I have had a little talk. I know what happened and I could do no less than support a worthy cause. The young man agreed to accept two hundred fifty dollars cash for the mare. Bridle and saddle are included."

Hester stared at him. In the little pool of silence she felt eyes fixed on her. She glanced at John and saw his mouth set in a thin line.

"Mister Bookman, I'll pay you back on Monday. As soon as the bank opens."

Alec Bookman brushed a fleck from his sleeve as if it were her offer and smiled.

"I believe Officer Bixler is anxious to get on with his duties."

"John. . . ."

"It seems I'm not needed, Hester."

She would try to sort it all later but right now she would have to act. Her thoughts tumbled like confetti.

She wished for one wild instant that John would step forward, speak for her. Instead, the horse-holding trooper called out.

"Hes, are you going to take this animal off my hands or aren't you?"

"Sure, Eddie. And thanks." She took the reins, and the mare moved trustingly to her.

"Mister Bookman, I don't know what to say. You did a kind thing, and I can't say you shouldn't have. I'll have the money for you, I promise."

"Please, Miss Brady, don't worry about it. I was glad to be of assistance." *Miss Brady* again. She noticed the odd, unblinking eyes.

"What are you gonna do with that horse, Hester?" Billy Haskell, skinny for his fifteen years, danced around the mare.

"Don't you rile her up, Billy. She's been hurt. You go up to the stables there by the track and tell Nate Parsons I'm bringing in a mare and can he keep her for the night?"

Alec Bookman had disappeared. The onlookers were drifting away. John, striding up the field, tall against the sky, somehow taking the sunlight with him.

She bent her head and felt the warm velvet of the mare's nostrils against her neck.

"Come on, girl. Maybe I'm not the best one for you. But it's you and me now. Against all comers?"

What had happened Hester Brady could neither name nor define. But she had made a discovery about herself, she told herself passionately, that she would resist as long as she lived.

Chapter Eight

Alec Bookman closed the volume in his hands, rose slowly, and stopped at a mirror to adjust his bow tie. The man who employed him had arrived home without notice and summoned him. Alec understood the value of taking his time. Ben Orlini was used to quick obedience. So his own success lay in not doing what Ben Orlini expected. Four weeks had already proved the wisdom of that.

The stocky, black-haired man, with his absurdly little hands and feet and his pointed shoes, was standing at the window, one of the floor-to-ceiling glass panels that characterized the Orlini house on Thatcher Ridge. The window dwarfed him, as did the voluptuous marble nudes that flanked the pool beyond the terrace. Ben Orlini liked to surround himself with artifacts and environs larger than life.

He had earned it, reflected Alec. And what a man earned was his. He too would someday earn the right to everything he desired. Someday. But for the time being. . . .

"You wanted to see me, Mister Orlini?"

"Of course I wanted to see you. Hello. How are you, Alec. Everything going well?" Ben extended his hand. Alec took it, distastefully. Too small. Too well kept.

"That's up to you to judge, sir."

"You're too modest, Alec. I've already seen my son. He looks well. Seems more willing to talk."

"Yes. He is taking an interest in things. The new car did that."

"He doesn't drive it?"

"Oh, no. No. I can't promise that."

Ben nodded and focused his glance beyond the terrace, the pool, the statuary, to the emptiness of the sky. A dreary place, this, in the approach of winter. He had built this house to please his wife. Now he and Julia lived their lives separately and kept their sorrows apart. Ironically it was Nick, the damaged man who was their son, who clung to the vast, sprawling estate in its chilling loneliness. Nick had refused to leave and Julia might have isolated herself with him had not Alexander Bookman come into his life.

Ben Orlini admitted little patience with or understanding of Bookman's skills, but his coming had appeared to end Julia's possessiveness. There was no doubt that Nick was the better for that. Recently he seemed to show improvement that Ben had not dared contemplate.

He motioned Alec to a chair.

"Join me in a drink while we talk."

"Just seltzer, if you please, sir."

"That's right. I forgot. Never drink on the job?"

"Quite so."

Ben Orlini regarded the neat, muscular figure and wondered how any man could undertake a twenty-four-hour-a-day routine. But Alec was being paid for it—and paid damned well. But then, with his knowledge and credentials, Alec Bookman would be paid well anywhere. The question was not how but *why.*

Ben remembered every detail of their meeting. It had happened by chance in the small overstuffed writing room of a Zurich hotel overlooking the lake. He had gone there in a fury after Julia had removed their son from the Swiss sanatorium where Ben had placed him. He had planned to drive the next day to meet with the doctors who he felt had let his wife betray him. Instead he had begun a casual talk with the sympathetic stranger and found Dr. Bookman seemed to have a better grasp of Nick's problems than the entire staff of the sanatorium. He had agreed at once with Orlini that the young man should never have been released unattended by professional care.

Orlini found it easy to talk to Alec Bookman. The man had a way of listening with complete concentration.

"I am familiar with that type of head injury, Mister Orlini. The body functions are restored to adequate use, but a personality change takes place that usual neuropsychiatric methods cannot always meet. Your son has changed?"

"Changed? My God, he's not my son. Before the accident, he was as handsome as any young man I ever saw. Sharp. Alert. Quick moving. Loved life and lived it. His mother spoiled him, but when I could get him away, we had a good time. Women were mad about him. I encouraged that. I wanted a man for a son. Not a mother's boy. You can understand that, Doctor Bookman?"

Dr. Bookman nodded gravely, his unblinking eyes fixed on Orlini. Outside, the wind keened, ruffling the steel-gray lake, making the red-upholstered room cozier. Ben Orlini was not given to confidences. Whatever you revealed gave a piece of yourself away. In the power game of his life, he wanted no man to find a weakness. But with a doctor. . . .

"It has been very hard for you, Mister Orlini." Dr. Bookman's voice was low with authority.

"I counted on my son. I am in corporate management. I travel a great deal. My son had a great career ahead. With me."

"And you feel robbed?" The voice was softly urgent.

"Robbed? Yes, by God, that's just what I do feel. Robbed of everything I wanted in my son. He's there. But he isn't. I keep hoping, then I see him. In that damned wheelchair!"

"A wheelchair? How long has it been since the accident?"

"Two years. Three next November."

"Hmmm. And your wife is with him?"

"She took him back to our country place. Thatcher, in Connecticut. Now he won't leave. And she won't be separated from him!"

" 'Won't' is an inconclusive word, Mr. Orlini. We all have hidden springs of persuasion. Well, it is an interesting case." Dr. Bookman brushed an imaginary bit of lint from his gray-striped trousers and rose, preparing to leave. "But unfortunate for you, sir. Most unfortunate. I am sorry the young man has been taken back to the States. I should like to see him. Perhaps had the opportunity. . . ." His voice trailed. He held out his hand.

Ben Orlini shook it. It was firm and dry, with a hard clasp that Orlini liked. His mind was working rapidly, but he had practiced caution all his life. It was needed now.

"I'm happy to have talked with you, Doctor Bookman. You will be at the hotel for a few days?"

"I am leaving on a ten o'clock plane for Berlin. I am making a speech."

"I see. Perhaps we could talk again before you leave. I don't ask for free advice, sir, but you seem to have a grasp—I found it relieving." Ben was not used to uncertainty.

"I understand. I shall be in the hotel until plane time."

Ben Orlini did not drive to the sanatorium. Instead he spent the afternoon in his room. Dr. Alexander Bookman's credentials were slim but impeccable, as Orlini's Paris office supplied them. He had studied at the Toronto College of Neuro-Medicine, at the Vienna Institute of Applied Psychology and served for three years in the Munich Clinic of Mental Disorders and Neuro-Surgery. He had written one book, *The Brain, the Body, and the Will*. Birthplace unknown. More information would come later.

But Ben Orlini had no time to wait. Nor would he confess to ignorance in academic matters. Without formal education himself, Ben had no way to appraise the institutes Alexander Bookman had attended. But the man had written a book. That said something.

Dr. Bookman was stunned, apparently, by Ben Orlini's offer.

"But my dear sir, I am involved in a great many things. I have a full schedule for the next eight months. While your offer is most generous. . . ."

Ben Orlini was at home with the pressure of money. In the end Dr. Bookman capitulated.

"My dear sir, only the most humane considerations could bring me to this point. I will see your son. But I must insist on two points. One, that if on examining him, I can hold out no promise of improvement, I shall return to my regular work at once. Two, that if I agree to take the case, I shall be allowed unlimited freedom to pursue my own tested methods." Dr. Bookman paused, then continued pleasantly. "You see, Mister Orlini, I do not wish to come to your son as a doctor. I wish to come as a friend and companion. You may use the word therapist but nothing more. No title. My work involves a good deal of physical activity, *mens sana in corpore sano* . . . a sound mind in a sound body, as the Romans said. That is where we shall begin."

Ben Orlini liked it all. The long buried tightness deep within his gut seemed to yield to this ephemeral touch of hope.

"One thing more." Dr. Bookman hesitated. "I say this with reluctance but it is essential. The lovely lady who is your wife, his mother, must understand that I am in charge. In fact she must be persuaded that separation for a while would be best for the young man."

"I'll see to that, Doctor Bookman."

"Ah, ah."

"*Mister* Bookman."

Ben Orlini congratulated himself on his good luck. From the beginning Nick, huddled, silent, and gray in his wheelchair, seemed willing to respond to the agile, energetic Alec Bookman. Alec, in turtleneck sweaters and good tweeds, settled into the huge winged house as if he had been born there. He instigated only a few changes. The Barkers, a Thatcher couple who served as housekeeper and groundsman, were replaced.

"They are too much a part of the town, Mister Orlini. Nick must have new faces."

A Vietnamese couple who spoke little English were installed, padding silently, almost invisibly, over the thick white carpets. But Ben Orlini had to admit the service could not be excelled.

Julia, to his astonishment, made no trouble. She agreed to come and go as a visitor for six months, provided Nick showed signs of contentment and improvement.

She even came to Ben's bed the night before his return to New York.

"It's been a long time, Ben." Julia had never hidden her needs, infrequent as they had become. She gave him a slow half-smile and that narrowed, knowing glance that had once driven him frantic. It was the first time he had seen her in anything but the gray silks and chiffons she had affected since Nick's accident.

She let an orange silk caftan that he vaguely remembered slide from her shoulders. Her loosened hair, iron-streaked, complimented the long sinuousness of her body. Half woman, half demon, he thought, she knew her powers of seduction.

Yet he did not want her. Desire was dead, or fed from the springs of younger, more pliant women. For too long had she shown her boredom with him and her obsession with her invalid son. The musky perfume that once set his blood pounding assailed him now as heavy and stale, reminding him of time hopelessly gone, making him feel old.

"I think you are right about Alec Bookman, Ben." Her long fingers stroked him lightly.

"I hope so."

"I think he is already doing Nick some good. He had Nick out all morning and when I came down Nick was standing. Standing, Ben! Beside his wheelchair. Not for long, of course, but. . . ."

He knew all this. Christ, had she come to talk about the boy all night? He moved from her.

"Stay if you want, Julia. But I'm leaving early. I need sleep."

Oddly the rebuff brought no response. She lay quietly beside him. Motionless. At last his eyes closed. When he awoke to the morning, she was gone. The episode was not repeated, but she had shown a willingness to leave Nick for days, then weeks with Alec Bookman.

It had all gone better than Orlini dared to hope. Now, as he regarded Alec in his neat flannels and bow tie he wondered how much longer the man would submit to this cloistered life.

"I wouldn't worry about it, sir."

Alec had an uncanny way of anticipating him.

"Worry about what?"

"Your son's rate of progress. It is better that we go slowly. As in physics, the dynamics of pressure can stimulate counterreaction."

"Okay, okay." Ben Orlini wished again that Alexander Bookman would talk in words that did not suffocate him. But he let the matter pass. He was alerted to a new sound, a car coming up the long private road from the base of the Ridge.

"Is my wife here?" His irritation showed.

"No, sir. She is not expected until next week."

"Then what's that?" Ben jerked his head toward the approaching car.

"A visitor, I believe."

"A visitor! Are you letting people come up there to see my son in his—uh—present condition?"

"Mister Orlini, when I accepted this case, I told you

I thought I could restore Nick to a full, normal life. In every respect. I believe that is what you want."

"Of course that's what I want. But are you telling me Nick is ready—?"

Alec held up a hand and nodded toward the window. Orlini swung around in time to see his son slowly, carefully crossing the terrace, a cane steadying his irregular steps. His face had lost some of its gauntness. Through the pallor Ben almost believed that he saw Nick's former dark handsomeness. He watched the halting progress in silence. When he turned back, his face was tight, his voice choked.

"I—I wouldn't have believed it, Alec."

"We've just begun, sir. I intended to surprise you when you arrived, but as you came so late last night and since his caller—?"

"Who is it?"

"A young lady."

"A woman?"

"A young lady. We met her one day when I drove Nick into town and we stopped to pick up a newspaper. I believe it is good for your son to drive into town, to establish some rapport with his former life."

"Yes, yes." Ben brushed the talk aside. "Who is the girl?"

"She seems to be a young lady who knew Nick once. Nick did not remember, but later when I prodded his memory a bit, he thought he knew her. Her name is Lowell Roundtree."

Ben stared at him. "You're crazy, Alec."

"She seems quite fond of him. I think the renewal of the acquaintance is quite beneficial to him."

"I tell you you're crazy. A Roundtree woman coming up here to see my son? You haven't been here long enough, Alec, to get the facts. The Roundtrees hate my guts. They didn't like this house I built up here on the Ridge. They didn't like my cutting down a three-hundred-year-old oak tree to make room for the drive. Who's land was it? They don't like my buying the

land down around Juno's Landing or my ideas for us-
ing that damned useless river out there. They owned
this town once. They think they still do. But I've got
other ideas. You tell me that girl—Lowell, is it?—
comes up here, hot for Nick?"

"I didn't say that, Mister Orlini. I said the renewed
acquaintance could be beneficial."

"God almighty, Bookman, I wish you'd use the English language the way other people do." Ben's shoe-
button black eyes narrowed. He paused and then the
pain showed again in his rounded features. "Alec, I
want a straight answer to a straight question. Do you
think Nick will be able to have sex again?"

"Mister Orlini, most of what we do in this world is
not a matter of body or mind. It is a matter of will.
Where I differ from my colleagues is that I separate
human existence not in two parts, physical and mental. But in three. Mind, body, and will. I believe you
know I have written a book under that title. Of the
three, I believe—in fact, I have proved—that will is
the most important. When your son has the will for
sexual activity—but of course when the damage is as
great as your son sustained, the will for any activity,
sex included, must be carefully recharged."

It was no use, Ben reflected. Alec Bookman was incapable of giving a simple answer to a direct question.
But there, outside, on the terrace was the evidence of
the man's success. Yet oddly, as Alec talked, a flicker
of memory stirred in Ben. Julia coming to his bed,
with glittering eyes and flushed throat. The first time
in how long? The memory slid away. She had not
come again.

He covered the moment of uneasiness with a sharp
laugh. It was high and thin and always surprising to
his hearers.

"Christ almighty, Alec. Maybe you've done it. Lowell Roundtree and Nick! Wouldn't that give old Martin something to worry about?"

He slid open the glass door to the terrace.

"Mister Orlini, I think it would be better. . . ."

But Ben's short, quick steps had carried him half-way across the terrace, his hand extended, as Lowell Roundtree, matching her walk to Nick's, came down the brick path.

Alec Bookman rose and went up the sweeping curve of the iron-railed staircase, walking so lightly he barely left a print in the deep whiteness of the carpet. In his own room he locked the door and walked to the window. Below, at the edge of the pool, beside the one headless statue stood Nick with Lowell Roundtree. Ben had gone. The girl was smiling. Nick's cane lay at the base of the statue, his hand rested on Lowell's arm.

Alec watched for a moment. Then from a locked case he drew a small volume. Nick could manage without him for another hour. Alec settled into the thick-walled silence of his own world.

Chapter Nine

"And what do you think she did, Mary? That nit-brained castoff of the Divil's fools—begging your pardon, Mary, but she's no daughter of yours or mine to be paying out hard-come-by money—?"

Mary Castle Brady smiled. "What's the mare's name, Hester?"

"I didn't ask. But Dad's named her already." Hester smoothed the pillow at her mother's back and concealed her impatience.

"That I did. With the roving eye of hers and the fancy way of holding her head high, she's a beggar's mistress for sure. A real doxy."

Mary laughed, and it was good for all three. "The Doxy! A lively name!"

"Lively or not, how long do you think Willard Roundtree will be willing to give her free keep and board in his own barn? And him offering out of a good heart?"

"As long as she needs it, I expect," said Mary Castle Brady. "I'd like to see her, Hester."

"You shall, Mom. I'll drive you out." Hester noted a soft flush in the thin, still lovely face and a brightening in the hazel-green eyes.

"And all you'll see, ma'am, if you go to the trouble, is a poor, gray, hock-bowed critter with a swollen belly and a gimpy off foreleg."

"Hester! Is she in foal? When?"

Hester hesitated. They had learned not to talk in terms of time. "The vet said in March."

Mary leaned forward eagerly. "I once saw a new-born foal. One of God's own beauties of this world. Now I shall see another. Mouse-gray it will be before it gets its rightful color."

Bantam turned gruffly to the door. "Pub's soon to open. Come along when you want, Hester."

Hester bent to kiss her mother. "You'll love the mare. I think she's got some Arabian blood. The prettiest little ears."

"And a neck curved like a crescent moon, and nostrils that fit into a teacup?"

"Not quite all that, Mom. She cost less than three hundred dollars."

Mary looked at her daughter. Her voice dropped to a whisper. "You paid for her yourself, Hester?"

"What else would I be after doing?"

"I think you did a good thing. And Tom knows it too. Once he's got over expressing himself."

Hester was conscious of a shading of the truth to her mother. For in the days that followed the money she had drawn from the Bollington bank lay burning a hole of uneasiness in her pocket and her mind. Alec Bookman had not returned to the pub. Night after night she found herself, eagerly then anxiously, looking past the regulars at the bar and the usual groups from the bowling lanes down the road. She found herself trying to keep free the side table Alec occupied. Not that she wanted to see him. But the debt had begun to balloon in her mind as something vaguely wrong, a burden, an evil she had assumed that had no foreseeable outcome. Later in her room she would recount the new bills and assure herself it was not a debt when there was the money to pay it. But how? To mail it involved a risk she could not define. To Hester the great winged house of granite and glass, the Orlini house, where she would have to send it, stood as guarded against the intrusion of mail as against outside visitors. How would she know that Alec Bookman would get it? So she waited, less easy, less open as the days passed.

"Now don't be wastin' yourself here every night, Hester. I never wanted that, no more than I ever thought I'd be needin' you here at all."

Bantam eyed his daughter narrowly. Whatever was bothering her, he would be the last to know. She should be married now and settled. Yet with the same thought, he knew he could not spare her or even face tomorrow without her. It surely was not Michael Roundtree she was still mooning after, with his dark bold way so long ago. He was gone and good riddance, and a lucky thing it was. The Roundtrees and the Bradys were not common salt and, if you asked Bantam, Hester was too good for the tribe of them, with the exception of Willard, a gentleman, a scholar, and a widower in his seventies. Bantam shook his head and glanced at the fine white arms of his daughter.

"Go along, Hester, and find yourself a proper suitor to be walking out with this evening."

"I'll make up my own mind about that, Bantam. Thank you." He watched her push a foaming glass across the bar to a craftily gazing young man, barely noticing him. Bantam sighed. Homer Midas had a future, in Bantam's eyes. Hadn't he built and didn't he own the new bowling alley? Wasn't it said that his father, Leo, Thatcher's only cobbler, had a tidy nest egg set aside? Bantam slid a bowl of dry cheese crackers at the heavy-faced young man and smiled benignly.

None of this missed Hester or bothered her. She had a decision to make and she had to make it soon. As she was usually honest with herself, she knew why. It was not alone for Alec Bookman she looked when the pub door swung open. John Roundtree had not returned to the pub since the fair.

"And the more fool you are," she told herself savagely. "Why would he be running back and forth to Thatcher when he should be doing his duty in Washington for the people who elected him? And why would he come here anyhow with Bantam making a silly fuss at him and him above it all?"

Yet she longed to see him. She had rehearsed the scene. She would find a way to toss her head and mention lightly that she had not only paid for the mare but an extra $25 to Mr. Bookman for his trouble. She would be that independent. And he would not turn his back and take the sunlight and leave her with a feeling she did not welcome and could not shake. "Bad cess to them all!" She wrung out her bar cloth. "And if you go on like that, my girl, letting Bantam's Irish temper and Irish words spill from you, you'll never get out of this place."

Someone rapped on the bar behind her.

Hester was in no hurry to turn around. She busied herself rearranging a hopeless vase of artificial shamrocks and daisies that was Bantam's joy. She addressed herself silently, carefully. "Miss Hester Brady. You have no excuse. You talk too much. You behave like a hoyden. You want the last word although you know it's the Irish stubbornness in you." She amended that. ". . . although you know it isn't always polite. You have a good schooling. The Sisters told you the past is gone. The future is ahead. And God in His wisdom will help anyone who helps himself. So let Him!" She set the vase back on the glass shelf and remembered. "Amen!"

She would act tomorrow. She would banish the debt and the weight and the foolishness that shackled her.

"Hi!"

She spun around.

John Roundtree sat with his quick smile, his hand extended. "I thought I'd have to ring the fire bell."

Hester's newfound determination wobbled and fell. She did not toss her head, she did not glance archly, she did not lean on the bar or extend her hand to meet his. She found something blocking her speech, a difficulty in swallowing.

"Hi." She had never realized how small the word

was. She found herself moving down the bar from him.

"Wait a minute!" she heard him call.

"Bantam. . . ." The heat was rising to her face. "Bantam, there's a customer."

In the dimness of the back room that was Bantam's office, Hester held her hands to her face. "You're a whey-faced coward!" She stormed silently. "And if you don't get over it right now, you'll have more of the trouble you've been born to all your life! And nothing else but trouble. You're a bargirl, remember. Just that! Go on out there and do your job!"

She bathed her cheeks and her eyes in the cold running water. She smoothed her apron. She gazed into the small cracked mirror with its greenish sheen. But she did not glance at her face. Instead, with a distant look, she closed one button higher on her blouse.

When she returned to the bar, John Roundtree had gone.

"Nick?"

The man huddled beneath a lap robe in the wheel-chair did not turn his head. But Julia Orlini knew that her son was not asleep. He had pulled the shapeless dark blue beret low over his forehead and was gazing motionless past the swimming pool, past the damaged statuary, past the untidy yews—to what? She did not know but it was always like this when she returned to him. In the city Ben told her glowing stories of Nick's improvement, of all that the man, Alec Bookman, had accomplished. Nick was actually walking now. Ben had heard him talking easily with Alec, even laughing once.

But when Julia came, it was always the same. Nick sat in his wheelchair in a warm corner of the terrace or propelled himself silently indoors and down the hall to Ben's former study that she had had converted to a bed-living-room for Nick. Not that she had expected anything more. The best brain specialists in Switzerland told her not to look for too much. There had been a personality change, some permanent damage, the motor functions—the frontal lobe—the technicalities had come thick and fast and wearied her with their futility. She had clung to the one straw a deeply emotional woman has—hope.

Yet now, when there were reports of progress, she became uneasy. When she should have felt only gratitude to the man responsible, she felt instead a curious revulsion and an inability to resist his unblinking eyes that looked through her as if seeing nothing. With her deepest woman's instinct, Julia Orlini sensed in Alec Bookman an enemy.

"Nick!"

The black-haired man with the shadow of handsomeness still on his lean, ravaged features lifted his head but did not look at her.

"Did my mother speak?"

The distant mocking tone she knew well but she had never grown used to his not looking at her. Her son. There came a time when that knot was tied in only one direction. She knew that in a full life of her own she would have accepted it, as all women learned to. But now all of her life lay slouched and bundled within the confines of that wheelchair. He must realize how much she had given and wanted to give.

"Would you like to move around a bit? With the leaves off the trees, the view is quite splendid and—"

A lift of his hand stopped her. "You'd like to push me, is that it?"

She did not answer. It was an old question and bait for his answer. "Haven't you pushed me enough, Mother?"

She walked alone down the terrace steps, one half of which were covered with a low ramp to accomodate Nick's chair. She followed the brick wall around the great house to the curving drive. The glass walls sparkled in the pale November sunlight and reflected a myriad of bared branches, green pine tops, and a silvery emptiness of sky.

She hated the house. She looked back in disbelief at her obsession once to build it. It was at a time when she knew she had lost Ben. Lost him to his overwhelming ambition and to the women his success had brought him along the way. Yet it was she who had brought Ben to Thatcher in the first place. Her own vague roots lay here. She had been born Julia Thatcher and in the seedy, impecunious home in which she had grown up, her high school-teacher father had filled her with stories of a Connecticut town that bore their name and a valley that was rightfully hers.

So she had lured Ben to Thatcher, she had pressed her claim and found it legally false. The Thatchers had long ago abdicated to the Roundtrees, and she could not even make her peace with them. Ben had quickly realized the beauties of the land and its river—for his brand of exploitation. He built this monstrous house on the Ridge to salve her own defeat and to seal his conquest.

Julia shivered in the mild sunshine. The Ridge had struck back with a savage cruelty. Nick had driven off the new driveway one dark night and plunged over the edge. The town did not soften toward them. Instead whispers ran like mice that the ancient Indian legend had come to life again. The Ridge was a place of the gods' anger. Intruders would be shrugged from it like fallen leaves.

In mockery of that legend her damaged son would live nowhere else. He had become not only the victim of the Ridge but its prisoner. And she with him. Until, of course, the arrival of Alec Bookman.

"Enjoying the weather, Mrs. Orlini?"

He was there now. He could walk like a cat and seemed to delight in approaching her and speaking without warning. In her irritability Julia snapped at him, and what she said surprised herself.

"Why do you persist in calling me Mrs. Orlini when you address every other person in this household by their first names?"

Alec's unblinking eyes fixed on her, his smile was slow.

"Grammatically wrong, but emotionally correct."

"I don't need tutoring, Mister Bookman."

". . . every other person by *his* or *her* first *name.* Singular noun, singular reference."

His eyes held hers too long. She was conscious again of uneasiness. She turned bruskly away. He was beside her.

"Your son has sent word that he would like to drive into town. Would you care to take him or shall I?"

She knew the answer. It was a little game Alec Bookman played with her whenever she came home to the Ridge. It was also a way of telling her the time had come for her to leave. She longed to drive Nick anywhere he wanted to go.

"You drive him, Alec. That is what he has asked for."

Alec smiled again. "Only with your permission, dear lady. Your wishes as you know are my command."

"Don't talk rubbish!" she wanted to say. But Julia Orlini, the tall, poised woman who had always been in command of her life and those who filled it had learned control, as iron-clad as it was barren.

"Take him for a drive, of course, Alec. It will do him good."

Alec Bookman nodded with an obsequiousness as transparent as the limpid light. It signaled triumph.

She did not return to the house. She wandered on the brick paths among the yews, the clipped boxwood, and the last glints of yellow among the sere leaves beneath her feet. November—the desolate days. But she would not think of winter ahead. She would think of Halcyon, the tiny island Ben owned among the Bahamas and which was now hers, a price, she knew, for his distance. If she could only take Nick there—alone.

If—if. That same treacherous little word had pro-pelled her to Ben's bed and her subsequent humilia-tion.

She would take vengeance for that night. She was not yet fifty, a woman in whom the fires of life still burned in the black hours of her loneliness. Who knows? She snapped a twig from a brightly berried bush. When a man is unfaithful, a woman can never feel the same toward him again. But when a woman is unfaithful, a man can find her more desirable. Yet it was not of Ben Orlini she thought, the blunt, some-how absurd little man who gave so much yet gave nothing. It was a faceless man, a silhouette as yet with-out definition.

She heard the low murmur of Nick's dark green sports car fade down the hill, Ben's latest extravagance at Alec Bookman's suggestion. As she turned back to-ward the house another sound struck her always alert ear, an approaching car—a thudding, uncertain motor that suggested intrusion. She hurried to the terrace. Any unwanted visitor she would dismiss on her ground and her own terms.

The car puffed and wheezed at the sharpness of the turn and stopped at last on the graveled circle beside the house. Hester slammed the car door behind her and gasped. She had seen the great house from a dis-tance, as all Thatcher had, glittering like an evil eye on the Ridge or black as a monstrous bird against a gray sky. An anathema in its newness and its differ-ence. But she had no idea of its stark beauty, its—Hester sought for the word—its *rightness*. Whoever de-signed it had understood the strength of the land that flowed in all directions from its site, the enduring blend of rock and sky, the power of the still unvio-lated tree-carpeted distances.

And the house itself. It soared outward and upward like an impossible dream. To Hester it was a splendor, a freeing from the imprisonment of all she lived with, the dimness of Brady's Pub, the tightness of the little weathered house that backed it.

She stood for a few moments, breathing deeply, gazing upward and outward at a magnificence that life had never before opened to her. The rambling white Roundtree house on West Street, with its multiple transformations and sureness of tradition had been to Hester the pinnacle of fine living. But this! This was tomorrow, the future, a world away. She would like to explore every prism of space behind those glass walls, angled in their columns of black granite. She would like—

"Are you looking for someone?"

The woman who addressed her stood as chill and aloof as the house itself. And as *right.* In a single glance Hester noted the rightness of the black-and-white tweed skirt and stole, the thick blackness of cashmere, the bulkiness of silver chain and pendant. Also the severity of an almost classic face, beneath iron-streaked black hair that might have fallen in fullness if it had not been so tightly bound back. She was as handsome as she was spare. Hester was prepared for none of this.

"I asked you a question, young woman."

It was not a tone one used to a Brady, of the County Mayo.

"I would like to leave something for Mister Alec Bookman."

Hester had intended to ask for Alec directly but she had identified the woman. It could only be Mrs. Julia Orlini, the reclusive and formidable legend. They said she no longer stayed in the big house since a companion had been found for her son. As usual "they" were wrong. She was here and she was haughty. Hester lifted her chin. "So if you could be so kind—"

"Who are you?"

"Hester Brady." The chin went a notch higher.

"Oh." The tone held recognition but not as much condescension as Hester had armed herself to expect.

"Tom Brady's my father. But maybe you don't know Brady's Pub."

"Of course I know Brady's Pub. It's been here as long as I have." Julia surveyed the auburn-haired girl with the hostile eyes and the proud lift of her head. "I've often thought it would be a pleasant little spot to drop into. Dim and perhaps quiet."

Dim, maybe, thought Hester. But God help us all if Bantam were at the bar.

"I guess you've seen better, Mrs. Orlini."

"How did you know my name?"

Hester searched for an answer. One could not blurt out to a woman the first time one met her the threads of gossip that stitched her name into Thatcher's life.

Julia Orlini sensed the refusal. Her voice chilled.

"What is it you wish to leave for Doctor Bookman?"

Doctor? Alec Bookman was that too? Hester held a reverence inherited from Bantam of anything that hinted of learning. But she wasn't ready to humble herself yet. If ever, she thought fiercely.

"Just this envelope, if you'd be so kind."

Unexpectedly Julia laughed. "I'm never kind, Miss Brady. If you listened to the gossip, you'd hear that too." She took the envelope. "I'll be glad to give it to Alec."

If she feels the crackle of new money, she'll want an explanation, Hester thought. It's not her business so she'll hear nothing from me. Yet she felt a lessening of her worry. Julia Orlini would deliver the envelope, sealed as it was given. She was a woman who did what she said she would.

"Thank you, Mrs. Orlini." Hester turned to the shabbiness of her car.

"Would you like to see something of the grounds?"

Hester turned in astonishment. "Me?"

Julia smiled. "Well, I don't see anyone else here, do you?"

Hester burst into a laugh, mainly because she wanted to. She wanted to like this strained-looking, gaunt woman as she had suddenly liked the house. Because everything here was different, unexpected. Hester was starved for whatever gave color and surprise to the numbness of her life.

She found herself talking easily to Julia Orlini. She had nothing to lose or to gain and she reveled in the stark, rich beauty everywhere, the glowing Etruscan red tiles of the terrace, the giant terra-cotta vases, the leaf-strewn elegance of the pool, and the jewellike Greek temple at the far end.

"Who knocked off the head of that one?" She pointed to the one headless statue among the eight larger-than-life nudes flanking the pool. Bantam should see those, she thought. He would banish such brazenness to hell but he would enjoy every curve in the process.

"It was an accident." A shadow crossed Julia Orlini's face. "I would have had it repaired, but my son doesn't want anything changed here. Anything."

It was the first time she had mentioned Nick Orlini. Hester walked quietly beside her because there seemed nothing more to say. She had hoped for a glimpse inside the great winged house. Instead Julia asked her to sit on the terrace, in a tone ending the visit.

"I'd better be getting back, Mrs. Orlini. I work in the bar. For my Dad."

"Tell me, Hester," Julia's smile was as friendly as her impetuous use of the first name. "How did you come to know Doctor Bookman?"

So that was it. The curtain that fell at the mention of her son thickened.

". . . that is, if you don't mind telling me?"

"Of course I don't mind telling you." Hester's friendliness matched her hostess! "Mister—Doctor Bookman—comes to the pub—uh, sometimes. My dad likes to know the customers."

"Of course. The regular ones."

The truth could trip you as often as a lie, Hester

told herself. "Well, thanks a lot, Mrs. Orlini. I've enjoyed seeing the place. It's—it's gorgeous."

"I thought so. Once." Julia Orlini rose, a flow of movement as graceful as when she had seated herself. Like a cat, Hester thought, a sinuous cat. Aloof. Unknowable. Yet the woman was as quiet as the thrust of granite behind her. "Perhaps you'd like to see more of the place another time?"

The simple question took Hester off balance. "Why, I would. I mean, that is—"

"I don't have many visitors. We'll see what we can do when I come back again." Julia spoke almost gaily. "Good-bye. I'll deliver your message."

"It isn't a message, Mrs. Orlini. It's just some money."

"Oh."

"Mister—I mean Doctor Bookman—loaned it to me at the fair when I bought a horse—" The explanation was becoming more tangled every moment. "It's all right—he'll tell you."

"I'm sure. Good-bye, Miss Brady." Julia Orlini's thin face had settled into the lines of winter.

Hester bit her tongue all the way down the long, winding drive.

Alec Bookman sat on a stone wall alongside the road, drawing circles with a stick at his feet. And listening. From where he sat, he could see through the leafless branches the dark green sports car parked on the rutted valley road. Lowell had been prompt, and for an hour Nick would be attentive. If he leaned forward he would see them sitting on a slab of rock in the pale sunshine. Talking. Everything satisfactory. Everything according to design.

But he had not anticipated a visitor. There were never visitors at the Ridge, without his knowledge. That had been one of his stipulations. The car rattled nearer. Alec swung a knee up on the wall, leaned his

arm on it, and looked into the distance, a country gentleman enjoying the last of autumn, indifferent to
the world.

The car thudded and slowed. Alec looked up too
soon. He jumped to his feet, his face pale with astonished anger.

"Hi!" Hester brought the car to a stop.

"What the devil are you doing here?"

Hester's irritation swept from herself to the rudeness
approaching her.

"I've got as much right on this road, as you have,
Mister—uh, Doctor Bookman."

Alec regained his poise. "Of course you have, Miss
Brady. Forgive me. I have a good deal on my mind. I
have undertaken a most difficult case here. My patient is progressing nicely but he must be assured of
absolute privacy and protection against outsiders."

"I've no wish to intrude and if I'd seen you at the
pub, I wouldn't be here this minute. I came to bring
you the money."

"Money?"

"Two hundred seventy-five dollars might be something you'd forget, Mister Bookman, but I can't. So
I've left it up there for you, with twenty-five dollars
extra for getting me the saddle and tack. And thank
you." Hester reached for the gas pedal. Alec's hand
was on the window edge.

"You left it? Where?"

"With Mrs. Orlini. She's got it for you." His unblinking eyes were fixed on her. She was aware of an
almost physical chill. The instant passed.

"I see." He dropped his hand. "You are an attractive
girl, as you well know. But you are stupid. I will give
you a little advice. Do not come back to this house,
Miss Brady. It is no place for you. Nor are you suited
in any way to the life here."

He turned abruptly, his stick swinging like a lash.
She pressed the accelerator in fury; the car shot forward, but not before she had glimpsed the unmistaka-

ble sheen of the dark green sports car, and the unmistakable sight of a man and a girl beyond it on the rutted dirt road.

To her relief there were no customers at the pub. She swung the car around the drive and up to the little house behind it. In the privacy of her room with its drab, fluted curtains, thin bedspread, and limp photographs stuck in mirror—Gus and Me at the Lake; Pete, New Year's Eve; Mom in the garden; Himself at the Lions' Dinner—Hester let out a slow breath. It was done, worse in the thinking about than the doing. As most things were. She cared little whether she saw any of them again. And she had in all likelihood lost the pub a steady customer in Alec Bookman. But it was over, her debt paid. She owed no man anything. If John Roundtree came in with that look again, she could give him an honest toss of her head.

She stood for a moment at the cramped window of her room. Instead of the passing traffic she knew, her mind held the sharp, strong outlines of the house on the Ridge. Once, long ago, she had had to read a poem in school, the syllables so strange that she stumbled over them until they were fixed forever in her memory. "In Xanadu did Kublai Khan a stately pleasure dome decree. . . ." She had no idea to this day what it meant. The house on the Ridge could hardly be called a pleasure *dome*, all juts and angles, glitter and glass. Yet the words floated and in them the great house. Not in color, but in the washed blacks, whites, and grays of a photographic negative. And with them, the woman. Aloof yet knowing, her gray-black elegance held fast in those prisms without life, that silence without sound.

Hester began to brush with vigorous, cleansing strokes the coppery wealth of her hair. She was not given to the imagery of poetry. If words had a lilt, give them a tune. If you hear a voice, answer it.

She changed to the fresh drip-dry blouse suspended

over the family tub. Alec Bookman was right about
one thing. There was no place for her in the Orlini
magnificence.

Yet late that evening she was not wholly surprised
when the telephone rang for her.

She was only surprised that it was Lowell Roundtree.

Chapter Ten

The plain little secretary with twinkling eyes glanced up from her typewriter as her employer passed.

"Don't let him get your watch," she murmured.

John Roundtree grinned. He liked Dorrie. She was friendly, honest, and loyal. But he had not yet caught up with her Washington-bred cynicism.

"It's being repaired."

"Good. Then keep your eye on his desk clock. It's two faced—what else? He expects you to watch it."

"Thanks. I will."

The meeting was not held in the traditional smoke-filled room of political folklore. It was held in the richly leathered, book-lined office of one of the most prestigious men in Congress, Representative Felix Twining, chairman of a useful balance of committees, molder of opinion, and swayer of votes. John had been flattered at the invitation.

Now as he sat in a low, deep chair, his feet squarely planted on the lushness of an Oriental rug, he was not so sure. Felix Twining had greeted him at the door, his smile wide with teeth and his handshake too quick for honest welcome. But he had graciously descended from his desk chair, come around to sit at John's near right, in a chair six inches higher, his head of full gray hair nobly backed by the flag in the corner, the stars and stripes gleaming so brightly that John found himself wondering whether the radiance was due to nylon, silk, or a hidden light. But it made Congressman

Twining look very good, as did the pictures of four Presidents smiling confidently down on them both.

For John soon learned that this was not so much a meeting as a tête-à-tête. Congressman Twining touched an invisible button on the arm of his chair. From a side door two aides appeared. John had already met them. In fact soon after his maiden speech Bill Fine had taken him to lunch. That, said new acquaintances, was a good sign. The other aide was a tortoise blonde with a chest covering of gold chains, Ms. Christina Hale.

The aides sat down with practiced ease on the long leather divan, Ms. Hale displaying a long, shapely excellence of leg and smiling at John just warmly enough.

Congressman Twining nodded benignly at the freshman.

"Well, John, I see you're beginning to settle in."

"I hope so, sir."

"I remember your maiden speech."

John regretted that. His own memory was painful. His mother and father, Uncle Will, Kim, Claude, and Lowell in the gallery. Not more than thirty-five members on the floor of the House. His own words growing in passion—all he belived in, the wealth of the natural land, the importance of the forests, the meaning in passion—all he believed in, the wealth of the One by one the Representatives had filed out. There were barely nine when he finished. But his mother's eyes had brimmed with proud tears. Willard had clapped him on the back, his voice breaking oddly. His father had concealed his emotion behind a quick invitation to lunch at the best restaurant John could name. The check for the seven of them had come to $218.69, and John had not yet found a way to pay the money back to his father.

"You talk well on your feet, John. You have a future. . . ."

John returned abruptly to the powerful stare of Felix Twining.

"Thank you, sir."

". . . and I notice you have already begun to feel your way." Obviously Congressman Twining did not care for interruptions. He opened a folder of papers in his lap and lifted one. "I see that you have suggested to certain members of the Appropriations Committee that it would be a good thing for Thatcher to have a new bridge across the Birch River." The congressman's tone sharpened. "Isn't that a state expense?"

"The bridge was new in nineteen-o-eight. The state and the county have paid for all repairs. But the bridge is no longer safe, and we cannot build a new one without federal aid."

"Quite understandable. Let me see. Thatcher population eight thousand . . . no industry to speak of . . . tax revenue chiefly from county seat of Bollington . . . Birch River no more than a hundred yards at its widest . . . again no industry. . . ."

"What has that to do with it, sir? People have to cross it to earn their living!"

Twining removed another paper from his folder.

"I see you have already let several members of the Energy Committee know of your opposition to the bill supporting new nuclear power research. Including the suggested building of nuclear power plant two miles downstream from Thatcher on the Birch River."

John began to see the master design, but he spoke evenly.

"I certainly do oppose it, sir. My part of the country is still unspoiled. Our lakes are good, our hills wooded, the river clean. Our people have no use for nuclear power. They don't want it. They believe that the ecology—"

"For God's sake, save that for the voters!" Twining tossed the folder of papers on his desk. A glance from Ms. Hale cooled him. He resettled his heavy features

into something that approached amicability, leaned
back in his chair.

"John, I like you. As I've already said, you're a man
who can make it big here in Washington. But you're
young. If I may make a bad pun, you don't see the
woods for the trees. In fact you don't see anything but
trees. You don't see people out there. People who want
homes, jobs—people who know the meaning of progress, who sense the greatness of this country!"

It was Bill Fine's turn to shift and cross his legs.
Representative Twining was slipping into his campaign speech.

"I see people, Mister Twining. I see—"

"Sure, John. You see a handful of people along
Birch River, a few old-timers in Thatcher." He lifted a
thick, well-manicured hand with a diamond-set gold
ring. "But you don't see the voters, the taxpayers who
want something more for their money than politicians
who just talk."

"Wait a minute!"

"John. . . ." It was a purr from Ms. Hale. "You
really should understand."

Representative Twining reached for the folder again
and put on his reading glasses. "Trees, my God, that's
all you have talked about. 'A nation that destroys its
forests, destroys the health of its land, the vitality of its
people, the very security of its future.'"

"That's biological fact, Mister Twining! Trees return natural humus to the soil. They hold it against
erosion. They are the purifiers, the natural air condi-
tioners. The oxygen a single tree gives off in twenty-
four hours combats the pollution caused by—"

"Oh, for Christ's sake! John. You've been here a year
now. You're coming up for reelection; we all are in
another year. Trees aren't going to keep you in office.
Not even the voters are, unless they know what they're
voting for. And that's got to be something big and simple. Something they can understand, no matter what it
costs them. Let me tell you a little story. You're an

admirer of Abraham Lincoln. Sure you are. It's the American thing to do. When good old Abe was in the Illinois Legislature he needed visibility. He put through a network of roads in Illinois, half of 'em never used, that left the state of Illinois forty thousand dollars in debt. Big money in those days, increased taxes. Did the people mind? Not on the day they cheered him off on the train to Washington, the next President of the United States. You spend big, you become big. And those trees you worry about aren't shaking down gold."

"They are! They—"

"Sit down, son! I want to tell you another little story. About your own town. Thatcher. In eighteen ninety-four the town was moving along. Like the country. Everybody talking progress. Everybody with big ideas. They had a plan to build a string of textile factories on that Birch River. Might have made Thatcher the capital of your state. The plan was blocked. You know who blocked it?"

Representative Twining had obviously done his homework. John waited in silence. He had begun to hate this ponderous man with his thick-mouthed distortions but he had been in Washington long enough to know that his future, any man's future here, lay through the channels of power. If he wanted that future.

"I'll tell you who blocked it. One Isaac Roundtree, richest man in the county. Ever hear of him?"

"Yes."

"Your great-grandfather, wasn't he? Not that it did him any good. The money went. The town faded away. Right? Until today—"

John had enough. "You don't have to tell me about my people or my district, Mister Twining. But I'll tell you, I didn't meet one of them that didn't support what I'm talking about. And if you think anybody, anybody along that river is going to agree to a nuclear power plant—"

"I'm sure they won't." Felix Twining smiled. "That's up to you, John. It's your job to make 'em. We think you can do it. Particularly if you want the new bridge."

Representative Twining and his aides withdrew through a side door. Christian Hale seemed to have forgotten her monogrammed gold pen. She found it in the folds of the divan.

"Don't fight him, John." Her whisper was husky as she passed. "He'll eat you alive. How about a drink, my place, six tomorrow?"

Dorrie Kellerman glanced up from her desk to catch John's distant nod. She followed him into his office and closed the door.

"Well?"

"You're right. But I wasn't carrying a watch."

"What did he want?"

"Me. My voters. My soul."

She nodded. "I'm sorry. I could see it coming. Hang around this town long enough, you get second sight or you don't swim."

"Christina Hale invited me for a drink."

"Step two." Dorrie laughed, a normal, easy laugh that might have been his sister's. "She's going to tell you you're making an enemy."

"She already has."

"But she'll help you?"

"She hasn't said that yet. How do you know all this?"

"Basic pillow plan. Known as 'the hot line' on the Hill."

"Christina and Twining?"

"Oh, come on, John. You know you shouldn't be left alone in Washington. If I didn't have two overmotivated kids and one oversecure husband, I'd help out. By the way, they're in a Thanksgiving play at school tomorrow. I mean the kids and I thought maybe—"

"Take the day off."

"The whole day?"

"I'm going up to Thatcher."

She glanced at him. "What about Ellwood—you know, Appropriations . . . ?"

"The hell with Appropriations. I need to breathe."

He thought about Dorrie as he settled into his plane seat the next day. He did not need to breathe. He needed to talk. He would have liked someone as friendly and direct as Dorrie, who would listen. Then he smiled wryly to himself. Who is kidding whom? He knew someone neither friendly, nor direct, who would not even listen. She'd toss her head, hang her apron on a hook, and walk out. Except once. The moment at the fair when he had seen the loneliness in her eyes. Then it vanished, behind the shadow of his brother, Michael, that stretched between them as long as Thatcher's Ridge.

"Fasten your seat belt, *please*, sir."

John watched the land diminish. Every dream he possessed seemed as elusive as the great white-domed city itself, now dissolving beneath him into the mists. Yet he felt no self-pity. His spirits lifted with the plane.

He was going home.

Edythe Roundtree, her face glowing from the sharp November air, pushed open the front door, snapped on the hall light, and listened to the silence. Martin had not yet come home from his office. Lowell had left by this time for the city. Kim was still at the veterinarian's where she had cajoled an after-school job. And the chill of the old house went to the bone, as it always did in the shadow of winter.

Yet she stood for a moment caught in its achingly sweet familiarity. She had come to it, newly wed, when Willard had written that it was much too big for a lone man and he preferred the farm. She had come, deeply in love with the slender, persuasive, brilliant

man she had married. She had come Edythe Temple-
ton Roundtree, but her maiden name had vanished
with the last wisps of girlhood, with the music she had
never sung, with the world she would never conquer.
She became Edythe Roundtree, molded slowly, irrevo-
cably to the role she had chosen to fill.

Any regrets became faint, warm threads in the tapestry. Actually she had none, except those of any woman
who passes into middle life with a new awareness of
time, of children growing and leaving, of a house
spreading from her, with newly dim corners and rooms
empty, waiting, too neat.

Not yet, she told herself fiercely. This was hers and
Martin's; their life together, thirty-two years of it, lay
within these walls. Not yet. She set her parcels on the
hall table, turned up the thermostat, and briskly lit
the lamps. Living room, dining room, hall, and staircase sprang to life. Edythe drew a breath of satisfaction. It was at last as it should be, fresh paint, renewed
wainscoting, refurbished upholstery, thick carpets, and
richly polished wood. She had even been able to rid
the exterior of the Victorian cupola. The fine old
house might have returned to its first splendor of Federal simplicity. But no one, not even Edythe, would
countenance the removal of the wide porches that still
clung like elderly and indignant relatives. The porches
that had witnessed decades of courtships and trysts,
farewells and hope, secret anger, hidden tears, and first
kisses. Architecturally misbegotten, the porches belonged. Like Martin. Like herself.

She turned on the two carriage lamps outside, bea-
cons for Martin through the deepening dusk, and said
a silent thank you to her remaining son, John, who
had made all this change possible. At what cost,
Edythe would not let herself think. There was a point
when one must accept the unpredictability of life or
cease to function. And function was the only weapon
she had against time.

She hung up her coat and went up the stairs as

lightly as she lived. On the landing she turned. The wide old hall now basked in a warm glow. The windows showed autumn-blue. But, for her, November was not a time of dreariness. Country living had taught her that. The bare-stripped trees brought neighbors closer. The early lights enlivened town streets and concealed their shabbiness. The short twilights promised again the gifts of faces and voices returning in the holidays ahead.

In the dim upstairs hall she was not prepared for what she saw, a pencil of light beneath a closed door. It was Lowell's room.

Lowell must have heard her, for she opened the door. She was dressed in gray slacks and a shetland sweater. She wore them well, her dark brown hair short and curled, her face thinner and prettier. But *older*, thought Edythe. Lowell had changed in the three years since she broke her engagement to Duncan Phelps. Secretly, after the shock was over, Edythe had not blamed her oldest daughter. Lowell had known Duncan too long. There were no new horizons there. But the abruptness of her flight, the night before her wedding, had hinted at something deeper, something Edythe now realized she would never know. Lowell had retired into a New York apartment, widely spaced visits, and a surface warmth. Lately she had come home oftener and stayed longer.

"I thought I'd stay over another day. Do you mind?"

The question was unnecessary. It irked Edythe. "You know we're delighted. I was just surprised. The house seemed so empty and then . . . but if Mister Carruthers—" She stopped. It was probing.

"Mister Carruthers has hired an assistant secretary. So when he's away, I'm not too busy."

Mr. Carruthers was away a great deal. "How nice, dear. Is that a promotion?" Again she was sounding like a parent.

"You could call it a promotion. A self-promotion. I wanted more time to myself; Mister Carruthers wanted me to stay on. So that's the way it worked out. Okay?" Lowell smiled with that open sunniness that Edythe remembered in her as a child, except that now it told her nothing.

"It's more than okay. It's marvelous. Your father will be so pleased to see you at dinner. I'm afraid he gets quite tired of me alone. And Kim's sick animals. That child does so enjoy clinical details."

"I may not be back for dinner, Mom."

"Oh?"

"I—I thought I'd see some of the old gang as long as I have time."

Lowell had gone by the time Martin arrived home. His face was set. His kiss slid past Edythe. She recognized storm signals.

"Lowell's staying over."

"Good. Good. If I had my way, she'd be home for good. Nothing in that city to compare with what we have here. Meet a good man, settle down. None of this off-on-your-own nonsense. Liberation. From what? That's what I'd like to know." Martin hung up his coat and marched stiffly into his study. Edythe followed.

"It's turned raw."

"Would you like some tea, dear? A little rum in it?"

"Not now." He thrust the newspaper at her. "Read that."

He sat himself upright in his black leather chair. She took her accustomed place in the cushioned rocker that John had dragged down from the attic for her. She had come to enjoy this brief interlude with Martin between dusk and dinner. A new habit. A new closeness. But now she recognized the clouds of crisis.

She opened the *Thatcher Standard*, read carefully as he expected of her.

"Oh, no, Martin!"

"It's only a preliminary list but there it is. Sites the government considers feasible."

"But Juno's Landing! It's unthinkable! I knew there was talk. But nothing so definite. This is Ben Orlini's work, isn't it? Buying up all that land. He must have known. But you're not going to let him get away with it, are you?"

He came near to a smile at her confidence.

"If it was only Orlini, we could deal with him. He already knows the townspeople won't stand for a nuclear plant in this valley. But I'm beginning to think there's someone behind Orlini. Someone we don't know. Someone we have to find."

"Martin, Ben Orlini has talked openly of building something down there that his son can run."

"Nick Orlini is never going to be able to run even his own automobile."

"Martin, how do you know?"

"Ask Jim Cartwright. He was the first doctor to reach Nick that night after the car went over the Ridge. He found the skull fracture, the brain damage. He says it's a miracle Nick's alive, except that all the liquor he guzzled probably saved him. But brain cells don't renew themselves. Nick's never going to be wholly right."

"It's a tragedy. When I think of that young man, so handsome, so full of life, dashing around Thatcher, dazzling the girls—"

"And breaking speed laws, buying off tickets, arrogant as they come. He never was any good."

"But you can still feel sorry for him. I remember the one time he took Lowell out."

"That wouldn't have happened if I hadn't been up in Bollington for my checkup."

"I admit I worried the whole night. It was a dance at the country club and I never saw a girl so starry-eyed. I thought she had a little crush on him but I was wrong. It was less than a month later that she became engaged to Duncan."

Martin reached for the newspaper. Woman talk always bored him, now it irritated him.

"But it's odd," Edythe continued. "I've heard very definitely around town that Nick Orlini is getting better."

"So have a lot of people. You can always trace it back to that fancy therapist who wants to hang on to a good job when he's got it."

Edythe laughed. "Martin, I've never heard you so cynical."

"I thought we had something a little more worthy of discussion than Nick Orlini." He put on his reading half glasses.

Edythe sat back in her rocker and eyed him directly. She knew the mercurial shifting of his moods and she knew the reason. Martin had come a long way back from his own black pit, and she could only be grateful. But she would not be submerged.

"Martin, can this nuclear thing be stopped?"

For an instant the graying weariness that pulled at her heart showed. Then he smiled. "You do put up with an old curmudgeon, don't you? No, my dear, it cannot. Not forever. Nothing man acquires or discovers in the name of progress can be stopped. But it can be channeled. It can be controlled. It can be directed. Not just with intelligence. There's plenty of that among our new bright minds. But with wisdom. With foresight. With a sense of the flow of history. That's what worries me. There's damned little of that around today. And damned few of us left to understand."

She felt the swift surge of pride she always knew in the balanced logic of his mind. She loved him. She had grown with him.

"Martin, sometimes I wonder if there isn't something to the old Indian belief that Thatcher Ridge is a place of anger. Anyone who hurts the Ridge or the valley will be punished."

He looked over his glasses at her, his eyes twinkling.

"I think you might better wonder how long a starving man can survive."

She rose. Impulsively she stopped and dropped a

kiss on the thinning gray hair. "I've spoiled you quite badly, Martin."

He touched her cheek. "Agreed." She was at the door when he spoke again. "Where did Lowell go tonight?"

"She didn't say."

"When will she be back?"

"I didn't ask her. She's grown-up now, Martin."

He made no reply, but in his silence she knew he faulted her. She wanted so much more for this daughter than he did. Lowell had spread her wings. Now she should fly. The world was much wider than in Edythe's day. Lowell was young, attractive, and the successful assistant to a man whose business ranged the globe. Instead, here she was, intense, secretive, putting limits on her future, coming home too often. What had they done to bind her so closely to this narrowing valley?

Suddenly, as she turned on the kitchen light, Edythe saw herself young again. She saw time telescoped into a cramped, old-fashioned vocal studio, cluttered with music scores and hope, on New York's West Side. She saw a young man, not more than twenty, who sometimes sang with her, sometimes listened. Their eyes met, their hands touched, their brief passion held the freshness of morning, before they took their separate ways.

For an instant Edythe gave herself to the faint embers of what-might-have-been.

Somewhere in the borderless November dusk was Lowell, this self-contained daughter, moving also toward that treacherous crossroad where what-might-be becomes what-might-have-been.

The valley held the last of the chill light.

Hester jolted the car over the dirt road leading to Willard Roundtree's farm. She was late but she did not care. She had not sought this meeting. She did not want it, least of all on Willard Roundtree's farm.

Lowell had named the place, adding that she wanted to see the mare—which Hester did not believe. But she had caught an urgency in Lowell's voice, a silent plea for help Hester could no more resist that than the cry of a child or the pain of an animal.

To her surprise Lowell was waiting on the porch steps.

"Thanks for coming, Hester!"

"It's okay. I thought you said the barn."

"We can go down there later. We can talk better here. Uncle Will has gone to Bollington. And the house is nice and warm."

Hester did not relish sitting in a Roundtree living room, talking to a Roundtree. It was one thing to accept a stall for the mare, another to come into the house as if she belonged or had forgiven. But she and Lowell had been close friends in high school. Before Michael, before—

"Come on, Hester."

Hester sat down on the bottom step. "It isn't cold. We can talk here just as well."

"If you like." The lamplight from the front-room window revealed Lowell's face, moth-pale, shadowed under the eyes.

"I really haven't any right to ask you for a favor, I guess, but I had to take the chance. I thought about meeting you somewhere for lunch, but this town is so uptight and so—" She stopped uncertainly.

". . . somebody would say, 'There's Michael's sister with Michael's old girl, the one who caused all the trouble.'" Hester finished silently. But she had not come to open old agonies.

"It's okay, Lowell. What can I do for you?"

Kindly, impersonal, brisk. Not what Lowell wanted, but she recognized the justice of it.

"I thought you'd guess."

Hester had guessed. But she waited, thinking what time could do, like rain or wind on stone, to human beings. Lowell in high school, with her short curly hair, her open sunniness, was voted the most popular girl by her class, "everybody's friend" in the yearbook. Now this thin, secretive, young woman, with her citified style and her foot-swinging nervousness.

"Maybe you'd better tell me, Lowell. Flat out."

"It's about—Nick Orlini."

"Oh." As Hester guessed.

"You saw me with him. Twice—up on the Ridge." It was a statement. It required no answer. "Well, you did, didn't you?"

"Yes. I saw you. What about it?"

"Hester, don't go off like that and pretend it's nothing. You know what my parents would think, what this town would say."

"I don't talk to your parents. They don't talk to me. As for this town, forget it, Lowell. I have."

"I know. And I think you've been wonderful about—everything. That's why I thought you would understand. Why I want you to understand. Hester, I need your help!"

The last rim of pewter light had faded from the hills. Hester was thankful for the darkness. She wanted this uncomfortable meeting to be over. She wanted to see as little as possible of Lowell's strained face. She sensed an entrapment. Lowell's voice threaded the dark.

"I knew Nick before his accident. I knew all about his reputation. He was spoiled, rich, and he drank too much. And he could get any girl in Thatcher he wanted. Then he asked me out to a dance up at Birch Lake Country Club." Her hands twisted in her lap. "My parents didn't like it but I went. Hester, he wasn't any of those things. He was sweet and considerate and exciting and he made a girl feel she was the only one in the world. And so handsome. He wasn't like anyone I had ever known. He belonged somewhere—" her arm flung out to the distance— "out there."

The silence hung muffled in mist. But Lowell's need to talk was as visible as a scar.

"He didn't call me again after that dance. I had a terrible sense of failure. I thought I had forgotten him. But I never really did. Then one day last fall I saw him. For the first time since his accident." Her hands went to her face. "He was so changed, Hester. I couldn't believe it. So drawn. So old. And yet somehow in a way—I don't know how to say this—in a way he was more like what I really thought he was. He remembered me. A few days later Doctor Bookman sent me a note, at home. Mom would have died if she knew what was in it. But it was so polite. Doctor Bookman apologized for intruding on my time, but Nick had spoken of me and Doctor Bookman thought if I might be willing some afternoon to drive up to the Ridge, it would help Nick in his loneliness."

Hester saw Lowell's face lift toward the new pinpricks of light in the house upon the Ridge. She herself could imagine the ghostliness of glass and granite taking shape. She wondered if Lowell had forgotten her presence.

"I went up there, Hes. Now, whenever I get back to Thatcher I let Alec know. He says I'm helping Nick more than anybody else could. Nick's walking, Hester! He gets out of his wheelchair now, which he never does when his mother's there, Alec says. Alec says maybe I'm the only chance Nick has. Don't you see? So I must go on seeing him. No matter what!"

Hester knotted her wool scarf. She was looking into the darkness at something vague, unknown, that made her uneasy. It was not her business, she told herself fiercely. She shrugged.

"Then why not? Do as you want, Lowell."

"You won't tell, Hes?"

"Tell? Who would I tell?"

"Anybody."

"Oh, come on, Lowell. You know me better than that. I don't tell anybody anything. Maybe it's not the smart way to live but it's the only way I know. If I get hurt, I keep that to myself too. So quit worrying. Do what you want. I don't talk."

"You promise?"

The need was raw.

"Yes. I promise."

"And John too? You won't say anything to him?"

"John. Your brother? What's John got to do with it? Or me?"

"He likes you, Hester."

"I don't see John. Sure, I promise."

Lowell rose. "I can't thank you enough, Hes. Even if you hadn't seen me with Nick, there isn't anyone else in this town I could tell it all to. Anyone who'd even try to understand. I know Michael treated you badly. I think my father did too. But I don't feel that way and I never have. Hester, can I come and talk with you again?"

This was a good deal more than Hester had bargained for. It was involvement like a string leading to a hidden snare. Yet she would not withdraw her commitment. She knew even better than Lowell the loneliness of failing to conform.

The red taillights diminished down the farm road. Hester had thought to leave first, but Lowell had hurried to her own car and driven off with a quick, nervous wave. Hester understood why. For the taillights had not disappeared onto the main road. Instead she saw the white glare of headlights flash upward. Lowell had turned toward the Ridge. In another moment the car would be lost in the black stand of pines that heralded the approach to the long climb up the Orlini driveway.

Hester shivered. From the faint glow crowning the Ridge, a chill seemed to drift toward her, mingling with the valley mist. She turned away and through the leafless trees saw a light in the barn. It reminded her of that inexpressible, sweet moment of childhood when she was lying in the dark, taut from a dark dream, and her mother suddenly opened the door, framed in light. Now no dream menaced; she was no longer afraid of the dark but in the loneliness of the place, the moment, the light beckoned. Where it shone there was warmth and the warmth was hers alone.

Charlie Redwing stood in the mare's stall, pouring grain from a bucket into the corner feed trough. The mare wickered. Charlie looked up, his leathered face wrinkled.

"Good. You are here. She wants you."

"She doesn't even know me yet, Charlie."

"She knows you. Come in the stall. That's right. Bolt it. Not that she needs it. She knows a good home. At last."

"Didn't she have one?"

Charlie pointed to rope burns on the silvery neck and shrugged. He thrust the half-emptied pail at Hester. "You finish."

It was good to be told what to do. Good too that it was small and kind and necessary. Hester poured out the remainder of the grain and stood watching the mare's contented munching. The stall was as warm as if it had been heated. On the rafter above sat a tame crow whose wing Charlie had long ago healed. On a shelf lay an enormous tiger cat who opened emerald slits of eyes to gaze at her suspiciously, then closed them. Stalker, the barn cat, she knew. On the partition of the stall crouched a newcomer, a smaller black cat with three white paws, poised to jump.

"Meow," said Hester with a grin. Charlie, on the other side of the stall, was watching her. "Who's that, Charlie?"

"I found her in the woods the day the mare came. She jumped on the mare's back and now that's where she sleeps. It is good for both of them. No, no!" He held up a seamed and powerful hand. "Do not leave her yet. Stay with her in the stall. She will go on eating. She wants you there." He slipped away.

The mare shifted, her flanks brushed Hester. Hester

leaned gently against her and found herself yielding to the warmth, the spell of this small natural world in its periphery of soft sounds and dust-yellowed light. What happened on the Ridge, what Lowell Roundtree did or did not do, had nothing to do with her, Hester. Here was a place she belonged, without conspiracy or dissemblance, where gentleness as well as ferocity had a meaning, an honesty.

"What do you think of this?"

Charlie Redwing had returned. He was leaning over the stall, displaying a polished piece of wood. Into its surface were burned the letters KIKIJEB.

"It's very nice, Charlie. What is it?"

"It's her stallplate. The name I've given her. It means morning. That is what my people called this valley—place of the morning, place of beginning."

There was no use telling Charlie Redwing the mare had already been named. The Indian no more bowed to opposition than did Irish Tom Brady. Let the clash come when it would, Hester wanted only this tranquility caught in its amber moment.

"I like it, Charlie."

"Good. I will nail it up tomorrow."

He disappeared. The heavy barn door slid open and shut on sweet-smelling quiet. The mare finished her grain, then swung abruptly to the other side of the box stall, to the hay rack. Hester moved too quickly to get out of her way, stumbled backwards in the unevenness of the bedding, and fell. For an instant a tumble of images crisscrossed her mind. The startled mare rearing and unwittingly trampling her or kicking out. She knew enough about horses to know that no horse would willingly step on the soft bulk of a human body. But she and the mare were barely acquainted. She held her breath. But the mare took no fright. Instead she only swung her head around with a soft look and then returned to her hay.

Hester picked herself up, brushing her slacks and her dignity free of grain hulls and hay wisps.

"Charlie Redwing," she muttered. "The curse of Crummel on you! If you think I can stay here all night, talking to a mare that's better fed than I am—"

A burst of laughter greeted her. She looked up. Outside the stall, his arms akimbo on the door's ledge, stood John Roundtree.

"Hi." His laughter faded into the softness of the word.

"What are you doing here?" she exploded. It was all that was left of the minuscule star shell that had exploded inside her, leaving her flushed and unsettled.

"I came to see my uncle."

"Did you?" She bent her head to brush hay fragments from her thick sweater. "And couldn't Charlie Redwing tell you he's gone to Bollington?"

"He could. But he didn't. Can I give you a hand?"

"No. Just let me through the stall door."

He slid open the bolt. "You've forgotten your pail."

"Oh." She retrieved the pail, clattering against the side of the wall. The mare pranced a step or two. "It's all right, girl. They're bent on giving the two of us no peace this day. So if you'll excuse me, John."

She slipped past him, shut and bolted the door, and found he had stepped in front of her.

"I said, if you'll excuse me, please. . . ."

"Hester, why are you treating me like this?"

"I'm not treating you in any way. I have my work to do. I'm late now."

"Can I drive you home?"

"I have my dad's car."

"Then I'll follow you. I want to see you, Hester."

"Isn't it enough of me that all of you have seen, you Roundtrees? It's no good, John. You're over on that side and I'm on this, minding my business and forgetting all of you as I wish you'd forget me. I knew no good would come of leaving the mare in this place, but when a poor beaten creature needs a home, it's no time to be sitting on my pride like a thorn in my backside. So she's here, God keep her. But I would have thought that the lot of you could leave us to ourselves in goodwill and—"

"Out of breath yet?"

"So if you'll let me by now . . . !"

"I've been doing that too long." He caught her, bent his head, and she felt his mouth firm on hers. Yet it was not his strength, nor his need that spread weakness through her. It was a newness, a caring, as if the first day of creation had come.

She shook herself free. "You shouldn't have done that!"

"When can I see you?"

"It's no good, John. I've told you."

"It's very good. I'lll come to the pub at ten when you're off."

"No!"

"Listen to me, will you, you stubborn little redhead! I don't have to come home as often as I do. I come because you're here, and you ought to know it. It's not my fault my name is Roundtree. You don't know how often in these past eight years I've wished to God it wasn't. But I'm sick of living with the past. It's dead and gone. If you want to tell me that you're still mooning over Michael, then say it now and I'll get the message!"

Michael! The blunt thrust of the name struck like a knife. It had been so secret, so hidden, a stone between herself and the world.

"Hester, I must have a chance to talk to you. To tell you how I feel. To find out what you think, if any man on earth can. Then you can tell me it's no good. If you still believe that."

He would have kissed her again but she stepped back.

"So, if you can stop thinking up bad reasons and worse lies for not seeing me, I'll pick you up tonight at ten." His smile turned boyish. "If I can wait that long."

She struggled against the thickness in her throat,

failed, and ran past him into the darkness, up the incline, along the post and rail fence, to where her car stood, alien as herself.

She glanced at the houselights on the Ridge. They were part of her entrapment. She started the engine and let in the clutch so abruptly that the car shot down the dirt road.

In the barn the mare tossed her head. The black cat leaped from the rafter to her back, soothing her. John leaned over the stall and thumped the silver-gray rump.

"It's all right, girl. It's something you understand. So do I."

He picked up the fallen pail. Charlie Redwing was coming toward him, the ancient and inscrutable wisdom in his face.

"Mister Will's coming in now."

Outside, a few stars were beginning to shred the mist. John did not glance at the lights on the Ridge. They had no more meaning for him now than the choked denial in Hester Brady's voice.

In the prismlike glow of the glass-walled living room, Alexander Bookman stood waiting. He toyed idly with a talisman he carried on a slim gold chain. He glanced at his watch. Only six minutes. But he had not yet conquered the nervousness he felt at the end of these visits.

He pulled a black silk rope cord. A birdlike woman entered on tiny, noiseless feet, black hair drawn tightly back from a skeletal Vietnamese face. Her advantage to Alec was her silent imperviousness to her surroundings. She knew no English. He had never heard her speak even in her own tongue. Whatever she had lived through had imprisoned her within the safety of herself. Only her sharp eyes, darting around the newness of her world, revealed understanding.

"I won't need you any longer, Dtoi." He gestured. "Or Weng either. Good night."

She bowed her head. He watched her leave. The couple lived in the servant's cottage. He always felt better when he had the house to himself. Yet it was a damnably desolate place to which his ambition had brought him. No, not ambition. Call it rather destiny. He could, no more than any man, resist the force of his own Karma.

Yet it was not going entirely as planned. He had had no intention of living through the endless, bone-chilling loneliness of a long New England winter. Nor had he anticipated the depths of polite resistance to him in this stubborn, provincial Yankee town. He had had to learn that Thatcher wanted no part of the Orlinis. It was something he could not have foreseen.

And he had made one mistake. The Irish girl. He had thought that, with her full-blown beauty so wasted in this place, she would be a willing conquest. Instead she had turned flint and fire and, he sensed, a certain suspicion. There was no room in his careful calculations for misjudgment.

The talisman, a two-inch gold penknife initialled A.B., swung on its fine chain around his forefinger once more. He deposited it in his pocket, crossed the vaulted living room, and followed the long hall to a closed door. He rapped lightly.

Lowell Roundtree opened it.

"It's time, my dear," said Alec Bookman softly.

"Yes, I know." She glanced back into the room. It was Nick Orlini's private study. He sat deep in a dark red leather chair, not glancing up at Alec's entrance.

"He seems overtired tonight." she whispered. Her own eyes were bright, her cheeks showed a faint flush.

Alec nodded. She went to the gaunt man in the chair, stopped, and gave him both her hands.

"I must go now, Nick. But I'll be back. And I'll find something livelier to read you than old Walt Whitman."

He drew her closer and freed one hand. With a

quick gesture he stroked it across her breasts, his eyes fixed on her.

"Thank you for coming."

Her face flamed as she passed Alec. He closed the door and accompanied her down the hall.

"He—never did anything like that before, Alec."

"Are you sorry?"

They had reached the living room.

"Sit down a minute, Lowell. I would like to talk to you. That is, if you are not in a hurry."

She was in no hurry. Tomorrow she would be back in the sterility of her one-room apartment and the monotony of her job. This man with his compelling intelligence showed her more understanding than anyone she had ever known. He drew the curtains against the cold blackness of the glass and seated himself opposite her.

"You must not be discouraged by his occasional fatigue or his changes of mood. This is a slow journey you and I are embarked on, my dear. Believe me. You will not be here tomorrow morning. If you were, you would see him brighter, stronger, full of plans, anxious to drive out. When I first came, he would not leave these premises. And his mother would have kept him that way, as we both know. But now! Progress, my dear. Such progress!"

"I wish I could be here to see that. Sometimes I think—"

"You think what?"

"If I gave up my job. If I were here—in Thatcher—"

"No. No, the time has not come for that. We are doing very nicely now." His smile was disarming yet oddly secretive. "I asked you a question earlier. Did it embarrass you too much to answer? No, I am sure not. We are allies, you and I. I will ask it again. Were you sorry Nick touched you as he did?"

She let the silence flow between them. Her "No" was barely audible.

"He is a man, Lowell. And you are a very attractive

young woman. And he was in love with you. Once."

She stared at him. "You don't know that!"

"My work is psychotherapy, my dear. My patients reveal many things to me that they are hardly aware of. I say he loved you. I think he still does and will, when he is healed. But it may be a long time before he tells you. You are a member of a family who has always shown hostility to the Orlinis, Lowell. You must know that. Nick never felt free to tell you how he felt. Perhaps you made him feel inferior."

"I? Oh! No. No! I couldn't! I never did. I—I. . . ." She stumbled over the words. This man with his inner power could confuse her, turn things she was sure of around. And yet . . . for an instant she saw the faces of her family, stiff, unyielding. And Nick, proud, handsomely foreign, hiding his differences from Thatcher behind arrogance. She shook her head.

"It wasn't that way, Alec."

"Well, we won't worry about it. That was the past. We are working for the future. For Nick's future." He paused. "Are we not?"

"Oh, yes. Yes."

At the door he stopped her, his question like an afterthought. "Did you happen to talk to the Brady girl?"

"Hester? Oh, yes. I saw her."

"Was it as difficult as you expected?"

"No. Not at all. She had seen me here with Nick. But she won't say anything. She promised. I don't think she really cares."

"Good. We don't need interference."

Lowell relaxed into a little laugh. "You won't get that from Hester. She keeps to herself. I think she's more interested in what my brother John does than what I do. Though she'll never admit it."

"No matter. Good night, my dear. I shall leave the usual message when Nick is ready to see you again."

"I'll come, Alec. You can be sure!"

He closed the door. He needed no assurances from

Lowell. But he would make very sure that Hester Brady did not come to the Ridge again.

He went down the hall, swinging the little gold penknife irritably. When he entered the study he found his patient, head thrown back, eyes distant, face gray.

"Nick," said Alec Bookman softly.

He began to swing the glittering gold talisman slowly and with purpose.

Chapter Eleven

"Congressman Roundtree's office. Oh, yes, Miss Hall. No, Mister Roundtree has not returned from Thatcher yet." John's cheerful little secretary cooled. "I know what I said, Miss Hall, but John—but the congressman has apparently been detained. Yes, I'll give him the message. Again."

She hung up but not before she heard the irritated click at the other end. She did not like Christina Hall, assistant to Congressman Felix Twining. She liked even less Ms. Hall's increasing interest in John Roundtree. John had come to Washington as naive a congressman as she could remember. Despite his lean, ruggedly masculine good looks, his outer affability, and his quiet but sharp humor, he was a hard man to know. He was single. He spent long hours in study. His life-style was almost Spartan. Now, with the announcement of the nuclear-power projects, he had become an innocently pivotal figure. Too innocent.

Dorrie tore up the telephone message. John did not need three of them. In fact in her opinion he didn't need any of them. It was past five. If he were returning tomorrow, she would have heard. With Congress adjourned, there was no pressing reason for him to return to Washington, but he had asked for a file of reports and given her a list of books on nuclear energy. They had been waiting on his desk for four days now. John Roundtree was as thorough as he was careful. She wondered what kind of woman had come between him and his self-discipline. For it was a woman.

Of that, comfortable, plain little Dorrie was sure. She had caught a new, quick vibrancy in the freshman congressman's voice. She turned out the office lights with a sigh. She loved romance.

In the chic starkness of her modern apartment Christina Hall stood with her hand on the gilt telephone receiver. She did not trust that snip of a secretary. Possibly out of self-knowledge Christina Hall did not trust any woman. Nor did she depend on them. John might be on the way to his own studio flat this moment. But she would wait before she called him there. She must relax. Annoyance showed as strain. Strain revealed lines. Past thirty, maintenance and makeup took more time. She would give herself at least an hour to finish dressing. Yet she could not put John Roundtree from her mind. At their first meeting she had decided she could make a great deal of this tall, young freshman with his unexpected courtesy and careful distance. She already anticipated the pleasure of coaxing him out of the thickets of his Yankee principles and through the minefields of Washington's social life.

Yet he had eluded her, deliberately or otherwise. Ordinarily she would have abandoned him to the bottom rungs of congressional hierarchy or else seen to it that he was permanently sidetracked to subcommittees on fish populations and commemorative stamps. Christina could wield such power and frequently did. But John Roundtree had become important. That, to Christina, was the operative word. She would be useful, not vengeful.

It had not always been thus for Christina Hall. Born Wenda Putly in a coal-mining township in West Virginia, she had come to Washington skinny, ambitious, with good face bones and the conviction that the place for a smart girl was beside or beneath power. She applied herself with the single-mindedness of a pointer hound to shorthand, modeling classes, speech lessons, and self-improvement. She submitted to the anonymity of the stenographic pool in a well-connected Washington law firm. In a matter of months, now as Christina Hall, she became secretary, private secretary, executive secretary. Then she found her goal. Congressman Felix Twining, known for his enthusiastic taste for chic women, needed a secretarial assistant. Christina saw that the right man suggested her name. Once installed in her own office, next to the congressman's, she promptly enrolled in courses in the science of politics, in executive psychology, and in the management and channels of power.

A year later secretary was dropped from her title. She became Felix Twining's chief aide, more valuable than the private list of campaign contributors he kept locked in his office safe.

It did not bother Christina that she was known as the Mata Hari of the cloakroom circuit. She was too smart to bed down with her employer, smart enough to choose her sleeping partners where it mattered. To Felix Twining she had become what she wanted. Indispensable.

Now as she sat at her dressing table, applying the last touches of hundred-dollars-an-ounce perfume, a gift of a grateful employer, she thought again of John Roundtree. He was not married. He never spoke of women. Yet his masculinity was as positive as it was near-virginal. He must have a girl somewhere. A little local thing, Christina guessed, with a mating call as sensuous as a wilted daisy. She could demolish competition like that. She had done it before. What she hoped to learn at dinner tonight should bring John Roundtree finally to heel.

She touched the perfume to her temples, earlobes, long throat, and small breasts. The hour had repaid her. Face creamy and unflawed; eyes subtly dark and luminous; full and carefully loosened, tortoised hair, and the clinging sweep of a coffee-rich silk dinner dress, cut strategically so that the eye followed only the arresting plunge of neckline. A chaste gold pendant hung deep in the cleavage. Christina called it her tabletop dress.

The buzzer from the hall lobby chattered. Mr. Gideon's car was here. Mr. Gideon would wait in the lobby. Explicit, Christina noted. Also prompt.

"Thank you," said Christina. She breathed deeply. She picked up a flow of black mink, let four minutes pass, lifted her breasts and her chin as she had been taught in modeling school, and glided out, leaving only one becoming light on in the dimmed apartment.

She had met Simon Gideon only once. He was one of that small coterie of men whose names to those who knew spelled the potency of unlimited wealth. He would slip into Washington, purpose unstated, visit brief. When he left, an invisible change would have taken place in the subsurface balances of power. He was said to live in California, but his addresses ranged from San Francisco to Paris, from the Bahamas to New York to Hong Kong. Little was known about Simon Gideon's personal life.

Felix Twining's orders to Christina had been specific. "Find out what he's after." She had managed to meet him at a minor embassy reception honoring a Kuwaiti dignitary.

Simon Gideon proved to be a large man with a balding head, shrewd eyes, and a deceptively hearty laugh. The talk followed the usual pattern of trivia, then he unexpectedly became direct.

"You're Felix Twining's—"

"Assistant," she interjected with a slow smile.

"I was about to say colleague. Do you like these affairs?"

"Not really." Washington's parties were Christina's lifeblood.

"Oil talk! A waste of time. Nobody can win. Twining's on the right track. Nuclear power. It's here. Waiting."

"He'd be glad to know you think so, Mister Gideon."

"I don't think he'd give a damn. But I'm curious about one thing. Where did he get that list of nuclear power projects? It's spread pretty wide. Oregon to—uh—Connecticut, for example."

"It isn't finalized, Mister Gideon. But if you're interested. . . ." she murmured.

They were interrupted but Christina was confident that she had not seen the last of Simon Gideon. To make sure, she called his hotel suite two days later. To her astonishment Gideon himself answered. She breathed an apology and said that she had the information he had mentioned. "Perhaps at dinner . . . ?" It had been almost too easy.

Now she entered Washington's most exclusive restaurant, which she had subtly suggested, a place where the rich and powerful were seen with the chic and beautiful but rarely their own wives. The maitre d' bowed low.

"Good evening, Ms. Hall."

Simon Gideon missed none of this. Nor the discreet corner banquette to which they were led. At the center in a cut crystal bowl lay an exotic, gold tinged orchid. Christina flashed a little-girl smile.

"Lovely, Phillipe," she said and allowed Simon to slip the black mink from her shoulders.

He had to admire the performance. The evening would have its points as well as its uses. Christina talked well, but not too much. Little threads of amusing gossip, the latest Washington quips, and questions that made it easy for him to talk about the still unspoiled vast west that he loved. After Christina had delicately toyed with quail and truffles and he had demolished a charcoal-broiled steak, Simon Gideon leaned back, his shrewd eyes drifting from the décolletage directly to hers.

"Well, little lady. What can you tell me?"

She opened her handbag. The list was neatly typed,

intelligently done. Each proposed nuclear power site was named, with its congressional sponsor, land available, estimated costs and value, and the public sentiment in the area.

"Very good. Very, very good, Miss Hall."

"Christina. Chrissie to my friends."

He apparently did not hear. "But there's one site missing."

"Is there?"

"Birch River, near Thatcher, Connecticut. Why isn't it included?"

Score one for Christina. John Roundtree should be grateful for that.

"I didn't include Birch River, Mister Gideon because there's a lot of doubt about it. The new congressman hasn't given it his support yet."

"I don't give a damn about the new congressman. Someone knows it's going through because there's a lot of land being bought up near the site."

"Really?"

"I think you know that, little lady. What's the real reason you left out Birch River?" He saw her hesitate. "I'll tell you. The real reason was to find out if I had any interest in the Thatcher project. What's in your mind I don't know. But why didn't you ask me straight out?"

"Would you have told me?" She saw that he did not like the question. She gave him a ravishing little smile. "Mister Gideon, if everyone in Washington asked direct questions and got direct answers, restaurants like this would go out of business."

Unexpectedly Simon Gideon threw back his head with a laugh that turned heads.

"By God, a man can talk to you. If he gets screwed, it's his own fault. But you put it on the table and that's what I like. I'm interested in Birch River—but why you care. . . ." He broke off as if he were seeing something beyond the walls of the room.

"It's not the biggest project on the list," she began.

"There's nothing that you can tell me about that area that I didn't know before you were born. The whole valley's dying of dry rot but with nuclear power. . . ." Again he looked into a distance of his own. "They're a stiff-necked bunch up there, but somebody's reaching them. Somebody knows Juno's Landing is going for a nuclear site. Somebody who saw to it that Birch River got on that list. I'm here to find out who."

Christina suddenly felt uncertain. She had started this little adventure on Twining's orders and pursued it for John Roundtree. But something sensual, primal had emerged between them, across the little table, an intensity, a driving physical power that took command. She could be attracted to Simon Gideon. She could also be afraid of him.

"Why don't you talk to the junior congressman from Thatcher? I'm sure he could tell you more than I ever could."

"You surprise me. If I had wanted to talk with John Roundtree, I wouldn't have come to you. I think we've passed that point Miss—"

"Christina," she said almost in spite of herself.

"I know, but I don't like it. Too fancy. Where did you get it?"

"Do you always ask women where they get their names?"

"Not unless I'm interested."

She was on ground now that she understood. The little byplay, the give and take. Here she could win.

"To be honest I took the name from a movie. I didn't like my own."

"What is your own?" He was moving to more personal ground. She began to wonder about the evening ahead. He was a man who would make the decisions. She had come prepared to attract, to flirt a little, to pay for whatever she learned with a show of glamor. But not to be dominated by the sheer animal magnetism of this man.

"Wenda Putly," she said bluntly. "I hated it."

"Wenda? Wenda." He seemed to be trying it on for his own use. "I like it. Direct. No frills. Fits you. It's a name that comes easy."

Christina studied her wine glass. "I do not come easy, Mister Gideon."

The laugh boomed. "Right! But I think you would, if it suited you."

"For the right man, yes," she said icily. "As it happens, I haven't found him in Washington. And don't expect to."

She was vulnerable. His tone mellowed.

"Let's get back on the track, Wenda. I apologize for any crudity. We're apt to talk loose where I come from. All I want to know is who pushed the Birch River site into that list of nuclear power plants. In return for that information I'll see that your man Twining gets the going rate in his political till. A deal?"

She was not ready to yield.

"Mister Gideon, it is only courteous to suggest consulting the interested congressman. Things go better that way in Washington. As it happens, you're right. I do know who got Birch River on that list. I have met him. A friend's house, a little dinner party. . . ."

He waved the small talk aside. He had enjoyed watching her work. The bright talk. The gold pendant. A lot of breast showing. Woman's game. She was smart enough to match wits yet remember she was a woman. He recognized the lure, the bait, the cast. This woman would understand trout fishing. But he was growing impatient.

"Well, is it a deal?"

"His name is Benjamin Orlini," she said quietly. "He is very rich and very bullheaded and you two should get on splendidly. I might introduce you but I don't know why I should."

"I make my own contacts."

"Good. So if that's all, I'll only add that I never eat dessert and I go home early." She flipped a credit card from a gold mesh handbag and beckoned the waiter.

"What the hell is that?"

"I believe I suggested dinner, Mister Gideon."

"Oh, no, you don't. I pay the tab, Ms. Hall. Make no mistake about that. I don't know what you liberated women think you're doing but no woman draws a credit card on me. If you've forgotten the difference between the sexes—and I don't for a minute think you have—I'll remind you. Waiter, give the lady back her card!"

"It was arranged, sir." The waiter looked nervously at Christina.

"You bet it was!" Simon Gideon opened his wallet, slapped two hundred-dollar bills on the table, and rose. He picked up her mink wrap, helped her to her feet, and, still carrying the wrap, led the way out.

In silence they drove through Washington's white night. He kept his head half turned, watching the bubble of the Capitol dome floating on a base of mist, the pristine shaft of the Monument knifing into the darkness. He knew the city too well, its jungle ruthlessness, its quicksand loyalties, its chimerical successes. Its women suited it. He was never sorry to leave it.

Christina's street was quietly fashionable. Without comment he helped her from the car and followed her into the discreet lobby. At the elevator he stopped.

"Well, Wenda. . . ."

Her futile anger was over. The evening was sliding away. It had both troubled and stimulated her. She was not ready to let go of it.

"Thank you for dinner, Mister Gideon." She paused. "Would you care for a nightcap? Or a peace pipe?"

He grinned, and for an instant she saw the young man in him. In the same curious flash of insight she saw herself, not Christina Hall, brilliantly successful, but teen-age, little Wenda Putly, tremulously longing for a first kiss.

She had never looked more beautiful.

"Thank you, little lady." Simon Gideon bent his balding gray head and with an unexpected courtliness kissed her cheek. "You'd better get some sleep."

Christina did not turn up the lamps in her silent apartment. Instead she dropped into a chair, her mink sliding to the floor. She might have told herself "Mission accomplished!" as she so often did. Instead she sat motionless, thinking about Simon Gideon, the tricks of time, and something she could not name that had passed forever. As Gideon and his magnetism faded another image replaced him. The painful and acute face of a younger woman whom, sight unseen, she hated. The girl who might be with John Roundtree tonight.

In his hotel suite Simon Gideon sipped a brandy and soda and waited for a long distance telephone call to be returned. It was not yet nine o'clock in San Francisco. He'd told the boy to stay in for his call. An order was an order. Yet he was no boy, this next of kin. God knows how he had lived or what he had done before Simon had taken him in. But he was of the blood, defiant, brooding, restless. Like Simon himself. Like Simon's own father.

He poured himself a second brandy. It was not only the silent telephone that irritated him. It was tonight's chivalry. He could have taken that ice-and-steel woman as easily as a sigh. He could have followed her up to her apartment, stripped her of that clinging brown silk. Her body would be too thin, her breasts too flat, her hip bones too prominent. It would be swift, joyless, loveless but, he guessed, primitively satisfying. Christina had a vulnerable earthiness. He would have left her surfeited and forgotten her.

Instead he found himself pacing the long living room of his suite, wondering why any woman wanted to pinch herself into the brittle sexlessness of a career. Put Christina on a ranch, get some flesh on her bones, clean air in her lungs. . . . He smiled wryly at himself. At sixty a man should give up thinking like a young stud. On occasion his heart thumped irregularly; he had been told to cut down on his brandy and his ideas were beginning to show a time lag. Today's women were a new breed.

Not that his father would have agreed. The old man had dominated Simon's life as he had dominated his Gothic-like mansion in San Francisco until the day he was carried out of it, dead at ninety. As corrupt and unrepentant a sinner as ever made the world his pigeon.

"Women aren't any different and never were, son. They get what they want. You just make 'em want it badly enough. Only way to manage 'em. But when you've had enough, you get yourself married. Doesn't much matter who she is as long as she's decent. Get yourself an heir, Simon. That's what matters. The blood goes on."

He would lean back in his invalid chair and chortle at a private joke. "I came west before the turn of the century because I had to, son. But I never regretted it. Frisco was wide open then. Wickedest city on earth. Know what my first job was? Bouncer in a whorehouse in the old Barbary Coast section near the waterfront. Those were the days! And the women!"

Simon had heard it all many times but he could never stop his father, nor did he want to. It was part of his heritage.

"The women. They got what they wanted, all right. There was Big Rooster Nell. Only that wasn't what they called her. Weighed two hundred pounds and eventually ran her own place. She loved the sea, owned a yacht, and never let a sailor get ripped off in her house. There was Petite Marie, known in the trade as Frenchie. Knew more tricks than all of the rest of them put together. Dainty as a valentine, never missed morning Mass. She had a trapdoor beside the bar for when the customers got too rough. Frenchie built an orphanage. They used to say she had to." The old man would chuckle and suck in his breath. "And there was Lady Daisy. Never forgot her either. All class. Always wore white and claimed she came from royalty. She hung the Queen's crest over her bed. Upside down. It didn't hurt business at all."

The old man would lose himself in time, gilded time. If Simon stood up to leave, he would open his eyes abruptly.

"Those were the days, son. I made good, all right. I moved up to bartender, then part owner. Before the earthquake hit Frisco, I owned half a dozen places. All high-toned, elegant. My own mother would have been proud." A shadow would cross the old man's face. Then he would go on.

"You know, son, a lot of people back East, where they take everything for the hand of God, thought the earthquake was a pretty terrible thing. But for this city and for me it was the best thing that ever happened. A lot of rot was swept away. And a lot of old records were lost. That was all to the good. The money was in rebuilding. I got into that. I knew all the politicians—hell, I had met them often enough."

Simon knew the story by heart. His father had emerged as political kingpin, prime power in the rebuilt city. And with that he had moved grandly into the respectability of a thirty-room mansion on the hill.

"But I'll tell you one thing, son. While I was running this city, none of those do-gooders, with their handkerchiefs to their noses, touched those girls. I protected the whole damned waterfront. I'm a grateful man. A lot easier on your conscience. But there was one place I wouldn't protect. Talk about women getting what they want! Miss Lucie Boggs kept a place just to please 'em. It was a whorehouse all right, young male prostitutes to serve well-born ladies from the hill. The ladies wore silk masks when they arrived."

Simon could still hear his father's sly, vigorous chuckle. "It was the only thing those ladies wouldn't take off!"

The old man's rowdiness remained undimmed to his last day. He had risen from his chair, shaken his cane at Simon. "I'm leaving everything to you, Simon, but you get yourself an heir. Hear me! It's the blood that counts. The blood!" With that he had toppled over and into the final splendor of a solid silver coffin.

Simon could live his own life at last, jet-propelled and worldwide. He parlayed his seven-million-dollar inheritance to where he no longer bothered to count. Even without marriage a twist of fate had furnished him with a legitimate heir. He needed only to make sure that the blood ran sound as well as strong.

The telephone spun him back into the present.

"Yes?" He sat down. The return call had come. "Hello, Mike. Where've you been?"

The short answer told him that nothing in life was easy, not even with those he held closest.

"Okay, okay. I've got the name of the man we want. I had heard of him. He's an operator but he's still on the way up, so he's got his price. I'm going to New York tomorrow to see him." He heard a background sound through the receiver, light, provocative, young. "Who's there with you, Mike?"

Again the answer was short.

"I told you to keep your wenches out of my house! Meet me at Boar's Head for the weekend. And don't bring her with you."

But when he put down the receiver, Simon permitted himself a smile. The blood was running true. He poured himself a last brandy and soda. He'd begin giving it up but not tonight. He stretched himself on the divan at last and reflected on an inner lost horizon. A valley made green by the Birch River, a town with a flag on a flagpole and five generations named Roundtree. For the sake of that name, he knew, his father had once killed a man. But when Simon was twelve, the old man had decided, "The name was not worth the keeping. I'm giving you your great-grandmother's name. Start clean." Simon had no idea who his great-grandmother was. At that age it hardly mattered.

Now at sixty, he discovered, to his own surprise, that a man shorn of his name was a man shorn of half his soul. As his father must have realized at the end, blood had a thickness beyond water, beyond common sense. So had a name; the time had come for Simon Gideon Roundtree to go home.

He and Michael.

Chapter Twelve

Big Moon's Diner in Juno's Landing was filling up with the after-work crowd. John Roundtree sat in the last empty booth, watching the door, occasionally glancing at his watch. The man he was to meet was late and John had a six thirty engagement in Thatcher. It was a date he would not be late for under any circumstances. Almost any. Yet here were circumstances enmeshing him again, like tanglefoot glue. He let Big Moon refill his cup from the enormous white coffee pot that was Moon's trademark.

"Cap'll be here, John."

"Sure." John returned to thoughts of Hester Brady. He had not been able to put her out of his mind since the evening he had come on her in Willard's barn with the mare. His impulse to take her into his arms, her sudden soft yielding, their kiss, as fleeting as it was unforgettable, had filled him with a happiness he had not dared admit to himself. She had not resisted that kiss. He was convinced of that. Yet he was not entirely surprised when he had gone to Brady's Pub three hours later as he had promised and found her gone. He returned the following night. She had left early.

"If it's Hester you want to see"—Bantam had eyed him sharply—"she's not around much these evenings. But if you go up to the house before six thirty, you might meet her coming down the path. She usually checks in to see how many's in the pub."

John had gone up the path. The result was less than happy. Her temper flared at the sight of him. "Why can't you leave me alone, John? Dogging my steps, getting in my way, following me. I don't want to see you. Haven't I made that plain? I can't and that's that!"

He was enough of a lawyer to know that 'can't' and 'don't want' are widely different. He did not move from the path.

"Okay. If that's the way you really want it. But every man has a right to his day in court. I'm going back to Washington the end of the week."

"I thought the Congress was over. . . ."

"It is. But the work isn't. And I'm not accomplishing much here." He restrained a smile. "So if you care anything about fair play, you will come out to dinner with me just once. If you tell me then that you never want to see me again, I give my word you never will."

"Isn't there some other girl you could find among all those fancy people in Washington?"

"Certainly. And I may just have to. Do I get my day?"

She had turned her head away, but John would not live on hope. He told himself he only imagined a glint of moisture in her eyes.

"You're stubborn, John. Too stubborn for your own good."

"Never mind my character. Do I get my day in court?"

"I don't know about that. But"—her head went up proudly—"all right. Pick me up here at the house at six thirty tomorrow evening. And don't be late, because my mind isn't very fixed on this."

He looked down at her with a smile that might have told her a great deal if she hadn't brushed past him and walked, head high, down the path to the back door of Brady's Pub.

It was now five thirty and he was still waiting for the one man he had to see before returning to Washington. He thought of Hester, dressing now for their date.

"Hi, John."

He would have risen and shaken hands but the two men passed on quickly to the counter. They were like the others, graying, shabby, still craving that after-five conviviality when they could no longer afford the cost of a bar. They were Juno's Landing men whose ancestors had farmed the land until the living had gone out of it, who had worked in the old brick textile mill now crumbling like some prehistoric monolith in their midst. They were like the oldest trees. While they stayed, the land held firm. Cut down, the land eroded and slid away. Now there was little work for them in Thatcher. They had to go to Pinesville or Bollington, as far east as Waterbury, or to the new plants fringing Hartford. John had made a campaign promise to change all that. He would, he told himself, with the help of God but without surrendering to the Felix Twinings and Ben Orlinis of this world.

Yet he was uneasy. He sensed a distance, a coolness. Even their greetings were brief. It was as if they were measuring him.

Big Moon leaned into the booth.

"Coffee getting cold, John?"

"Sorry about holding this booth so long."

"It's yours. As long as you want it. Cap'll be coming. He likes to keep important people waiting."

"Me? Come on, Moon."

"Especially since he lost his job."

"I didn't know that."

Moon dropped a hamlike hand on John's shoulder. "You've got a lot of friends down here, John. Don't forget that. But they're in trouble. They're looking for you to do the right thing."

"What do they think that is?"

Moon did not answer. Cap Tunbridge scuttled into the booth like a testy crab, a wizened man with three missing front teeth and the gnarled hands of a man willing to work at anything.

"Glad to see you, John. Glad to see you. How's Washington? They still robbin' one pocket to fill the other? Nope no coffee. But if you'd asked me to meet you over at Pete's, I'd have welcomed a glass of beer."

"Next time, Cap. Pete's doesn't open until six."

Cap took out a richly foiled cigar, unrolled it, and lit it with an elaborate gesture.

"You don't mind, John?"

"Nope. Looks like a good one."

Cap Tunbridge leaned back. "What's on your mind, son? Guess I should say Congressman but it comes hard when I remember you in short pants, whaling the hell out of the Blodgett kid for setting fire to a cat."

It was apparent that Cap Tunbridge's tardiness had involved a stop at a more hospitable tavern. John caught a breath of whiskey through the cigar smoke.

"What's on your mind, son?"

"Juno's Landing."

"It ought to be. Things are bad here, Johnnie. When my great-uncle run the old Juno across the river, this valley was the best place on earth for a man to live. Good farms, good cattle. Plenty of work. Why, my great-grandpop made harnesses and saddles he sent all the way to England. Tunbridge Saddlery. Stood right down the road where the used-car lot is. You didn't know this valley then, boy."

"There's a lot I don't know about it now." John glanced at the clock. He could only hope Hester's willingness to see him included a little mellowing patience.

"Cap, I understand there's a lot of land being sold down here. Who's selling?"

"Who's selling?" Cap blew an expansive drift of smoke. "I can tell you, John. I'm selling. Yep, Cap Tunbridge, sixth generation in this valley. I'm selling because there comes a time when a man's a fool to turn down honest cash for something that ain't around anymore and won't never come back. I don't hold with this here nuclear power. The Lord put the sun up there to make seeds grow and to keep us folks warm. Them fellows with their white coats and gadgets who don't even have a window to look out, fur as I can see, ain't satisfied with the Lord's work. They got to find something new even if it blows us all to hell. But the world's spinnin' too fast for me. And when a feller comes around and offers me forty thousand dollars for a house that ain't worth twenty-five—"

"Orlini?"

"Orlini up the Ridge? Hell, no. We haven't seen him around lately. This is a city feller. Don't give his name. Says he represents interests. Sure does. Got the darndest talk you ever heard. He says he'll buy up the four whole square blocks above the old factory, forty thousand dollars for every house, if every house is sold."

"Everybody willing?"

"Nope. Some don't like it. Sounds slick. But we're talking to them. I told Widow Ellie Gates I'd marry her if she'd see the light."

"That's a powerful persuader, Cap."

"She told me that wasn't her idea of a bargain." Cap flicked the ash from his cigar. "That city feller was handing these out three at a time. Best I ever smoked."

"Well, thanks for telling me, Cap. Keep me posted, will you?"

"Sure. But look here, Johnnie, I told you how it is. I got a right to ask where you're standing on it."

"I'm not standing in your way to sell your own house."

"I mean this nuclear thing. You ain't opposing it, are you? You ain't going to try to stop it down there in Washington? If that's what's making this land worth something again, I'm for it. And a lot like me. I tell you if you try to stop it, we're going to fight you down here, all the way."

John was conscious of the silence that trailed him out of the diner.

It was six fifty. He had two miles yet to drive to Thatcher.

Mary Castle Brady opened her front door.

"Why, Jonathan!"

"Haven't heard that for a long time, Mary." John Roundtree stepped into the little front room, bending his head to the low lintel.

"A fine, distinguished name. You never should have let them whittle it down."

"I was in no position to argue with my draft board." John grinned. He knew Mary Brady's soft-voiced firmness from the days when she came with what she called her pie basket to help out at Roundtree celebrations. She was woven into the texture of their lives. That was part of the trouble.

"You're pretty as ever, Mary."

"Oh, go on with you, Jon!" Her smile was girlish. He was delighted to see her chair empty of bed pillows, the quilt neatly folded. And the faint pinkness in her cheeks. She was holding her own.

"I'm late, Mary."

She saw him glance up the stairs.

"Hester's gone out."

"Where?"

"She said you wouldn't be coming anymore this late and she wasn't going to sit around the house." Candor and worry mingled in her look. "I don't know what's in the girl these days. She's not herself. She says one thing and does another. One day she's going to run out on all of us. The next she won't leave Tom alone with the pub. Why, the pub's never done better. Tom's got all the help he needs and he's finding out he can draw the next breath without pouring whiskey after it." Mary's candor was part of her courage. "That's not the worst of it. She tells Tom she's staying here for my sake. Why, I'm feeling fine these days. Besides, I've got that mare out at your uncle's place to worry about. The foal will be coming along soon. I wish Hester would get away from here. Maybe go back to that job in Bollington, in the dress shop. She made a lot of friends there. If I thought she was staying around here for me. . . ."

He heard the unsteadiness. He put an arm around her thin shoulders. "Don't blame your daughter, Mary, if she's as strong-minded as all the Bradys. Where did she go?"

"I hate to tell you. Gus—you know, at the gas station—called her just before seven. Asked her if she'd like a lift down to Pete's. That disco sort of place down at the landing."

"I know."

"Not inviting her, mind you. Just giving her a lift. She went without so much as a look back. When she'll come home, I don't know."

"She'll come home with me, Mary."

"She's as stubborn as a Donegal goat."

"So am I."

Mary laughed. She must have been a very pretty girl, John thought. She had given Hester that fine white skin and that way of smiling that could invite a kiss and break a man's heart at the same time.

"Don't you worry about her, Mary. I'll find her. I asked her to have dinner with me. I intend to keep the date."

Mary Brady closed the door behind him and stood thinking. The fearful, uncontrollable complexity of life. Eight years ago, she had closed the door on another Roundtree. She had never been easy with young Michael, dark and secretive and so sure of himself, looking at you as if he always had more important business behind your back. Hester had never seen that in him nor would it have made any difference if she had. Blind and heedless and in full bloom, she was that mad for him. Mary had kept the worst of it from Tom, even that wild November night, when Michael had stood at the very same door in the beating rain, the anger as low as the black hair on his forehead. He had come to tell Hester he was going away, and Mary, God forgive her, had told the only mortal lie of her life. Hester, she had told him, was out at a party. When the truth was that Hester had driven to Bollington to bring Tom home, dead drunk from a Hibernian wake. How little Mary had known then. But if she had it again to do, she'd tell Michael the same thing. She could find no peace in Hester that summer. Only the young summer madness.

Well, Michael had gone, and here stood John, a fine, true man that any mother would want for her daughter. But a Roundtree. It had never been a part of Mary's plans to mix Hester's life into the Round-trees's. But whoever made plans for their young that didn't unravel the day they took their first step from home? John could hurt Hester without even knowing it. As for Hester. . . . Mary pulled her shawl around her and sighed. Who knew what lay in Hester's mind after these eight years? Hester had buried her pain with a shrug and a laugh. Mary Brady knew how that was done.

It was early for Pete's Rock but a few strobe lights were already fingering the walls and the rock group— four of them, with Pete taking the drums and beating out a low, heady rhythm. John found Hester at a table for six, Gus beside her and four youths around her. He did not know them nor did he waste time admitting it.

"Excuse me, gentlemen. Sorry to keep you waiting, Hester. Let's go, shall we?"

She eyed him stonily. "I'm not going anywhere, John. I'm here. I don't wait more than thirty minutes for any man." She looked white and withdrawn.

"No reason you should. Unless you temper justice with patience."

"Take the weight off your feet, John." Gus was enforcing his priority. "Always room for one more. Move your butts, guys."

"Thanks, Gus." John's smile was easy. "But I have an engagement to take Miss Brady to dinner. I was delayed. I appreciate your looking after her."

"A real pleasure." John did not miss the smirk.

One young man hitched his chair nearer. "Aren't you Roundtree, the congressman?"

"Right."

"Guess you don't know me. I come from upriver, Pinesville. So does Joe here and Fred and Hank."

"How do you do?" John remained standing.

"We voted for you. Now that you're here, we'd like to ask you a few questions."

"Sure, why not?" He could smell the beeriness. They had been here quite awhile, he guessed. "What do you want to know?"

"Oh, for heaven's sake!" Hester sat upright. "We're here for a little fun. If you're going to talk politics, I'm moving out. See what you started, John?"

"We've only got one question. I guess the congressman has time for that."

"What is it?" John felt a chair pushed under him.

"It's just this, Congressman. Yes or no. Are you for this nuclear plant thing on Birch River or against it?"

"I'm against it."

"I don't believe you."

"I'll let that go. This time. There's a lady present."

"A lady?" Eddie grinned. "Where? I don't see any lady. Do you, Hank?"

John half rose, his hands clenched. "Do you want to repeat that? Outside?"

"Sit down, John!" Hester tugged at his sleeve. "They're looking for trouble. Eddie, you big ape, what are you trying to do? John . . . please!"

John already felt his fist in the fleshy jaw. But he could not lose his temper, not here, with Hester beside him. He had faced hecklers before. He knew the rules.

Eddie hunched forward. "Congressman, weren't you

down at Moon's diner tonight talking to Cap Tunbridge? And doesn't Cap and his deadbeat pals stand to make a pile of bucks if the plant goes in?"

"I wouldn't say that."

"I am saying it. Old Cap and a few other people. High and mighty. Now we don't want that plant. And neither do most people in this valley. We don't want its poisons and we don't want its dangers."

"Neither do I!"

"What are you doing about it?"

John thought of Twining and his threat to Thatcher's badly needed bridge. He thought of the tired, shabby old men at the diner. This heckling roughneck had probed to the core of his dilemma. John also understood the hostility. It had nothing to do with the power plant. It was a resentment born into the valley since the first settlers had come, some to own the land, others to work it. How little they understood him. He was aware of Hester's eyes on him. He spoke quietly.

"I am opposed wholly to the nuclear plant. I will do everything within the power of the law to prevent it. But I will also see that fewest possible people are hurt in the process. Does that answer the question?"

Eddie drained his beer glass. "How much are you getting, Congressman, for that?"

A chair fell backwards. Hester was on her feet. "What do you mean by that, you idiot! John Roundtree's the best, the most honest, congressman this place ever had, and you're not good enough for him to spit on! Everything he does is for the good of this valley, and if you haven't found that out, you better go back to the bushes where you belong! Come on, John! Let's get out of here!"

She was on her way out the door. John had no choice but to follow.

It was not until John's car was headed north, well out of Juno's Landing, that Hester allowed herself to sink back in the seat. John gave her a sideways glance.

She was pale and tight within herself, staring straight ahead.

He touched her hand. "Thanks, Hester. With you and a full tank of gas I'd win every vote in Thatcher County."

To his inexpressible astonishment she burst into sobs.

"Wait a minute, Hes." He reached for her hand. She withdrew into the far corner. The sobs continued, long, shaking sobs, torn from her body. He drove silently, bewildered, yet he felt a tenderness that filled his throat. This girl who put such a wall between herself and the world, so alone in her bravado, would never be alone again, he told himself.

Her sobs lessened. John put his arm around her and felt her body, still shaking, curve and relax against him. He drove expertly through the darkness. At last she sat up, slid from his arm, and reached into her bag for a handkerchief. He handed her his own.

"We've passed the pub," she said.

"Certainly."

"Where are we going?"

"Dinner. Remember?"

"No, John. I can't."

He took her hand firmly. "Hester, stop trying to fight the world. In the first place you can't. In the second place it's making a mess of you." Her free hand flew to her hair. "And in the third place you can eat or you can watch me. I'm hungry."

"Those—punks!"

It was not the heckling that had brought those sobs. But he let that go. Some other time he would try to understand them. Just as some other time he would explain to her that his tormentor had been right. He, John, must make his position clear, unchallengeable. But tonight her hand lay curled in his. He tightened his grasp. Had they at last come to a very small place, tenuous as it was, that they could make their own?

They stopped at a roadside tavern twenty miles beyond Thatcher. They sat on a shabby glass-enclosed porch, with a gutted candle on a wine bottle, a checkered tablecloth, and the neon sign outside flashing red and yellow on their faces. They ate manicotti and drank raw red wine. Hester said almost nothing, yet John sensed that she was not unhappy. The bravado was gone, with the flashy smile and shrug. Something simple, youthful remained, something that John knew he wanted beside him for the rest of his life.

He ate hungrily. "Not bad."

"I can make better."

"I didn't know you cooked Italian."

"I cook what they want at the pub."

"Doesn't Tom have a chef?"

"Yes, but most of the time he would rather drink with him than cook for him."

He had an answer to that but not now. He started on a side dish of spaghetti.

"You're a good doer, all right."

"What's that?"

"A horse with a good appetite."

"Thanks. I mean, I think so."

He grinned, emptied the red wine into their glasses. Their eyes met, a sweet, slow look as if the world went no farther than the checkered tablecloth. Again the tenderness choked him. She looked away first.

"Let's play something on the jukebox."

"Sure. You choose."

"No. You."

"Come on. We'll both choose."

He dropped four quarters into the machine. They alternately pushed buttons, once on the same button. He held her finger down.

"Ours."

They laughed and returned to the table.

"I like it here, John."

He nodded.

"Because here you're not a congressman."

"Can't you forget that?"

"No. That's what makes it all impossible."

"You want to talk about it?"

"We have to, sometime. I like seeing you. I guess I don't hide that very well. But I can't. And you know it."

He pushed the half-finished spaghetti from him. "Okay. Let's have it out. I don't know why you can't see me and I'm sick of the word. Can't. Doesn't fit you."

She spoke deliberately as if each word were meant to tear an invisible fabric.

"I can't see you, John, because I'm Michael's old girl that he walked out on and you're his brother with a big career ahead of you."

"Did you enjoy saying that?"

"No. But it's the way it is and nothing's going to change it." Her voice trembled. She stiffened to control it. "You found Michael and me up there on the Ridge. You told your father. If you hadn't, maybe he wouldn't have hated me so. Maybe Michael wouldn't have walked out on me."

John drew a long breath. He wanted to tell her how wrong she was. How she was hurting him. But something much deeper had surfaced. They had come to the only fact that mattered.

"I never told Dad anything. I saw you once on the Ridge with Michael. I hated his guts then. I still do. My own brother. He took whatever he wanted. I never dared. But I never told on him. That doesn't matter now. Nothing matters except one thing, Hester. That I have to know." He hesitated. He had postponed the question as long as he could. The answer when it fell, like the Greek sword, might cut him forever from all he wanted.

"Are you still in love with Michael?"

"No."

"Is that because he's been gone so long?"

"No."

But he was not satisfied. "If he walked into this place this moment, what would you—"

"No, John! I won't answer any more questions. I shouldn't have come out this evening. What happened, between Michael and me, happened! And nothing can change it! You go your way, John, and I'll go mine. That's the only thing that's possible! Please drive me home!"

He had his answer. He did not really mind. In the face of her anger he tried to conceal the new hope he glimpsed. He believed her. She did not love Michael. But it would take time. Time was on his side.

He drove her to the parking area of the pub. But he did not release her.

"I'm going in, John, to see if Tom's all right."

"I'll go with you. In just a minute." He put his arm across her to hold the door latch. "I asked for my day in court. I'm going to have it. I don't care what happened between you and Michael. I've lived with it. I've got it behind me. I love you, Hester. I want you with me for the rest of my life. Will you marry me?"

"Marry?"

She stared at him so bleakly that he wished she would cry again. He could deal with that. But whatever had shaken her before drained away. He saw only a numb incomprehension in her face.

"Marry?" she repeated. "You—marry me?"

"Tomorrow, if you say so."

But she was fighting something inside her, fighting it alone.

"Hester, what is it? If you're holding on to something dead and gone in the past, then I'll fight it with you. The past is over. Nothing that happened then could make any difference today. I love you. I want you. I'll wait as long as I have to to marry you. I want you, Hester, every way a man can—lover, mistress, wife."

"Don't, John. Just—don't! I can't marry you."

"Because you don't love me?"

"Because—" her shoulders sagged—"because I do love you."

The parking area was not quite dark enough for him to take her into his arms. Her face was at once stricken and yearning, fearful and innocent. He would win now or he would lose forever.

"Hester, I have to go back to Washington. I'll be here on Thanksgiving. I have two weeks after that to myself. If you won't marry me now, will you give us a chance to be together? Just the two of us. No Thatcher, no past. You and I, Hester. . . ."

She was so silent that he wondered whether she understood. Yet he knew she was as aware of him as he was of her, of a powerful desire binding them together as it had over the shabby little table in the tavern.

"I know a place we can go. It's a ski lodge up in the mountains, a good hundred miles from here. It belongs to a friend of mine. He was going to develop a ski resort"—he was talking to fill time, to keep her beside him—"but the money ran out. He doesn't come north now. I have the key. I want to go up there for a few days. Hester, it's the cleanest place in the world! Clean snow. Clean mountains. Clean pine trees, fifty feet tall. And the silence. That's clean too. Will you come with me?"

She looked past him to the pub. One light had gone out. It was nearly closing time. The cramped little house behind it was still bright with waiting. The familiar present, the binding past.

"If you don't want marriage yet, Hester, that's up to you. Someday you'll be my wife. But give us a chance now, my darling!"

She started to answer but his fingers touched her lips. "No. Don't tell me tonight, I'll be back Wednesday. We'll go right after the holiday."

He kissed her, realizing that she did not respond. She sat stiff, unmoving in a world he could not reach.

He opened the car door. "I'll walk you up to the house."

"No, please, John. I'd rather go alone." She gave him a ghost of a smile. In the half-light she looked young, untouched. Again he wanted to take her in his arms. But she had set a fragile distance between them. He would give her time.

He waited outside the car, watching her climb the path to the house. She had given him no answer but she had not rejected him. Nothing on earth would come between them now.

As she closed the door behind her Hester heard the car's engine start, build to a crescendo, and fade, like the beating of her own heart.

Soon after, Tom Brady closed down the pub for the night. He had seen the figures in the parking area. The silhouette of John's head. Hester's tossed hair. They had stayed there too long to suit him. Tom Brady was a humble man, born in a famine-humbled place, the County Mayo, God help him. But he knew who he was. He would fight any man who looked down on him or his family. Or hurt his girl in any way. Especially a Roundtree. One was bad enough and that one had cleared town long ago and good riddance.

But as he climbed the path he knew he would have little to say. Hester was a grown woman, nostriled and spirited as a Galway mare. What was worse, he knew nothing about her nowadays.

As he opened the door he heard Mary call from the downstairs bedroom.

"Yes, it's me, Mary."

"Hester's home. I heard her."

He grunted a reply.

"There's a warm meat pie in the oven, Tom."

"I'll find it."

Instead he climbed the stairs. There was still a crack of light under Hester's door. He turned the knob, then changed his mind and knocked. She was hardly even his own child anymore. Like a guest. Or maybe a bird that might fly before dawn.

She was sitting on the bed, still dressed as she had come in from the evening. Her eyes were as bright as coals, her face milk-white. He felt awkward.

"Just come to say good night."

"Good night, Da."

He lingered. "Have a nice evening?"

"I went out with John. A spaghetti place."

"I saw you come back." But any question stuck like a fishbone in his throat. He cleared it. "Your mother's looking better."

"Yes."

"Good night, girl."

"Good night."

That's all he would ever know, Bantam told himself, from his only child. He went downstairs, carried the meat pie to his sagging chair in front of the television, and drew from his pocket a pint of Irish whiskey. Age was a lonely business. He should have brought a quart. But a pint showed character.

Hester undressed slowly, turned out the light, and walked to the single window in her small room, made smaller by the slope of the roof. The pub's sign was out, thank goodness. Only the streetlight remained and the glancing lights of an occasional car. All too occasional, before the night revealed its emptiness.

She was Hester Brady. The past stood fixed and unchangeable. The present lay at her feet like a trap. Tonight, as they had left Pete's, she had wanted to fling herself into John's arms. Instead she had wept. He had asked her to marry him. *Marry* him. She would never forget that. There would be time ahead to remember that. And to remember a distant white and mystic place glittering with snow and sun and love where for a few days she had been with John. A few days that would hurt no one, not even themselves.

Hester knew her answer too before she fell asleep. The radiance of her decision lay like peace on her face. A few days with John.

To fill the rest of her life.

Chapter Thirteen

A spearhead of wild geese flew so low under the leaden sky that Willard Roundtree, on the porch of his farmhouse, could hear the brush of their wings. The valley lay cold, silent, and waiting. Any moment the first flake of snow would spring the trap of winter. Three or four crows perched in ruffled black in the maple tree. He liked crows, handsome, hard-working birds who cleansed the land and the roads of small carrion.

But he had no time this morning to dwell on the completeness of things. It was already nine o'clock. By one the house would bulge with every Roundtree he could summon for his long-established celebration of Thanksgiving. It was not only the occasion to display a Yankee feast of his own cooking, it was his special time to take stock, count noses, scent out rifts, and generally see that if family affairs were not advancing, they were not backsliding. He had not many years left to serve as ballast. He counted on John to take over. He had not seen enough of John lately.

A first flake fell on his coat sleeve, then a second. Fine, dry, triangular, and lasting. It heralded a heavy storm. In the old days that meant hospitality, overnight visitors. Today it meant traffic worries. As he turned into the house he heard the car. In another moment it had rounded the curve, black, less than new, but sound of engine as befitted a congressman from Thatcher County. John was early indeed. He came up the path carrying a lumpy bundle and followed Will into the kitchen.

"Thought I'd bring the governor over early; I have a few things to do. What's it going to do out there, Will?"

"Snow, the same as you've known every winter since you were born."

"The radio says heavy-storm warnings."

"So do the crows. If you listened to those radio fellows, you'd think nobody should set a foot out of the house unless it's seventy degrees in full sun. And then the windchill factor could frighten you back. Where do they broadcast from, those people? A feather bed in a subcellar?"

Willard briskly unwrapped the old quilt around the bundle. What emerged was a fifteen-inch bronze replica of the famous nineteenth century statue of the Pilgrim Father, broad hat, flowing cape, and buckled shoes.

"The old boy looks as tough as ever."

"He believed in God, administered justice, and prayed for the next supply ship from England. And if he'd ever had that much cloak to wrap around him, he'd have asked forgiveness."

Willard carried the statuette into his old-fashioned parlor. The furniture had been pushed back and a long, tressled table took up the length of the room. It was covered with a coarse gray cloth and a long-running centerpiece of dried goldenrod and swamp grass, red and yellow corn, and a lavish sprinkling of hazel and hickory nuts. Willard set the statuette in the center. The Pilgrim Father indeed looked at home.

"How many coming this year, Will?"

"Not more than a dozen. Though I've set for fourteen. I hope each year Lili will get some sense and join us, she and her man. Claude's in some playacting group in Denver and writes that the show must go on, whatever that means. Hutch is flying freight to Hong

Kong. It doesn't sound like much of a marriage to me. But then times have changed."

John concealed a smile. Willard Roundtree's homespun style, adopted on these occasions, concealed the shrewdest legal mind in the state and the most knowing.

"Lowell's driving up from the city this morning." Willard rested a fine, strong hand on a ladder-back chair as if Lowell were already seated there. "Hope she left early. There's Ariel, up beside me, and baby Susan—I got the old highchair down from the attic. Duncan'll say grace. Emily's coming with them. Duncan's taken good care of his mother since Harlan died. But Emily's faded. Married to the old rascal thirty-eight years. I guess a woman doesn't let go of that so easily." Willard shook his head. "I wish it were going better for Duncan. Fine a man as you could meet, but I'm not sure how far you can push a square peg into a round hole. Sometimes I wonder if he shouldn't cut clear out of the ministry. The young folks like his ideas when they've got time to think about them. But it's the old folks who support that church. Well, I keep my ideas to myself until somebody wants to hear them. Ariel's too thin but more beautiful than ever. Put her in her great-grandmother's dress and she'd be Henrietta to the life. Hard on her here. But anything Duncan does is right. So I guess it doesn't matter if the wind blows through that house they live in." Willard completed the circuit of the table.

"This will surprise you, John, but at my age a man can't postpone things he'd like to do. I asked Mary and Tom Brady and Hester. We've got one member of that family down in the barn now, and a fine mare she is. Seems the rest of 'em ought to be up here too. Martin might get a little dyspeptic, but a hot rum will take care of that. In my view that's what Thanksgiving's for—to mend fences. Well, I didn't expect they'd come. Tom Brady's the only Irish porcupine I ever knew."

He gave John a sharp glance but John seemed to be studying the table.

"Well, maybe it's just as well, Johnny. Tom drove Mary over here to the barn last week, and when he saw the nameplate Charlie Redwing had put on the mare's stall, he drove right home and brought back his own. He said Kikijeb was no fit name for an honest, God-fearing horse. I'm not sure Doxy is any better. It may just work up to the first Irish-Indian war in history."

John laughed and shifted restlessly and regretted it. "Charlie will be here?"

"It's part of our contract. I told him he needn't ever set foot in my house or my kitchen with any company he didn't want. Except on Thanksgiving. His people were at the old governor's first Thanksgiving. Charlie's going to be at every one I hold. Right there." Will nodded toward the end of the table. "Well, there's Clancy wanting to go out."

The huge red Irish setter had emerged from his place near the stove, wagged courteously at John, and moved to the front door.

"All right, Clancy. Sometimes I think you hear the snow before it falls." Will opened the front door. The great dog trotted out.

"Here I am standing around as if I hadn't three bass to clean for steaming. Dinner's at one, John. Come early as you like. I don't hold with cocktails spoiling a man's taste but there's hot rum and mulled wine. . . ."

"Thanks, Will." John controlled an impulse to talk about Hester to this all-seeing, all-knowing old man, to trust him with the radiant turn his life had taken. But not yet. Not until Hester stood beside him. "So it's bass today?"

"And venison, wild duck, currant stuffing, white and yellow turnips, spiced beets, barley loaves, corn pudding, gooseberry and squash pie. All authentic and from that land out there. I was going to add squir-

rel stew," Willard's eye twinkled. "But I didn't think
the ladies would sit still for that. And no turkey. No
use telling them there hasn't been a wild turkey in this
valley for nearly a hundred years now."

He watched John walk down the porch steps and
get into his car, telling himself he had kept the young
man too long. And yet he had not brought himself to
the subject that bulked largest in his mind. The letter
had come yesterday and now lay in his wallet. He was
old. He had no right not to share it with someone. A
man could die suddenly and what he knew, what he
believed, would die with him. Willard turned back
into the living room, angered at himself. He was not
ready to let go. That was the crux of the matter. He
had held the family and the land together against all
cracking and splitting, just as he drew them to this
house and this table on this annual occasion, by his
willpower.

He drew the letter from his wallet. It was brief,
blunt, handwritten.

My dear Willard,
    As my late father said, there is only one Round-
tree now in Thatcher with enough sense to remain solvent. I would like to meet with you. I
think it would be of advantage to us both. I shall
be coming east in mid-January to stay in my New
York apartment for four weeks. During this time
I hope to consolidate and advance my interest in
the Birch River valley, to the mutual gain of us
all.
    As you may or may not know, Michael is with
me. He has been with me for three years. He will
stay with me. Whether you care to divulge this
information is of no interest to me, but I hope
you will see the wisdom of our meeting.

                           Yours truly, sir,
                           Simon G. Roundtree.

He should have been more surprised than he was. He had seen Michael once himself and kept the secret. What Michael had become could give no reassurance to his family now. Nor to Martin who waited in the deluded hope of reunion, of apology and reinstatement. Michael was the true spawn of Isaac Roundtree, as was old Simon and this second Simon, all inheritors of the brooding darkness of that fierce, demon-possessed man lying now for more than fifty years on the hilltop of Thatcher Cemetery, beneath festooned granite. It was inevitable that his line would return. It belonged here long before the fire and light of young Henrietta came from New Orleans to warm it.

Willard folded the letter abruptly into his wallet. Time was pressing him. But not now, not today. There was John, standing in the door of the future, with a new light on his face.

Willard went into the kitchen, tied a butler's apron of striped ticking around his waist, and took three large silvery bass wrapped in brown paper from the ice, flapped them on to a board, and began expertly to scale them.

Willard enjoyed the work in hand, as he enjoyed this day of drawing his family back to essentials, his mind running ahead of them like a keen-nosed Irish setter.

"We are omnibuses in which all our ancestors ride." Did anyone read Oliver Wendell Holmes anymore? The old words returned now, oddly consoling. Do what he could, the blood would run wild or dark or sweet again. He could only temper it with compassion. He had been right not to show Simon's letter to John. The challenge was his, Willard's. As long as a challenge remained, he would endure.

As the lucent scales flew from his knife he began to whistle. It was an Irish air, and he remembered where he had heard it last. It was a tune Mary Castle Brady had hummed as she stood gently rubbing the mare's cheek, Hester's mare.

* * *

A powdering of snow was already coating the road as John slowed his car at the fork to the Ridge. He turned toward the main road but not before he had seen the tire tracks of a single car headed up the Ridge. Or down. He could not tell which.

Ultimately he would have to confront Ben Orlini on the nuclear issue. But he had faced Orlini before and discovered that the slippery, black-haired little man in his pointed shoes was not so much ruthless as frightened. Whatever tightrope Ben Orlini walked was of his own making. No, it was not Orlini who held the last threat. It was the unknown. The nameless stranger with invisible resources who had come to strike at Thatcher's being.

With that John pushed the matter from his mind. A great deal had cleared for him since that last evening with Hester. He had the eagerness of a schoolboy to see her now. He would not press marriage too soon. He would only beg her for a time for themselves. This snow would turn the haven he had chosen into a private Eden. They would drive up there on Tuesday. The roads would be passable, the snow deep and virginal, silencing the earth, hooding the pines, and wrapping the lodge in the white radiance of their first hours together.

He swung the car into the pub's little parking area and took the path up to the house in long bounds. To his surprise she slid out the front door, in parka, slacks, and boots.

"It's better this way, John. I saw your car."

"Anything wrong?"

"Oh, no." She laughed. It was light, easy, and John found his heart pounding. She had not come in this mood to say no. "Da's still at his sausages, in his socks. Mom's doing the corned beef."

"Corned beef. On Thanksgiving?"

"And cabbage. He doesn't care what else is on the

table but it's no holiday without that. The way she caters to that man!"

"You're against it?" It was banter, but his voice was deep with warmth. She had never looked lovelier to him. The snowflakes sprinkling her rich, auburn hair, her face fresh and glowing as the winter morning.

"What do you think? There's no man on earth I'd cook two dinners at once for. Turkey for us, and something special for him. Always special."

"Remember that, my girl." John pulled the car door shut and resisted kissing her. He sensed that something more than Tom Brady's tastes lay behind her quick escape from the house. He headed the car onto the main road and turned west, away from town.

"I didn't expect you this morning, John."

"Why not?"

"Holiday. Your family. All that. They wouldn't think much of this."

"Hester, I live my own life and it's going to be—" He stopped. He wouldn't press her yet. It was enough that she was here.

"Where are we going?"

"Out to the lake. We can get in as far as the boathouse. I have a present for you."

She was content to sit in silence and watch the falling snow starburst against the windshield. She was content to let him take her hand. When he put his arm around her and drew her close, she was content too. It was all he had hoped for, this prelude to their future. Their long, bright future, without end.

The road into the lake was barred with a chain. He parked the car and took a long, flat package from the back of the car.

"What's that?"

"It's for you. I'll show you."

The boathouse was locked. The frozen lake was whitening. Sharp-edged fir trees and the lacy web of bared branches thrust into the gray sky in silhouetted black.

An occasional roof along the lake's edge emitted a
feather of pale smoke.

"It's pretty."

"Not a patch on Snowgoose."

"What's Snowgoose?"

"The ski lodge we're staying in next week." It was a
sudden parry but John could not wait in suspense any
longer.

"I don't know how to ski."

"You won't have to. That's why I brought you a
present."

He tore off the outer wrapping. Under that it was
gift-wrapped, and he let her finish, her face as young
as he had ever seen it. She burst into a sudden laugh,
and a little of the skeptical Hester returned.

"Snowshoes!"

"It's the best to get through the big woods in deep
snow. And that's what I want to show you. The forest,
Hester—white, with the sun slanting through the great
pines and the smaller trees bent over beneath the snow
like women in shawls or even nuns. I used to think
that. And not a sound. Except maybe a woodpecker or
a slide of snow. And the animals' tracks. I can show
you where a field mouse has crossed the path of a rabbit and a fox has dragged his quarry." He broke off,
aware of her eyes on him, lingering, serious.

"Here, let me put the snowshoes on you and you can
give them a try. They're not too long, or too wide. You
won't have any trouble. The Indians didn't need skis
like the Norwegians for long, open mountain slopes.
They used these for tracking through the woods. See?
Just a tough branch of hickory bent clear back on itself. Strips of caribou hide or deerskin for a mesh. And
there you are!"

He knelt beside her, took her booted foot to place
into the leather thong. His hand slid above the boot,
and suddenly the touch was more than he could bear.

"Hester. . . ."

He stood up abruptly, and she was in his arms, willingly, clingingly. He kissed her lips, her eyes, her face.

"Hester. . . ."

"John—John. . . ."

His hands would have groped through her thick outer garments but at the sound of a distant car she moved from him. They stood looking at each other, the snow blinding yet oddly intensifying their vision. Her eyes filled with tears.

"Hester! My darling girl!"

"Don't you see, John? It's always going to be like that. A car horn and we—we jump apart! As if it were all wrong. And we were guilty."

"Do you think we are?"

"No."

"Will you come to Snowgoose with me next week?"

"Yes."

He took her in his arms again, and their kiss was long and deep with promise.

"I'm not good at waiting, Hester."

"Neither am I."

But they would wait a little longer for the place that would be their own. He picked up the snowshoes and reached for reality. "I'll pack them with mine. You'll love them once you get the hang of it. The trick is to slide one inner edge over the other as you walk."

"I see."

They said little or nothing on the drive back. It was enough to hold hands and to let the awareness of love fill the little car.

"I'll call you tonight, Hester."

"No. Please. Don't call me. Where do I meet you?"

He sighed. Now the lies would begin, the lies he hated. "I'll pick you up at your house Tuesday."

"No. All right. I'll tell them you're driving me to Hartford. They want me to get away."

"It won't always be like this, Hester."

She did not answer. Her face was set expressionless toward the whirling snow.

"Want to stop somewhere for coffee?"

"No, thanks."

At the pub she hastily opened the door on her side. He reached for her hand.

"I love you, darling."

"I must go, John." She managed a small laugh. "Who's going to press Da's corned beef if I don't?" She slid out so quickly, he barely managed to meet her in front of the car.

"Hester?"

"Please, John. . . ."

"You won't change your mind? You won't let anything happen? You'll come with me?"

She nodded. Then he saw the mask of indifference settle on her face, heard the light mockery in her voice.

"Be seeing you, John. Happy turkey! Don't ask for the part that goes over the fence last!"

She was gone, the soft yielding girl who was veiled in snow at the lakeside. She was Hester Brady, bright, valiant, hard-edged, running up the path and shaking the snow from her hair. There was so much she did not know, so much of gentleness, of safety, of beauty he longed to teach her. One lifetime would not be enough. But he knew that with the happiness she brought him, she could break his heart. As she turned from him he had seen the glint of tears in her eyes.

It was ten minutes past one when John entered Willard Roundtree's crowded living room to meet the delectable odors of roasting duck and spices. And, unmistakably, a curious, quiet tension.

"John, where've you been?" Kim, the youngest of the Roundtrees, caught his sleeve. Her brown hair was cut short, and now her chubbiness was lengthening into grace. She's going to be pretty, he thought.

He ruffled her hair. "Busy, peanut."

"I wanted to come here with you when you brought the governor over but when I got downstairs, it was gone from Dad's desk." She stopped, uncomfortable in the silence.

"Bad planning. Sorry I'm late, everybody."

"It's Lowell, John." Edythe spoke nervously. "She isn't here yet."

"She called us from New York, this morning at eight. Said don't worry." Martin had his pocket watch in his hand as if it were to blame. "She would be here before the snow. It takes two hours and a half, not five, from New York." His father looked blanched in the afternoon light. Beside him Duncan stood tall and serious. Ariel had drawn little Susan close. They were all looking at him.

At the small-paned windows the snow pressed closer. Willard emerged from the kitchen, small Emily Phelps encased in the butler's apron behind him.

"You stay there, Willard, with your family. I'll tend to things on the stove. Though in all my days I never saw anything to match what you've got in those pots. One good twenty-pound turkey would have taken care of everybody." She felt needed. Her artificial cheerfulness was her own gift to the crisis.

Willard was direct. "I've called the police, Martin. There's no report of an accident. I've sent Charlie down in the truck to the state highway. The snow's dry and blowing off the roads, so far. Lowell's a good driver. Sensible. She's not really late yet. John, how did you find the driving?"

No secrets, thought John. Everything must be present and accountable. Still he was more concerned than he would show. This was not like Lowell.

"Not bad, sir. Not bad at all. Lowell probably got a later start than she intended."

"If she'd taken the train to Hartford and then the bus, we'd know when to expect her. This long driving for a young woman alone. . . ." Martin's worry showed in irritation.

"I'd count on her to be all right, Mister Roundtree." Three years ago Duncan would have sounded presumptuous. He had been engaged to marry Lowell, when she had abruptly broken it off. The tissue of family ties had overgrown the scars but no one had forgotten. No one, thought John, ever forgot anything. He wondered what it would be like when he brought Hester into this close circle. Maybe he should take her to the other side of the world and escape from it all. "I like the treason, I hate the traitor," winged through his mind.

"I think we should have dinner, Will." Martin snapped shut his watch case. "If she isn't here in half an hour, I'll call the police myself."

The ritual began as always. Willard drew a piece of paper from his pocket, rose and looked down the table. They had heard it so often. Today he knew they would be barely listening. Yet nothing must be changed. At the far end of the table Charlie Redwing sat in stiff, silent courtesy. Tolerance, thought Willard. Tolerance for a lesser wisdom. He settled his glasses.

"From the account of the first Thanksgiving, from Edward Winslow. Massachusetts Bay Colony. December eleven. The year sixteen twenty-one." Willard held them with a glance and began to read. " 'You shall understand that, in the little time that a few of us have been here, we have built seven dwellinghouses and four for the use of the plantation. We set last spring some twenty acres of Indian corn. We sowed some six acres of barley and peas. We manured our ground with herrings and shads. Our corn did prove well, God be praised. Our barley indifferent. Our peas not worth gathering. But our harvest being gotten in, we rejoiced together after our labors, many of the Indians amongst us and their King Massasoit, whom we entertained for three days. Although it is not always so plentiful, yet by the goodness of God we are so far from want that we wish you partakers of our plenty.' "

Willard folded the paper, nodded to Duncan who rose.

John snapped back to the present with a start and wondered if his truancy had been guessed. Willard's well-worn and polished words had been a shield while he sat imagining Hester beside him, her bright direct-ness winning them, lighting the table, secure in the as-surance of his love. She would make the twelfth at the table, a good round number. She would fill the empty chair. His mind was playing tricks. Years ago Willard had set one empty place at the table, in the tradition of the isolated Yankee farmers for a traveler who lost his way or needed shelter from a storm or rest for his horse. After Michael's disappearance there was no longer any empty chair. It had suddenly become only mute and painful evidence of defection. Michael. What if he were here now, the thirteenth, the odd one . . . or was John himself the odd one? John felt his chest tighten. He was looking straight into the di-lemma he had so far refused to face. Michael, sitting opposite, looking at Hester in his bold way. Hester smiling back, caught again by his dark appeal. Both remembering—remembering. John's fist came down on the table. Eyes, suddenly startled, stared. He caught his father's frown, his mother's incredulity, Ariel's warm-eyed surprise, Kim's throttled giggle. John bowed his head, as Duncan's voice rolled richly on.

". . . so on this Thanksgiving Day, in the year of nineteen seventy-three, we thank Thee, Lord, for all the gifts from this land. May we serve its strengths and its freedoms our forefathers found here. May we dedi-cate ourselves again to the harvest of those strengths and those freedoms for the benefit of all men."

The ritual was over. John lifted his head again, not to reveal his chagrin but because these were words he believed in. There was the usual split second of silent deference, followed by the usual burst of talk as if each were slightly embarrassed by this exposure to sen-timent and faith.

The women rose to start serving, Edythe dropping a hand on Ariel's shoulder.

"Sit down, dear, and liven the table. Your turn will come. Kimmie, the mare will still be in the barn after dinner."

Martin's eyes were on the window. "Snow's getting heavier."

John felt a compassion toward the thin, fading man who was his father, his sense of purpose outdated, his fine hands feeling the slipping of the reins.

"If you're thinking of Lowell, Dad, I reckon she's turned back to the city. There have been traveler's warnings for some time now."

"Of course I'm thinking of Lowell. Whom else would I be thinking of? She's never heeded warnings of any kind. Any more than any of your generation." His anxiety took a testier turn. "What's going on down at Juno's Landing these days? Are you going to let this nuclear thing go through?"

"I'm going to do everything I can to stop it, sir. You know that."

"I expect you're as capable of compromise as the next man. There's no room for that."

"John's in a difficult position, I would think, Martin." Willard, gently uncorking a wine bottle, concentrated on his task. "If he opposes the bill too openly, he stands to lose federal funds for the bridge we need."

"Rubbish. A man stands for what he stands for."

"I agree with you, Uncle Martin." Ariel laid a light hand on Martin's sleeve and smiled ravishingly. "Compromise is the hobgoblin of little minds."

"Consistency, my darling. Not compromise." There was a burst of laughter, including Ariel's.

"You must excuse my wife, gentlemen." Duncan took Ariel's hand. "Her Paris upbringing taught her many things, more than she should have known, probably. But English words of more than three syllables were not among them. To my relief."

"Golly, Duncan," Kim had never lost her youthful adoration. "You hardly ever sound like a minister."

"So the parish seems to think."

"Duncan. . . ." Ariel leaned over and kissed him.

Marriage, thought John. Marriage. It was what he wanted more than anything in life now. Marriage to Hester.

Willard's fish chowder arrived on the table.

Suddenly, without warning, Charlie Redwing rose to his feet. He said nothing. They waited in surprise.

"Listen! Do you hear?"

Faintly, from the distance, came Clancy's deep-throated bark, repetitious, grating.

"Clancy's treed something, Charlie. Maybe a raccoon. He'll get tired," Willard waved a hand.

"No." Charlie pushed back his chair and went to the door, flinging it open.

"Charlie, you'll freeze us out!" Someone called.

Charlie closed the door, went to the closet, and came back in his thick woodsman's jacket.

"What is it, Charlie!" Willard rose. "You think a deer's caught on the ice?"

"It is something different." Charlie opened the door again. The bark was nearer. "He's coming to us. I will go meet him. He will show me." His eyes met Willard's. He went out into the driving snow.

"I'm going with him. John, you come." Willard spoke quietly. "The rest of you stay here. We don't want to have to go looking for you in this storm."

"Will, your lovely dinner!"

"Edythe, how do you keep steamed bass warm?"

"Martin, you and I better work on the hot rum. They'll need it."

The door closed on the tide of voices.

Across the field Willard and John could see Charlie Redwing running in the distance. The big dog was racing toward him. They saw Clancy begin to run in circles, away from Charlie, back to him. As Willard and John caught up with them the dog broke away, galloping toward the Ridge. His heavy paw prints were not difficult to follow in the deepening snow.

Clancy was soon lost in the curtain of the storm but the tracks held sure and steady. They led into rougher ground of cattails and frozen marsh, and finally to the edge of the icy swamp.

"Oh, my God, Will!"

Half in broken ice, half on the wet bank, Lowell lay, her face bruised, her parka torn. She was unconscious but she was breathing.

Chapter Fourteen

Ben Orlini rocked back and forth on his small, neat feet and looked out his bedroom window at the bleakness that was Thatcher County. It reflected the bleakness in his own soul. He had asked Alec Bookman to meet him in his study in ten minutes. But this time he would keep Alec waiting. With pleasure. He did not intend to consult with Alec. He would ask one question only, then he would announce his decision. It brought him relief but no satisfaction. He stood, on this Thanksgiving Day, at the highest peak of his career. His name was known, his advice sought in half the world's capitals. He had aligned himself with a prestige beyond his most youthful imaginings. And yet the moment brought the taste of ashes to his mouth, the exhausted grayness of this winter sky.

Thanksgiving. At home that had meant eight or ten children, a score of aunts and uncles, grandparents, a new baby somewhere in the house, a kitchen full of chattering women, an ancient one sitting shawled by the stove. It meant the smells of a roast mingled with pasta sauces, it meant. . . .

He started to draw the heavy drapes against the whirling whiteness outside and thought better of it. That would only encast him in the dead whiteness of this bedroom. White, browns, rust, blacks. Julia had said the house must be a background for the view. And he a man with the love of color burned into his heart. But he had given in, as he so often did, for the peace of going his own way. Now their ways were the world's width apart and widened further each passing year by the son they had somehow managed to destroy. Not that Ben Orlini would accept that guilt. The indulgence had been Julia's, as it still was. But if he had stayed closer. If? Would he be where he stood now, able to offer Nick his shattered life restored and whole?

Nick had improved steadily. His setbacks had come always after a visit from Julia. Alec Bookman did not need to tell him that. Ben could see it for himself. This weekend he had forbidden Julia to come to Thatcher. He had come himself to take Nick out of this cotton cocoon. He had told Simon Gideon any agreement between them must include a place for Nick. Alec himself had said Nick might be ready soon.

Alec Bookman was standing when Ben entered the elegant little study with its walnut paneling, its studded red leather chairs and its shelves of matched sets of unread books. Alec was as careful in his deference as he was in his tailoring. The dark, patterned silk handkerchief stuffed in his blazer pocket added elegance to his cashmere turtleneck sweater and managed to irritate Ben unreasonably.

"Well, what happened?"

"When, sir?"

"You heard it and I heard it. Is Nick home?"

"Oh, yes, he's in his room, resting. He had an excellent walk. He does quite well on his own now."

"What about that cry?"

Alec smiled tolerantly. "There was no cry, sir. What you possibly heard was a large bird, a crow, or perhaps the yelp of a dog."

Ben had not asked Alec to sit down. He took his own chair.

"I don't 'possibly' hear things, Alec. I heard a woman's call. More like a scream."

"There is no sign that anyone has been up on the Ridge. I went over the whole route that Nick usually takes. Down the drive, to the path at the bottom of the

Ridge, along the edge of the valley, then up the path behind the herb cellar. It's a walk he enjoys even in this weather. It does him a great deal of good."

Ben studied the wall behind Alec's head.

"Sit down, Alec. I believe you, of course. But I must know every facet of my son's behavior. Particularly now. Any irregularity would be most unfortunate for us all."

"I assure you, Mister Orlini, Nick is as normal as I had ever hoped for in this relatively short time we have worked together. I should of course like more time."

"Does he still see that girl? The Roundtree girl?"

"You were in favor of it, sir."

"I was in favor of his seeing women. My God, he's a man, isn't he? But I think we can dispense with that one. He'll meet plenty of others in New York. His own type."

"You've quite made up your mind to this move, sir?"

"I'm driving Nick back to New York with me tomorrow. I want him to get used to the city again, to the apartment. I want to get him some decent clothes, take him to a few shows. He is to meet Mister Gideon next month. I want him to be ready."

"Are you planning to drive him down alone?" The very flatness of the question managed to convey a note of warning.

It was exactly what Ben had planned. Yet, in the eerie emptiness of the vast house, his nerves jumped. He heard again that quick, single distant cry. He was not mistaken about it. And he had seen Nick returning to the terrace, reaching for his cane. Did he, Ben, want too much, too soon? But the powerful westerner with his fabled wealth had come to him. Ben had learned that Simon Gideon approached few men first. Ben himself had already lost interest in Birch River valley and Thatcher. He would gladly release his holdings on the condition that Nick—Ben was aware of

Alec's eyes on him, fixed and unblinking. Damn it, the man could be hypnotic when he chose. Ben knew beneath his turmoil of conflicting thoughts that he had begun to take a very real dislike of Dr. Alexander Bookman.

"No, Alec, I very much want you to come with us. I have a busy schedule. I think Nick would like to have you."

Alec sat back and crossed one well-creased-trouser knee over the other. He had the slightly tolerant smile of the victor.

"I think that's very wise, sir. For the first trip."

"If all goes as well as I hope, there's no reason why you can't end this exile and get back to your work in Zurich."

Alec made a deprecatory gesture. "My work will always be there."

"I'm sure. But this has been pretty lonely. You will of course receive the full amount of our contract including the optional extensions. No man should be penalized for doing a good job. Thank you, Alec." Ben rose. "Tell Nick when he's rested, I'll be in the game room. The young devil used to beat me any time he wanted to, at billiards. I'll bet he still can."

Ben Orlini went silently out through the long halls, silently on the white deep-piled carpeting, silently back to his own room, wanting to believe he at last had a son. His son.

Alec entered Nick's ground floor room without knocking. Nick was seated in a deep armchair, his eyes open. Alec approached him directly. From his pocket he drew a short gold chain. Slowly he began to swing the miniature gold penknife suspended on it. Suddenly he snapped his fingers. Nick shook his head and yawned.

"How do you feel, Nick?"

"Fine, thanks. What time is it?"

"A little after two. Your father wants to play billiards with you."

Nick stretched his arms. His face bore traces of former handsomeness but it had the shrunken gauntness of a man whose life had been lived.

"Billiards. He never learned to play the game but he keeps trying."

"Would you rather not go downstairs?"

"I don't mind." He started to rise, then slumped back.

"Take your time. Did you have a good sleep?"

"Too long. I sleep the morning away, then what do I do in the afternoon?"

"You went out for a walk, Nick."

"In this weather? Are you crazy?"

Alec's voice grew softer, more persuasive, as if reading to a child. "You went down the swamp path and you met a girl. A girl you were once fond of."

"I met a girl? This morning? I haven't left this room. What are you trying to tell me?"

"Your boots are wet, Nick."

"What did you do? Borrow them?"

Alec began to breathe easier. It was working, better than he had dared hope.

"Your father's going to take you to New York tomorrow."

"New York?" For an instant fear flickered in the clouded young-old eyes. "Away from here?"

"You don't have to go if you don't want to."

"You're wrong, Doctor Bookman." Ben Orlini stood in the doorway. Neither had heard him. Alec cursed himself for his momentary carelessness. He must have left the door unlatched. Orlini went to his son's chair. "You're coming with me, Nick, because I wish it. You've been up here too long. You're almost well now, and it's time you got out and enjoyed yourself. I want you to meet a friend of mine. He's a big man, Nick. At the top. He can mean a lot in your future. I've got plans for you, son. I want to talk to you about them.

We'll run down to the city, the way we used to, see a few shows, take in the town. Just the two of us."

Ben clapped a small puffy hand on his son's shoulder and felt him flinch. Nick sat staring straight ahead, his face dead-white.

"Haven't you heard me, Nick?"

"I heard you."

Ben whirled furiously at Alec. "What the hell's the matter with him, Alec?"

"He was out a bit long this morning, sir. Bad weather and all. Perhaps he overdid."

Nick sprang from his chair. "I never left this house this morning. Why do you tell lies about me? I didn't leave it and I'm not going to. Tomorrow or any other time. If there's any peace in this world for me, it's here. Where it's quiet. Where—where—" His voice broke, rose to a thin scream. "Alec, don't let him. Tell him I won't go!"

Ben Orlini turned from the room rather than see his son collapse weeping into a chair.

Alec Bookman followed him out. "I'm sorry, sir, this is one of his bad days."

"I thought he was over them."

"He's gone for weeks without a spell like this. But one never knows."

Ben Orlini took stock of the dapper, smooth-voiced man to whom he had entrusted his son. The dislike he had begun to feel blazed into sudden jealous hatred. He longed to tongue-lash this smug outsider, then fire him, to rid his life and Nick's of this encumbrance. Then what? The old helplessness, the only real link he had with Nick gone. Ben Orlini always knew when he had no options.

"I'm an impatient man, Bookman. I like to get things done. When I see no progress—"

"There's been great progress, sir."

"He went out this morning. I saw him."

"He'll remember when he's rested."

"I won't leave for New York until he's ready to go

with me." His voice sharpened. "But I want him out of here before his mother arrives next week. I expect you to see to that."

Alec Bookman watched Orlini down the long, silent corridor and felt almost sorry for the man. But he was satisfied. He had secured at some trouble the place he coveted in the Orlini scheme of things. He had no intention of being pried from it. There seemed little likelihood of that now.

The snow fell steadily into the night. The Bollington radio predicted a twenty-four-hour storm. Tom Brady looked out and would not be dismayed.

"It's a holiday weekend. They'll come. What can a man do in this weather but console himself with a drop or two?"

Hester dreamed herself through the small festivity Mary Castle created with a turkey, paper tablecloth, matching nut cups, and stubbornly the matching drinking cups.

"I'm not putting good beer, good whiskey, or even a shaving brush into one of them things," Tom announced as expected. "And I'll take the pope's nose and a drumstick, if it pleases you, along with me corned beef. And a little of the stuffing with me cabbage."

How she indulges him, Hester thought. And then smiled. If it were John, wouldn't she—? She tried not to think of the large family table at which he was probably now sitting. The laughter, the closeness, the family jokes and teasings she would never know. But next week would be theirs. She tried to imagine Snowgoose and saw a confusion of modern ski lodge and turreted castle.

At six Gus called. Did she want to go down to Pete's disco? But she was past that now. John would call before the day was out and when that happened she would become whole again.

By nine he had not yet called. She went to bed, because there she was free to think of him and await the telephone ring that would shatter her delicious dreams with the heart-stopping insistence of his voice.

The silence thickened, broken only by the stinging snow against the window and the distant blatancy of Tom's ritual TV. Hester heard her mother's bedroom door below close. She would not look at the time; John would call. They had made a commitment. He would not let the holiday pass.

She lay in the dark warmth of the old goose-down quilt that had comforted her since childhood and thought of fate. If there was such a thing. Or was it some perversity within herself that had managed to twist her life to this moment? She had known the Roundtrees since school days. Jonathan Roundtree had been nearer her age. She had laughed at his name. It was so Roundtree, proper and stiff like them all. Her mother had taken her down for saying so. "They're good people, Hester. They've done a lot for this town. And if they've fallen on lesser days, they haven't changed their manners. It wouldn't hurt you to learn a few of them!"

Hester had been intrigued but resentful. She had dismissed Jonathan but she could not dismiss Michael. She was already showing a woman's bloom. He eyed her with bold, persuasive assurance and went off to law school to heights she could only guess. He returned with summer and leisure. Michael the lover, Jonathan the traitor.

And that was her weakness. Lying in the dark cocoon of the quilt and her own body, Hester knew she had no room for small emotions. She loved, hated, envied, or despaired at full passion, as if there were no middle ground. She had brought herself to this moment.

And to John. She had despised him. Suddenly that cauldron of emotion had erupted into something beyond her own understanding. John. Not a Roundtree. No brother to Michael. No part of the past but abruptly and inexplicably the only man who could fill her life. Today, tomorrow—she flung away from the glimpse of the future. He had not called, but she could think of him now and bring her to him. As he had looked at her in the first fall of snow at the lake, as his hand had moved when he bent to strap the snowshoe, as he had swept her into his arms.

She could think of that yet unknown pitched and raftered lodge, with its glass windows slanted to the stars and its great fireplace adding its soaring radiance to their own. There, alone, beyond time and identity, their lovemaking would begin. She fantasized its beauty. The gentleness with which he would touch her. The slow, lovely exploration of each other. The deepening awareness. The perfection of discovery. The burst of need, of love.

"John!" The cry broke aloud from her. She stifled it beneath the quilt, her body aching with unspent longing. But the very sound brought her back to reality. He loved her. For a little while she would live in that security, But he was John Roundtree. Beneath that, for all time, lay the quagmire of self-knowledge and secrecy. John, the lover. Michael, the traitor. Michael had taken her in a whirlwind against her diminishing resistance and had never let her free herself from him again.

Hester turned her face into the pillow and let the tears come. She loved John. That would never change. She loved him for everything that was right and kind and decent. She loved him beyond that without any further definition. Only with him could she escape the entrapment of the past. Yet she could never marry him. She would never marry him. Marriage would bring to her the fullness of love, to John anguish and defeat.

The house had chilled. She reached for her watch. Twenty past midnight. John would not call now, wherever he was. As Michael had not called that night so long ago before he had vanished.

She fell asleep at last and dreamed of a two-faced mask, one smiling, the other cruel, tumbling headlong like a snowball down a bottomless hill.

The snow fell steadily through the night, the next day, and the following night. The second morning dawned clear and brilliant. Standing at a downstairs window, Hester felt the dazzle sting her eyes as she looked out on a hushed, obliterated world of white silence, mounded shapes, peaked drifts, where nothing familiar remained except the roof line of the pub. The parking area had vanished. The mailbox, like the fence posts, was lost under a dunce cap of snow. On the west side of the pub an eight-foot snow wave curled to meet the roof.

The Bollington radio announced the heaviest snowfall since 1894 and warned the citizens against too much shoveling of drifts. In 1894 a man had gone to the Ridge, heedless of the storm and had never been found. As he bore the honorable name of Thatcher, the citizens noted the warning and, with time on their hands, remembered and embellished the old story. Wasn't it that Thatcher, young Colin, and Henrietta Roundtree? . . .

"The water's off." Mary was emerging from the kitchen. "Tom's lighting the kerosine stove and says we're running short. Which anybody could have known three weeks ago by looking at the empty can. I told him we can always burn some of that Irish whiskey from the bar. My, isn't it a beautiful world, Hes? Pure and white as angel wings."

"It is. I better do some shoveling, Mom."

"To where? The best thing you can do is go out and bring me in a pail of snow. It makes the best coffee in the world."

"Now where in the world did you take that notion, Mary?" Tom, with soot on his face, came from the kitchen.

Mary pinked. "Mr. Willard said so. Snow is like soft water. It has fewer or more nitrates, I don't remember."

"I'll take what comes out of the tap, thank you."

"Then you'll have to ask for a miracle, and I don't think you have the knees or the patience for that."

Hester escaped with the pail. As she opened the door a mist of tiny white crystals blew into her face. She drew a deep breath of the sparkling air, wondering if she and John could leave on schedule for Snowgoose. She had put away her night's hurt at his failure to call. There were reasons. Good reasons. She had only to wait. She took another deep breath, and the air, like her love, filled her with its cleanness.

Then she heard it, a sound like a rusty knife cleaving the morning's purity. With a clanking and a rattling a dilapidated snowplow hove into view on the drifted highway. To her astonishment it turned into the parking area and with a final gasping thus came to a much-needed rest in a ten-foot drift.

John jumped down from the driver's seat.

"John! Oh, John!" Hurt evaporated into silvery light. Hester ran toward him, floundered, fell, picked herself up, floundered again in the drifted snow, and finally lay, laughing and half-buried when he reached her and fell beside her. Their arms went around each other; they kissed, their bodies close as if heaven had decreed this unlikely spot. Then suddenly too aware, they struggled to their feet, hip-deep in the powdery whiteness.

At the window, Mary Brady turned away.

"Oh, John, isn't it glorious? It won't stop us from leaving, will it? It will be even deeper at Snowgoose, won't it? Where in the world did you get that contraption? If worse comes to worst, we could drive it all the way up there. I don't see why not. And if we get stuck we could sleep in the cab. I'd pack plenty of food and coffee and things. Oh, John I—thought you'd call."

"I wanted to, Hester. Let's get out of this drift before you're soaked through. Where can we talk?"

"Not in the house. It's been an absolute prison. Like Thatcher. Like everything!"

"Take it easy, there. I hate to tell you, but nobody's going very far today. They haven't even gotten the power lines back. Are you people warm enough? I mean Mary."

"She thrives on emergency." Hester heard her own impatience. His face was so serious. Had he come all the way out to talk about the weather?

"Let's go sit in the cab. I have something to tell you."

"What, John?"

"No patience. But then neither had I until Dad labeled it self-restraint. Here, let me give you a hand." They had reached the snowplow, squat and lifeless in the drift.

"A beauty, isn't she? I'll probably have to get a wrecker to tow her back. I borrowed her from the fire department. They've got new equipment, and the bets are twenty-to-one she'll never make it home."

They were in the cab, protected by the snow-glazed windshield. He put his arm around her again and kissed her.

"Oh, God, Hester."

"What's happened?"

"Lowell."

"Lowell!" She felt the chill of presentiment. "What about Lowell?"

"She had an accident on Thanksgiving Day. She drove out early from the city and went up the Ridge road to see the view. She misses the country now, I guess. She left the car and walked down along the swamp path and apparently slipped and had a fall in the swamp."

Hester was staring at him.

"She lay there for more than an hour, I should guess, before we found her."

Hester had to say something. One question lay uppermost. But she dare not ask it yet. "Is she all right?"

"She's in the Bollington hospital. She has a broken ankle. The exposure was bad. She's been run-down. Too thin. No resistance. Yesterday she developed pneumonia."

"Oh, John!" But beneath her compassion Hester knew an instant of blinding resentment. These Roundtrees who could order their own lives to the twisting of others! She saw Snowgoose vanish; she saw John drawn away from her. It was as plain as the emptiness outside the cab window.

"And she was all alone out there, when she fell?"

"If anybody had been there, she wouldn't have lain in that broken ice. Clancy found her first. He came back. Charlie Redwing and Willard and I went out looking."

So neat. Strong men and enveloping family to save you from your mistakes. She could hear Lowell's willful words. "I don't care what anybody says, I'm going to see Nick. I know I can help him. That's all I want. To help him get well." Now she had brought them all down—or would if it were known. Hester hated herself for her thoughts yet she could not break out of their tightening circle. She was aware of John's sudden, sharp glance.

"I am sorry, John. Truly I am. What a Thanksgiving for you. I knew there was a reason you couldn't call."

"There's something else, Hes. I know you have never been close with Lowell. But she wants to see you."

"Me? Why?"

"She keeps asking for you. She was half-delirious when she first came to. You were the first one she asked for. And the only one. She doesn't seem to want to see anyone else. I came out for you as soon as I could. Will you go with me? The highway to Bollington is clear enough once we get into Thatcher."

So this was why he had gone to such trouble. The worn-out snowplow. The risk of drifts. For Lowell, for the Roundtrees. For the wholeness of the family.

"John. Tell me just one thing. I can take it. What does this do to Snowgoose?"

He took her hands gravely, his eyes warm with love.

"What do you think, Hester?"

"I—guess it's out."

"Would you want me to do anything else right now?"

"No. No, of course not. I want you to be you, no matter what."

"I love you, Hester. I love you with everything I am, everything I have. For better or worse." His voice deepened. "As long as we both shall—"

"No, John. Not that! Please, not that!"

She pushed open the cab door, jumped, fell into the softness of the drift, and found an excuse to laugh.

"I guess I'm the snowgoose. I just forgot it was deep."

He was beside her. "My darling girl. . . ."

"Don't be tender, John. I can't stand that. Here, brush me off and try to start that thing up. I'll mush back and get my bag and tell them not to worry."

As she pushed up the hill in her own tracks, she heard the engine grunt, stall, and turn over.

She would see Lowell. She would wear the mask of kindness.

As it happened, John had been overoptimistic in his hope of driving Hester to Bollington. It took another day to clear a lane on the highways, and a day longer to restore telephone and power lines to the blanketed area. The ancient snowplow truck had grumbled a hundred yards down the clogged road and surrendered. John had walked Hester back to the house and after a listless good-bye had given himself over to the job of getting into Thatcher.

"We're only postponing Snowgoose, Hes. You know that."

She had nodded and gone indoors, as subdued as a child with a secret.

Martin Roundtree opened his front door and looked at the neat path shoveled to the sidewalk.

"How quickly a man can lose his usefulness." But he did not say it aloud. Edythe was standing beside him and for the first time in four days she was smiling. "John did a good job."

"Yes. He says you're not to touch a shovel, Martin."

"Did he? Well. The old man is to take his orders now?" But he said it without malice and tried to provide the twinkle he knew Edythe would expect.

"He didn't mean it that way, Martin."

"Edythe, where's your sense of humor? My hair may be thinning and my mind too, but my skin isn't. Now that he's dug the path, I'll do him the courtesy of walking on it. Good to have the boy home. Now especially. Well, it looks as if we won't have any trouble getting to the hospital today."

"Martin, I've just talked to them."

"Yes? What?" The words were clipped with anxiety.

"Lowell's getting better, as they told us yesterday. She's past the worst of it. . . ." Edythe hesitated. What she had to say was not easy for her or for Martin.

"Yes. Well—go on. I can hear there's more. What else did they say?"

"They suggested that we don't come to see her today. Maybe tomorrow."

"Why not?"

"Because she doesn't want to talk."

"All right. She doesn't have to. Neither do I."

"Martin, we can't just sit looking at her again."

"She managed a few words with John. I guess she can manage at least a glance for her father. If you don't want to come with me, Edythe, say so. But I'm

not letting some officious busybody keep me from my
own daughter. Too many orders these days. That's the
trouble. Too many orders when a man reaches my
age."

He put on his overshoes, took his hat, overcoat, and
cane from the closet. As always Edythe watched his
erect, frail figure down the path. She held her breath.
But it was needless. John had not only shoveled the
path, he had cindered it well into the sanded street
where pedestrians now had to walk. Edythe turned
from the door, thanking whatever dim and forgotten
political wisdom had ordained that congressmen were
free to be with their families these particular weeks.

Lowell lay with her face toward the window where
a louvered blind dimmed the winter glare. It was easier to lie like this, very silent, very still, eyes closed and
the world shut out like the sky itself. Easier not to
talk, easier not to think, though the latter was impossible. For it came back in quick, broken glimpses,
shards of glass cutting into her consciousness. The
walk through the new snow to meet him. His almost
shy smile, his hesitant outstretched hand and then,
then something happened, so swift, so meaningless. She
groped for it in her mind, opened her eyes, and then as
quickly closed them. There was sudden hurt and then
nothing. Nothing at all. A hole in time. A blackness.
No one to tell her, no one to help. Until she found
herself here.

They kept asking her foolishly if she knew who she
was. Of course she knew. But there were plenty of
other people to tell them. She did not have to answer
that. She was Lowell Roundtree. That was all they
would learn and not from her. No one knew she loved
a man, no one but herself. It was a secret that lay in
such deep pain within her that she never needed to
open her eyes or talk again.

A nurse entered the room, looked at her for a long

minute, then bent over the bed and whispered something.

Lowell's eyes opened. She pushed herself upward. "Here? Now?"

The nurse nodded.

"Yes. Of course." Lowell touched her own face. "How do I look?"

"As if you could walk out tomorrow."

Lowell sank back. She was not ready for such normalcy.

Hester entered and stood with her back to the closed door. John had urged her to go in alone but he had not prepared her for the white stillness in Lowell's face. She lay half raised against the pillows. Only the dark intensity of her eyes, the short curly mass of her dark hair seemed alive.

"Hester!"

"Hi. How are you feeling?" Friendly. Careful. Distant. Hester had come as she had promised but she wanted no involvement. Yet she sensed it was there. Invisible. Threatening. She remained at the edge of the room.

"Hester, I thought you'd never come. Bring the chair over close. I—I can't talk to you over there." She lay back. She was expending her energy too fast.

There were flowers on her bedside table, the windowsill, everywhere. Hester made no comment. They were no more than a punctuation to the irony of the moment. She pulled a chair closer to the bed. Then she saw the blotches on Lowell's face.

"I'm sorry about the accident."

Lowell closed her eyes, her hands clenching the bedcover.

"It was not an accident."

Hester felt not so much surprise as the first presentiment of her own defeat.

"That's what I've got to tell you, Hester. Because there's no one else I can talk to about . . . it."

The bleakness in Lowell's face touched her. Compassion for anything hurt or wounded had always robbed her of commonsense. "It's all right, Lowell. Tell me."

"You won't tell anyone else? If my father knew—"

"You asked me that once before. And I never did."

"But you have no reason to be nice to any of us, really. Hester—it was Nick."

She should have been more surprised. She saw the dark eyes swim with tears. She waited while Lowell brushed her hand across them.

"I was supposed to meet Nick Thanksgiving morning. Doctor Bookman called me in New York—he has my phone number. It was the only way Nick and I could make our dates. He said it was a lonely holiday for Nick, and if I could come up early enough to see him. . . ."

She talked more rapidly. The release itself gave animation and a hint of color to her face.

"I drove up and got there and walked along the path to the swamp. It had begun to snow. I thought maybe Nick wouldn't come. But he's so much better these days, Hester, you couldn't believe. Anyway, there he was standing on the path when I got there. So still, so dark in his heavy coat that it made me think of a tree that would never move. I knew we couldn't stay there long. I ran to him. Hester, I do love him. I think I always have loved him no matter how many bad things they used to say about him. And I thought maybe he loved me. I know he'll always be something of an invalid. But I'd take care of him all my life—if he'd let me. At least—at least that's the way I thought. Until Thanksgiving."

A shiver ran through her. Her face had gone ashen.

"Lowell. . . ." Hester touched her hand. It was icy.

"Let me go on, Hester. I must. I ran toward him on the path. He never moved. He looked at me as if I were a stranger. He wasn't Nick. He was someone else, someone who hated me. It was a terrible look. I never saw anything like it in my life. As I reached him his hands suddenly went to my face, then—then to my throat. So tight, so choking. I tried to break them away. But I couldn't. He was so strong, Hester. As if something possessed him. As if he *had* to—" Lowell's hands covered her mouth. Her shoulders shook with dry sobs. Hester glanced with alarm at the closed door.

"No, no, Hester. Let me finish! Please! I tried to break his grip. I knew he was terribly sick. He didn't know what he was doing. I think I screamed. He struck my face and then suddenly let me go and pushed me away. I fell backward, down into the swamp. I don't remember any more. Except one thing. Just one thing. And then I'm not sure. As I fell I saw someone—I think I saw someone standing on the slope above. A man. That's what I thought. I'm trying to be sure. Maybe it was a tree. But it wasn't, Hester. It wasn't a tree. I know!" Her voice sank to nearly a whisper. "It was Doctor Bookman. I saw him. Just standing. Standing. Watching. He didn't help me. He didn't move. Hester, what's happening up there? What's happening—to Nick?"

Her whole body was shaking.

"Lowell, honey. Don't. Don't. Maybe it's a nightmare. Maybe it's something—"

The door opened.

"Lowell, you have another visit—" The young nurse broke off and ran to the bed. "What is it?" She filled a glass from the table with water and dropped a capsule in it. "What's upset you? Here, take this. You must be quiet." She spun around to Hester. "What upset her?"

"No, no, nurse. It's my fault! I was talking." The glass of water in Lowell's hand spilled.

"I'm afraid, miss, I'll have to ask you to leave. The patient needs absolute quiet."

Hester rose. "I know. I'm sorry."

"Excuse me." It was masculine. It was a command. Hester turned to see Martin Roundtree standing in the doorway. Behind him loomed John, unsmiling.

It seemed to Hester that her whole life had drained to this single moment. The slight, gray, immaculate man, emotionless, dry, was her enemy. Her old enemy. If this at last was to be the confrontation, let it. Better than the barrier of silence. *Let him tell me what he thinks of me. And have it over.* But deep and latent she felt the stirring of a proud fury. Separately these Roundtrees had asked for her love. Her return was this disdain. In her anger she lumped them together and braced herself for Martin Roundtree's attack.

He looked past her. "Nurse, I seem to have intruded."

"Not at all, Mister Roundtree. Lowell has overtaxed herself. She needs rest, but if you want to stay with your daughter, it might be comforting for her."

Lowell turned her face to the window.

Martin made a slight old-fashioned bow. "No. I think, nurse, rest would be better. My wife and I will come tomorrow."

"Any time, of course, Mister Roundtree. She's getting stronger every day."

"Thank you, nurse."

The doorway was clear. If John had tried to meet her eyes, Hester was unaware of it. He had gone, this thin, fragile man with courtesy, like quality, bred into every bone. He had come and gone, and he had looked past her as he had looked past the wall. There would be no confrontation now. There never would be. For Martin Roundtree, Hester realized, she did not exist.

Yet because she was Hester she would never forget she had seen pain for a moment in his eyes.

She permitted John to drive her home. She had learned her lesson in self-control. She sat hunched in silence on the far side of the car. When he tried to take her hand, she drew it quickly away. She stared blankly out of the window, unwilling even to see his glance of compassion.

The parking area of the pub was cleared of snow now. John had seen to that.

"Hester, darling—"

She shook her head. "I saw, John, and so did you. I know where he stands and I know where I stand."

"Hester, try to forgive Dad. He—"

"You don't forgive a man for being what he is. You respect him. I've been told that all my life."

"We may get to Snowgoose next week."

"Oh, John! John, don't you see? There's nothing for us. There never could be. You're with him. You belong there. It's what you are, and you can't help it. All I'd do is take you from him. Maybe for only a little while. But there it would be. Hester Brady again. Just like today." Her thoughts went from Martin to Lowell's stricken face. She would keep Lowell's secret but that was over, too.

"My darling, no one blames you. Dad—"

"Blame? Blame! I could take that. Blame you can fight and shout down and clear away. That's not what your father feels to me. Maybe once but now it's something else. Something I can't live with. You too, John. You'd like to sleep with me. You say you love me—"

"I do love you!"

"No, let me finish! Maybe you would. For a little while. And then you'd think of Michael and pretty soon you'd despise me. Your father thinks of Michael and he despises me. He did once. But now—now . . . no, John, no man on earth can look through me as if I were dust blown into his face."

"Hester, I'll call you tonight. . . ."

"If you do, I shan't be here. Or the next night or the next. Don't touch me. This isn't easy for me either!"

"You're wrong, Hester. About everything. I'm not my father. It's us, you and I. *Our* life!"

"Tell me something. Honestly. If you had known your father was coming to the hospital this afternoon, would you have driven me over?"

His hesitation was minuscule, but she was waiting for it.

"Thanks for being honest. You're part of them. You

always will be. Or you wouldn't be here now. But I'm not. And I couldn't ever be! That's all there is to it. No. Don't touch me! Good-bye, John." Her voice shook.

She was out of the car and up the path like a flame that could only burn itself out alone. He could not bear to think of the ashes of her hurt.

He loved her. He would find her again. He would offer her everything he had. But he knew that it would be very little. Even as he had seen Lowell's crumpled body in the snow, he had known that his future was once again not his own.

John turned his car into the snowbound road. He was not yet ready to go home.

Martin Roundtree, as thin and ailing as Edythe had ever seen him, paced the restricted length of his study, his hands white-knuckled behind his back.

Edythe stood rigid. "Martin, please. I'm sure it wasn't John's fault that the girl was in Lowell's hospital room." Her voice was as soft as she could make it to conceal her own disbelief.

"Before her own father saw her? If it wasn't John's idea, whose was it?"

"But, dear, you told me, John said Lowell asked for her."

"Was that a reason? Or is this whole family in a conspiracy against me? Every one of you knows the sordid affair with that girl that dragged Michael into the gutter until he no longer knew where he belonged. Today I find her there beside my poor, desperately ill daughter, arrogant, brazen, defying me . . . ! I did not trust myself, Edythe. I turned and left. I'm waiting now for John to get home and give me an explanation."

"Martin dear—not John."

Martin turned, took a short breath, and sank into the black leather chair. "I'm all right, Edythe. No, I'm all right. Let me be." He drew a deeper breath and straightened. "There are some things, Edythe, on which you and I do not agree and never will. I must ask you to leave this matter wholly to me. I have had no occasion to mention the girl's name in eight years. I hope, after this day, I will never have to again." He lay back in his chair and closed his eyes, the ashen skin tight across his fine features, the hair grayed too soon above the high, intellectual forehead.

Anger has aged him, she thought. Anger and a crippled pride. With an intuition deeper than she realized, she sensed that this frail, highly principled man she loved needed a focus for his hurt and his disappointment. Heaven knew, she had tried to gentle him, to heal the scars of that night so long ago when she had stood in this same hall and heard the savage words Michael had flung at his father, the rising, demonic temper she had failed to channel in their son. Michael, their beloved firstborn.

"You don't like Hester Brady because you don't think she's good enough for the Roundtrees! Well, let me tell you she's got more guts than this whole family put together!" Martin's answer was inaudible. "No, I'm not going to marry her, Dad. But I'm not giving her up either. If I whistle, she'll come whenever I want her. Okay, I've shocked you. But it's about time. I've gone your way until I've had a bellyful of it. Maybe you should face a few facts. Look around you. Look at this house! Look at that crummy office of yours on Main Street! Look at this town! Dead of dry rot like its ideas. This is a different day, Dad, and you better understand it. I don't believe in what you believe in. I'm not taking orders to salute the flag, kneel down in church, marry the right girl, and get sucked into all the crap that's put the Roundtree name on every stinking monument in this town. You don't like what I do! I don't like what you do! The difference is that I'm honest. You're kidding yourself. You're through, Dad, and I'm beginning. And it's my life!"

Then Edythe heard Martin's voice, so thin and high she barely recognized it.

"Get out, Michael. Get out and stay out! Don't come back until you've brought an apology for every word you've spoken in this room tonight!"

The slam of the study door, the slam of the front door. And then—the sudden, terrible crash in Martin's study.

"Martin!" she had screamed.

It would never go away. The nightmare lived on beneath the surface of their lives, a monstrous invisibility waiting to spring at them, unchained, when the moment came. Now Hester Brady had brought that moment.

Edythe slowly climbed the stairs. It was not easy to find forgiveness for the image of the girl at her daughter's bedside.

John returned late in the afternoon. He had helped the snow-shoveling crew down at Juno's Landing, where the snow had drifted nearly roof-high over the low, huddled houses. He felt better for the hard outdoor work. Better but for the face of Hester that seemed to dance just beyond him in flurries of tossed snow.

The green lamp was lit in his father's study.

"That you, John?"

"Yes, sir." He would rather have gone directly up the stairs. He was startled by his father's pallor. "We're digging out, Dad, but it will take time." He took the desk chair opposite his father's black leather one. This was as good a time as any to announce his plans. "I'd like to be able to pitch in for the whole job but I'm going back to Washington tomorrow."

An instant of silence. "I thought you were staying up here two or three weeks."

"I get a lot more done there. There's a lot of homework for this nuclear business."

"Quite. John. . . ." Martin's mouth was tight. "Did you bring that girl into Lowell's room today?"

"If you mean Hester, Dad, I already told you. Lowell wanted—"

"Did you take her there; did you drive her?"

"The driving is still tough. . . ."

"Don't put me off, John. You know what I'm asking. How long have you been seeing her?"

"Hester is not what you—"

"So you have been seeing her."

"I'll be glad to talk to you about it when you're willing to listen."

"I don't want to talk about it. First Michael, then you. The daughter of a saloonkeeper, known for her— shall I call it—willingness. We had another name for it in my day." Martin's face whitened in anger. "Slut!"

Eight years blazed between them. John's fists clenched with inner fury. He was the second, the lesser son. He had played that role all his life. It was part of his father's belief in traditions of existing order and self-discipline, of unchanging values of excellence. One by one his children were failing him. Michael, Claude, now himself. *We have to,* thought John desperately, *or we'd smother. Right here in these four walls.*

Martin, sunk deep in his chair, had drawn out his handkerchief and was wiping his brow and his mouth.

"I regret I lost my temper, John. It's been a bad day. A shock. Lowell's illness. I—I lost track of time."

John waited until the handkerchief was pocketed.

"I guess I understand. I've tried to. I didn't want to talk about it. But you had to know. Maybe I want you to know." His eyes were fixed on his father. He hesitated, only because words gave a finality he could not yet endure. "I asked Hester Brady to marry me."

"You—"

"She refused. Not because we're not in love." John felt himself pounding against the invisible tyranny of his life. "She refused because I'm a Roundtree. And for the first time in my life, in that hospital room today, I was ashamed of it!"

The room throbbed with the ticking of time, the ghosts of spent angers, past defeats. Martin sat staring from his chair like a man who had suddenly seen the outline of his own grave.

The compassion that was his weakness turned in John's stomach.

"I'm sorry, Dad. But that's how it is."

He was at the door when Martin made his supreme effort. With that slight wave of disdain that John remembered from childhood, he dismissed the ugliness that was beneath him. John saw again the self-discipline of a man who had fought defeat all his life and would not bow to it now.

"I'm sure you've already regretted what you said, John. Before you go back to Washington tomorrow, I should like to talk to you about this nuclear energy business. It's a good deal bigger than anyone around here understands. One plant costs a billion dollars to build. One flaw in that plant could destroy half of New England. It's not a matter of the land now. It's the enormity of responsibility. Who's to take it? That's the question you must ask, John. And *you* must answer."

Command returned. Order restored. John escaped. The words were a kind of apology, he guessed. He would come to their meaning later.

It was enough now to face the days ahead without the anticipation of Hester. He had no regret for revealing his feelings.

Three days later Bantam Brady, polishing glasses in his pub, looked up to see a figure in black across the bar, a tiny man shorter even than himself. He knew little about Orientals and the few he had ever met disconcerted him with their polite calm. They gave him the feeling they knew something he didn't. "Which wouldn't be hard," Bantam had told himself.

"What'll it be, y'r excellence?" Respect was the only safe avenue when you were unsure.

The little man held out an envelope. It was thin and gray and Bantam could sniff its elegance. On it in a fine, strong hand was written: MISS HESTER BRADY.

Bantam accepted it with a nod. "Have one on the house, excellence?" From behind the bar he produced a dust covered bottle of saki. "Very good. You like rice wine?"

The Vietnamese gentleman bowed and smiled. "I prefer Scotch," he said almost without accent. "But not in working hours."

It was four o'clock when Bantam took time off to trudge up to the house with the letter. To his relief Hester was home. He had seen very little of her in the last three days. To a simple question of where she had been she had snapped, "You and Mom are always telling me to get out of the pub. I'm looking for a job."

Now he found her in her room, doing, as well as he could judge, not much of anything.

"For you, Hes. Came by Chinese delivery." He waited for some relief to his curiosity.

"Thanks, Dad." She closed the door.

The letter was brief.

> My dear Hester:
> When we met some time ago, I said I hoped to see you again. I'm here on the Ridge for a few days, quite alone, and it would give me great pleasure if you would have tea with me. Shall we say four tomorrow?
>
>   Faithfully,
>   Julia Orlini

Hester reread the letter slowly. Then a third time. It breathed elegance, even to the word *faithfully*. She had never seen that. As she held it in her hand it took on a kind of magic glow, a chink in the prison of her thoughts, a crack widening to something distant and mysterious. She had no thoughts beyond its simple invitation but even that broke the tight encirclement of her life. She had no concern that it was from an Orlini. She had never had anything to do with the people in the glittering house on the Ridge, except the day she went to repay Alec Bookman. For an instant she remembered Lowell, but loyalty, like love, were part of the past.

Hester had never drawn back from an opening door. She would not now.

Part Three

Halcyon Cay

Chapter Fifteen

An unexpected ripple of laughter rose from the beach below, scarring the crystal silence of the morning. Julia Orlini looked down from the balcony outside her bedroom with an inner sigh of relief. Whether it was impulse or the face of loneliness ahead, it had been a stroke of good luck when she leaned across the teacups that pale, wintry day in Thatcher and asked Hester Brady if she would like to come to Halcyon with her.

"What's Halcyon?" It was the girl's third visit to the Ridge and she had not yet broken out of her curiously artificial restraint.

"It's an island in the outer Bahamas. My husband bought it years ago and built a house there. It's mine now. It won't be very exciting. We don't entertain the way we used to. In fact it's very quiet. But there's the sea. And the beach. It's very beautiful."

Hester had stared for a full moment out on the gray snowbound valley.

"I don't know if I could leave," Hester seemed to be talking to the valley.

"Think it over. I won't be going for a month or so."

Julia rose.

Hester jumped to her feet, rattling the tea table.

"I have thought it over, Mrs. Orlini. I—I never had an invitation like that. Ever. I don't see how I'd be hurting anybody. I mean at home—my mother's not too well—but a week wouldn't make any difference. She always said, 'Go. Go when you get the chance and then you won't have regrets.' I hate regrets. I hate being sorry. Don't you? I hate—oh, I'd love to go!"

The rush of revelation had taken Julia aback and left Hester embarrassed. But in the vacuum of Hester's departure Julia was not unpleased by her impulse. The warmth of companionship, someone to talk to, someone not *paid* to talk. Halcyon had once been an idyll for Ben and her, then an emptiness, now a place of exile. If it worked well, she might persuade Hester to stay longer. There could be visitors again, a reason for them.

Julia rubbed warmth into her long, fine hands. She had always been able to arrange her own life and she would again. She had deferred to Ben too long. Once again he had taken Nick from her. Eventually Ben must face his own failure. Then she would have her damaged son back, to care for as only she could. Whether it was Hester Brady's burst of spontaneity or her own urgency to survive, Julia Orlini could not tell, but her spirits lifted. Hope had become more than a wind-tossed straw.

The time was at last come. Scorning the Orlini's private jet, they had flown by commerical airline to Nassau, on to Eleuthera and by water taxi to a small irregular island with a cluster of white buildings and a lighthouse.

"Welcome to Halcyon," said Julia as she stepped onto the white dock.

Hester had managed a thank you and stared. Could one man, one little man whom most of Thatcher ridiculed and despised, own all this? Thatcher began to dwindle.

The first two days at Halcyon had been a near-disaster. Hester had been stiff with uncertainty and the unaccustomed idleness. Julia had seen how little they had in common, this vibrant girl from behind the bar of a country tavern, and herself, the careful product of twenty-five years of sophisticated purpose. Julia displayed the marvels of her breathtaking house, set in levels in the blackness of porous rock. They walked the beach, which she loathed, and lingered at the private pier so that Hester might see the white-sailed skiffs of the tradesmen bringing their loads of pomegranates and lemons, tomatoes and cucumbers, fish, turtles, crabs, and octopus.

"Try one, miss?" A bronzed man with a blond beard held up a four-foot specimen, gray, eerie, and writhing. "They make fine soup."

"Quinn, don't frighten Miss Brady. She's new to the cays."

Quinn touched his captain's cap.

Hester smiled fleetingly and followed Julia up the steep coral path to the house. Julia could only wonder whether the girl was overwhelmed or bored.

"You're a friend of the Roundtrees in Thatcher, aren't you, Hester?"

They were dining on the terrace of the vast blue-and-white room that opened to the sea. In the distance a ship pinpricked the dusk with its running lights. Hester watched it, expressionless.

"My mother once worked for the Roundtrees a long time ago."

"Would it interest you to know that I am related to them?"

"You are?" For an instant suspicion flickered in Hester's eyes. "I didn't know that."

"My maiden name was Thatcher. Oh, a very distant branch. Plainfield, New Jersey. My father was a high school teacher. I once believed I owned the valley." Julia laughed. "But I learned that I didn't. It's all Roundtree. If they have the sense to hold on to it."

Hester did not answer.

"The reason I brought the subject up is that I believe one of the Roundtree girls, Lowell, has been visiting my son, Nick. Not that I mind. Years ago, before the accident, he had taken her out. But it is tragic unless she realizes. . . ." Julia's voice trailed.

"But we can talk of something else. I try to forget

all that down here. It's the place to forget, if you're my age. If you're young, you haven't lived enough to forget. I wish there were more entertainment for you. We are isolated here. You may be bored."

"Bored!" The change in Hester's face amazed her. "I've never been bored in my life. My mother always said the Bradys couldn't afford it. But I'm sorry if that's what you think. I can't explain it to you. I've never seen a place like this in my life. It's all magic. As if somebody made it appear out of the air and if I closed my eyes it would be gone. Yet it's been here all this time for anyone to see. Two days have already gone, and I've been pinning it all to my mind."

The girl's intensity pushed at the deepening dusk.

"I misunderstood, Hester. I envy you."

"It's nothing to envy, Mrs. Orlini. It's just that it's different for you and for me. I'll never see it again but I love it here. I would never mind even being alone."

"Then be alone, Hester!" Julia felt the air clear. "Do what you want. I didn't ask you here to attend to me. You're free, my dear girl. Be free. Maybe you can teach me how it's done."

That was last night. In the early morning, as she stood on the balcony, Julia told herself Hester had taken her advice. She was standing below at the sea's edge, her full, cotton skirt blown back, her head and body erect, outlined in the sun's new light and sea's new glitter. It suits her, thought Julia. She belongs here. She heard another ripple of voices but the roof's angle cut off a view of Hester's companion.

She's lost no time, thought Julia. But she did not mind. The house had been silent too long. She rang for coffee, opened a closet door on a riot of unworn colors, and wondered if her face had become too drawn, her hair too gray. Time was not the only thief. What a woman did with it scarred as deeply. She drew a brilliant fuchsia caftan from the depths of the closet and avoided a mirror. Perhaps it was not too late.

* * *

"How far away is the horizon?" Hester turned her face from the sea toward the blond, bearded man in white ducks and a white captain's cap with its fouled anchors in weathered gilt thread.

"Twenty miles."

"From here?"

"From wherever you are at sea level. Given a clear day." He had come unexpectedly on this girl from the north. She was direct, without self-awareness or guile. He liked watching her, the full-flowing lines of her body, like a wild bird paused in flight.

"And if it isn't clear?"

"My dear young woman, if you can't see the horizon what in merry hell difference does the distance make?"

She laughed. The water rippled across her bare toes. She curled them deeper in the sand.

"I think it makes a lot of difference. If the only thing that mattered was what you can *see*—"

He waved a muscular, tanned hand.

"Too early for metaphysics. Besides, I'm a working man."

She nodded.

"I can see that doesn't interest you."

"I don't know any other kind."

"So your name is Hester, and you're visiting the lady up there, and you've never seen the ocean before. And you're obviously carrying around some deep secret."

"What makes you say that?" Her tone was sharp.

"Guessed it, didn't I? Easy. Because you don't give away any part of yourself. And because, although I am a personable man albeit pushing middle years, you don't give a damn what I do or when I leave. Most girls want to run naked in the moonlight the minute they reach the islands."

"Well, I'm not like that." Hester had begun to dislike the conversation.

"I respect you for it." He touched his cap, and his

smile was broad. "But you obviously can't sit here on Halcyon for a whole week. As I don't spend all my time delivering fruit, fish, and mail, I could show you a little more of the sea and the nearby cays."

"Keys. What's that?"

"C-A-Y-S. Bahama for island. I have a trim little sloop. I'm quite reliable. Just ask for Quinn."

"I'll speak to Mrs. Orlini."

"Why?"

"It's polite. She might like to come too."

He grinned. "Mrs. Orlini does not sail in a twenty-four-foot sloop-for-hire when she has a sixty-foot cruiser in the slip. Barnacle-bottomed as it is *now*. Do what you like. I'll be along tomorrow." He touched his cap again and disappeared around the curve of the beach.

Hester turned her face to the sea for one more draft of this vast and lovely emptiness. She had been abruptly sheared from everything plain and prosaic that had made up her days. Only once had she been swept out of its monotony. Michael had possessed her. And gone. Suddenly, in the dazzling clarity of this air, she saw what she had let her life become. A shield against all reality, a lock on her innermost nature. She had lived without living, telling herself that it would be different someday, translating time into waiting, and hours into a jigsaw of small chores.

Even her love for John, poignant and deep as it had been, had flowered only within her imaginations. Words and partings and more waiting had been its substance.

Now, after two days of numbed transition, she was standing in the early brilliance of this translucent morning. Every sense, every pulsebeat was alive. She was not imagining the enormous, mysterious splendor around her. She could bend and touch the soft pink sand, feel the silvery water frothing at her feet. She could breathe the dancing air. It was real. She was liv-

ing it. As other people had before her. It was hers. As
if it had always been here waiting for her.

Quickly, buoyantly, she ran up the white steps to
the fairylike house that too had emerged into reality.
She was no longer Hester Brady. She was an innermost
nameless self, at last burst free.

"By all means let Quinn sail you around the cays,"
Julia Orlini had said. "He knows more about them
than anyone around here."

"Who is he?"

"I've never really known. A Britisher, I think. You
come back and tell me." Julia was satisfied. This was
what she had sought. Filaments into the world. The
electricity of contact through other eyes. Young eyes.
Eyes, she noticed, newly luminous and eager.

Quinn handled a boat as if it were an extension of
his arm. The mainsail set and drawing, the jib alive to
every pull and pressure of his hand. He sat back and
surveyed his passenger. Not the perfection of beauty
but surely its enticement. Her white slacks fitted well
but not too close, her dark blue jersey right by chance
or design. She was not the usual run of self-loving,
free-offering girls on holiday, surrendering themselves
to sun or man, whichever came first. The name Hester
Brady gave no clue. No elegance. No pretense either.
He liked that. Nor did she talk too much. He liked
that too.

"I don't enjoy being stared at, Mister Quinn."

"Quinn. There's no Mister to it. Never was. Down
here. Of course if you care to go back, you'd find a
knighthood about the time of James the First. Being
Scottish, he set about endearing himself to his English
subjects. By making as many of them as possible knights.
That included a worthy family of honest yeomanry
named Quinnly-Bush. The knighthood faded but
a family sense of class remained. I've spent the better
part of a misguided lifetime betraying it. Quinn will
do nicely."

She hadn't the faintest idea what he was talking

about nor had she listened too carefully. The plashing of water against the boat's side, her fingers trailing in the coolness, Hester was busy living. Yet his voice was deep and pleasant and he seemed not as middle-aged as he'd hinted. She felt oddly, inexplicably safe.

"The Bahamas," he began, "are seven hundred up-thrusts of coral and basalt rock. Do you want the long version or the short?"

She sighed and stopped living for an instant. "I was never any good at history. I just like to look. And feel. Where are we going?"

"How many days will you be here?"

"Five more. Four and a half."

"Then I think we'll go to the cemetery first."

"A cemetery? Oh, no!"

"I quite agree but some of these cays—"

"Islands?"

"Some of these islands were settled by New England Yankees, bloody royalists, actually, who were run out by the American revolutionists and came here lock, stock, barrel, pigs, horses, shipyards, and all. They lived, prospered, died, and were buried. Most Americans like to look at a cemetery or two. Where are you from?"

"I live in Thatcher, Connecticut."

"No doubt you'd find a Thatcher in a grave or two."

"Thanks but no thanks." If that sounded rude, it was no ruder than this unexpected knife thrust of yesterday into her new-found confidence. "I hate cemeteries. Honestly I'd rather just sail. If it's all right with you. It's wonderful, isn't it?"

"I always thought so." He glanced at her and saw only the back of her head. She was trailing her hand in the water again. An odd girl. No tricks. No guile. No undersurface demands. "So we'll sail. Suits me fine. I'll take you to meet Odella. She's a legend in the islands. When she's done with the tourist crowd, if she likes you, she'll give you goatsmilk and spells.

Then, if the weather holds, we'll go out tomorrow to Boar's Head. Very private. Very posh. But I can bring a friend. If I ever find one."

Hester lifted her face to an invisible horizon. Happiness was much simpler than she had thought. Thatcher had vanished. The trade winds carried a singing silence. As the breeze stiffened, only one name, one face lingered above the boat's dipping bow. Then John Roundtree, too, slowly dissolved into the hypnotic light.

This, Hester told herself, was the beginning of a second life.

The hours passed like spilled seashells. Hester was content to sail, to let the sea flow past her, the sun warm her, and the great white belly of canvas fill and stiffen above her with the wind. Sometimes Quinn gave her the tiller to hold, which she did with surprising competence. Once he handed her the mainsheet. He respected both her silence and her lack of knowledge. Quickly she came to recognize the force of wind power on the small sloop. He would talk of the mysteries of currents and tides, the pull of moon and earth, of soundings and sea bottoms. She would listen gravely.

"How deep is the sea?"

"At its deepest it measures more than the world's highest mountain."

"Here?" The question was nervous.

He laughed. "Oh, no, we're over a part of a shelf. Islands are tips of reefs and undersea mountains."

She joined his laugh. "I guess it really wouldn't matter whether you drown in ten feet or a hundred."

"I think it would. Below us it's quite splendid. Beautiful plants. Moving creatures. Light. But elsewhere, six miles down to a total blackness, no man knows."

She shivered, partly with pleasure. This steady, friendly man, about whom she knew so little, never

made her feel stupid, as Michael had. Or inferior as
Martin Roundtree had. Why, why would that return
to her now? But she knew she would remember forever
that one quick glance John's father had given her in
Lowell's hospital room. It had slid from her in an instant but its anger, its contempt, had stripped her
bare.

She shook her head like a water spaniel.

"Bad thoughts?" Quinn looked at her closely.

"Not too. It's over now."

It was not as easy to shake free of John. If she let
down her guard at any special glimpse of magic, John
materialized. He would as long as she was unable to
stifle her longing to share it with him.

"How would you like a picnic tomorrow?"

"Wonderful! Where?"

"At a tiny cay that has no name. But it's rather different. You can give it a name if you'd like."

"Shouldn't you be—well, I mean you have a lot of
things you do, and you haven't let me—I mean, you
know, you just don't give all your time away, do you?"

"If you're trying to say, Miss Brady, that you'd prefer to hire my boat by the hour instead of sailing as
my guest—"

"I didn't say anything like that! My, you are
touchy, aren't you? But I'm taking a lot of your time
and if I don't know a lot of things about a boat, I do
know what's right and fair. And I don't like just ac-
cepting things."

"We are being the proud queen of the western seas,
aren't we? If I assured you that you are a moon of
constant delight to me and I am in your debt, would
that square things?"

"It would if I knew what you are talking about.
What's that?"

Hester pointed aft to the horizon where a low black
line was visible beneath a lemon-colored sky. The
wind had risen to a keening cry.

"A squall is blowing up. They come up fast. But

we're running ahead of it and if we're lucky, we'll make Halcyon before the worst of it."

The sloop was heeling over now as the tiller held her steady, a little off the wind. Hester clung to the rail, and when he thrust the jib sheet into her hand, she hung on to it like a lifeline. She was frightened but exhilerated, as if the elements were drawing together to pit her own strength against them. Little as she knew him, she had an odd, total trust in Quinn. He sat braced in the cockpit, holding the pitching sloop in his hand, giving it its head, urging it through the rising seas. Like a Thoroughbred, she thought, ridden to a victory both man and horse knew lay ahead.

She heard a hissing sound and felt the sudden sting of rain. He glanced at her and held two fingers in a V for victory. She laughed and felt the water plaster her shirt and slacks to her body. The wind rose to a scream, the dark squall enfolded them.

It was over as quickly as it had come upon them. Under a mother-of-pearl sky they rode into the slip at Halcyon. Rain and wind had swept the little pier dripping clean.

Quinn tied up the sloop to a cleat on the pier, then nodded toward the west. The full arc of a rainbow reached from horizon to horizon, its colors deepening to an unearthly brilliance. They watched the climax in silence. As the colors paled he held out his hand. For an instant she misunderstood, then realized he was helping her up onto the dock.

"Excellent," he said. She did not know whether the words referred to her, the sea, or the rainbow. But they held an honesty she needed.

She ran up the path. He had not set an hour for their picnic. He did not have to.

They were no longer strangers.

Chapter Sixteen

"I envy you," said Julia Orlini.

"Me?" Hester laughed. Laughter came easier these days.

They were sitting on the terrace, with its pots of pink hibiscus, red bougainvillea, the changing yellows of lime and banana trees that some skilled hand had translated into a riotous garden above the incredible green-blue silk of the sea.

"Then come on the picnic today."

"My dear girl!"

"I mean it. Quinn asked if you'd like it."

"Quinn has a talent for saying the right thing. Partly because he's British and partly because it keeps people at a safe distance." She gave Hester a sharp glance. But the girl's face, glowing as it was, showed no emotion. "I said I envied you because in less than four days you've let go to the spirit of the place. It's becoming."

"I love it here," said Hester so simply that the older woman knew she meant it.

"That's how I felt when we bought the cay. I named it Halcyon. My father was a high school teacher and he used to quote something about the halcyon sea. I didn't know then what it meant, but it sounded lovely. I never forgot it."

Hester sensed a new willingness in Julia to talk. Perhaps a need. It would be another hour before the man named Quinn rounded the beach, his cap low on his head, his nod as brief as if he had found her by accident. All of which suited her. Forgetfulness. Without demands.

"What does it mean? Halcyon?"

"It's Greek. I think it was originally a kind of bird, a kingfisher who builds his nest on the water. So the sea has to be calm. So that's what it came to mean. Tranquil. Smooth." Julia gave a little unexpected laugh, and her face lit up, the dark deep-set eyes, the strong bone structure. Gaunt as she was and without makeup, her black hair streaked with gray, her long body skeleton-thin, Julia Orlini showed style. Hester realized that she must once have been a strikingly handsome woman.

"Hester, was that name ever a mistake! Ben was never happy unless he brought planeloads of people down here. All business. All status. He would take the men off marlin fishing. He'd leave the women to me, to see the sights and buy everything that wasn't nailed down. But I understood him. He was terribly ambitious. I became quite talented; I knew the name of every fish taxidermist in the islands, all the men who stuffed and mounted the poor creatures. And I could serve dinner for thirty on four hours notice. It helped Ben." She was talking now to the rim of the sea.

"The children didn't like it. Not the way Ben wanted. We have three, you know." Her eyes shadowed. "That is, Ben and I have two. Twin sons. Tess, Theresa, is Ben's daughter. By a girl he married before me. The divorce hurt Ben. He's so Catholic when he thinks about it. He's never accepted the divorce idea. But I was quite willing. The child was sweet. At first. Then she left home. I haven't seen her for years. She seems to have an extrordinary skill for finding young men to live with but not to marry. The latest believes that God set men and women on this earth to copulate but never to work. He is a part-time janitor if Ben's check is late. Ben cannot deny money to any of his children. It gives him height."

In the bright silence a sequined hummingbird hung

at the ample spread of a hibiscus blossom, in another moment it had made its penetration, its wings vibrating to a music beyond human ear. Then it was gone. Hester was caught in fascination by the tiny dazzler.

Julia stirred on her chaise. "Forgive me for talking like this, Hester. I never do. Family stories are such bores. Like travel slides. No one cares except for their own."

Hester waited in the silence, partly contrite, partly relieved. Through Julia's light, bitter chatter, she had begun to sense other depths, a pain Julia wanted to touch but not reveal. For an instant Hester remembered Lowell's white face against the pillow. "Something's happened to Nick. Something awful!" But Hester had broken off with all that. That was why she came away. Not to think of the Roundtrees ever again.

"Twins!" said Julia so sharply she might have come out of a reverie and afraid she might not be heard. "Biovular. Do you know what that means, Hester? They came from two eggs. Two eggs within my own body, that I warmed and nourished and sheltered equally. And loved. Yes, I loved them equally. I tried to." Again her eyes were on the horizon, her thin hands played with the folds of the sun-striped caftan. "But how could I?" It was more a cry than a question. "Bruce was short and squat. Thin, sandy hair. His hands were too big and his shoulders too thick and he was strong. Oh, so strong. He didn't laugh. He went away and got mixed up in that cult in San Francisco. When Ben went out to get him, Bruce had his head shaved and wore rope sandals and called himself a Brother of Light. But he didn't come home. Not even after Nick . . . after." She drew a tight breath. She seemed to have forgotten Hester. "And I was glad. Glad. I had Nick. Why should a woman love all her children the same? Oh, if you had only known Nick. So dark. So handsome. So charming. He could have any girl he wanted. There was nothing he couldn't do if he set himself to it. He even learned to play the balalaïka one year." Julia gave a shy, almost girlish laugh. "Tennis, golf, swimming, dancing—he danced like a dream. The girls threw themselves at him. He adored dancing. We often danced together."

She rose in one quick movement, her hands clenched. "Hester, my son will never do any of that again. I know! I've seen every great specialist in the world. His brain was damaged when that car went over the side of the Ridge. That can never be changed, never restored. But I could give him peace. And contentment. I could bring him here. I wanted to bring him here. Ben has taken him away from me. With that awful man. Alec Bookman isn't helping Nick. Nick follows him around like a dog and does what he's told. Three times this winter Ben took Nick to New York. Ben wants him in his business. His son and heir. He thinks Nick's getting better all the time. That all he needs is toughening. Do you know that Nick wouldn't leave the apartment in New York? He was too weak. Alec Bookman took his place at those meetings. . . ." Her mouth opened as if to cry out, and she put her hand across it. No sound came, but her eyes stared wildly at nothing.

"Hester! What are they doing? I would rather see him dead!" The cry broke from her. She ran across the terrace and disappeared inside the house.

The sun was rising into the cloudless sky. The day was growing hotter. Hester shivered.

On the beach below, a stalwart figure stood erect, motionless, face to the sea. Quinn made no appearance of waiting, he was simply there as if time had no place in his scheme of things. Hester picked up a light sweater and went slowly down the steps. She could not have explained even to herself why the stillness, the silent brilliance of sea and sky seemed to menace.

All that feeling vanished as Hester sat braced in the sloop's cockpit, her feet against the hull's planking, her hands gripping the tiller. Quinn had taught her a great deal about the subtleties of handling a sailboat.

"Temperamental as a woman. Head her the wrong way and she'll leap out of your hands."

It was a measure of her detachment that she let that pass. She liked the steady strength of this blond, bearded man. She liked being with him. But he was part of what would be gone. What excited her were the tides that seemed to rise and fall within her, the sensual power of wind and sea that unleashed, would overwhelm her. But now she held them at bay, at her will.

"Look there! You're luffing!"

The sail was flapping overhead. She released the tiller to Quinn.

"Will I ever learn this?"

"Not in forty-eight hours, my girl. Men have spent millenia mastering the sea. Most of 'em have left their bones on its bottom."

They beached on the nameless cay, which Hester saw to her delight was feathered with green. Slim trees rose from a tangle of bushes that seemed at first glance impenetrable. Without a backward look, Quinn plunged into them. She followed and almost immediately found herself on a thread of path that widened as the light dimmed to a leafy translucence. She caught her breath. At their feet lay a pool, motionless as glass, of a green so deep that it could not have come from reflection.

"It comes from the sea. It's nearly bottomless. Slightly brackish, high mineral content. At night it glows like a moon from phosphorescence. I call it the Eye of God."

Her fingers touched the water and sent a scurry of ripples across it. It was warm.

"Take a swim. Marvelously refreshing."

She remembered. Her bikini lay in a mesh bag on the terrace at Halcyon. Julia's outburst had swept it from her mind.

Quinn's eyes met hers. "Go ahead. Try the pool. I

have to go to the other end of the cay and count the parrot population. I'm never sure if anyone has disturbed them." To a crackling of branches he disappeared.

Hester hesitated, then, caught in the spell, slipped off her clothes and as quickly slid into the Eye of God. If she intended to swim across the pool and back, its buoyancy surprised her. Its warmth permeated her. She floated on her back, her body shadowed marble, her hair fanning out, in the most delicious lassitude she had ever known. The dark green water embraced her. The treetops, bending to the winds, mesmerized her. All that had stung or tormented her drifted away. She closed her eyes and lay in the pool as if it were the cradle of eternity and time had no meaning.

A crackling in the bushes awakened her. Her eyes flew open. The man she knew so casually as Quinn was coming to the edge of the pool. She jackknifed into the water.

"I thought you weren't coming back."

"How long did you expect to keep the Eye of God to yourself?"

She flung sprays of water around her, and her body was lithe and beautiful as a fish.

"If you'll just go back to the bushes so I can get to my clothes, you can have the whole pool!"

For a fraction of a second he hesitated.

"Go on! If you wanted to go nude bathing, why didn't you say so, and I wouldn't have come on this trip. You can go look at your parrots again if there really are any parrots. . . ." She dived under, came up, and found him gone.

She climbed out, dressed quickly, and sat on the bank, shaking out her dark, wet hair. She wondered why she had made so much of it. She was no prude. Nude people swam together. She had done it herself in the Birch River in a daredevil, teen-age abandon.

But this was different. The overheated seduction of the place, the intense, erotic privacy, the unknown

scents of tropical greenery mingled in the heady moisture. Her whole body was alive to it. She imagined the
night, the pool become a moon, the sweetness of desire
after loneliness. And a man. The name burst inside
her like a cry. John! *John!* The one man without
whom there would be nothing.

Quinn returned to find her standing near the break
in the bushes. "Mind if I have a swim?"

"I'll go down to the beach."

"The picnic's stowed in a basket in a box of ice in
the hatchway."

"I'll find it."

It had become again all quite ordinary, yet subtly
changed. He had seen her body, and the knowledge
lay uncomfortably between them. They ate in near-
silence. Cold crawfish, fresh bread, fruits she did not
know. Pomegranates and papayas, she learned. At long
last the Eye of God began to fade.

"You were really quite brave this morning."

"Let's not talk about that. You were quite rude."

"No. I mean really brave." Quinn reached into his
back pocket for his wallet and handed her a photo-
graph. The picture was greenish in color and what she
saw made her gasp. "The Eye of God is also a drinking
hole."

She stared at the picture. A huge scaled head lifted
beside a tree trunk. The powerfully bowed legs were
clawed. An elongated body ended in a long spiny tail.
Malevolent eyes above a wide predatory mouth, and
from it unmistakably a tongue of flame.

Hester sat bolt upright. "A drinking hole! You
mean that thing is on this island? Back where you left
me?"

"I took a chance."

The Eye of God evaporated in Irish fury. "You left
me alone! I could have been eaten alive! What is it?"

"A lacertilia, distantly related to the crocodile and
other saurians. Even more distantly related thirty mil-
lion years ago to the dinosaur."

She sprang to her feet. "I want to get out of here! How big is it anyway?"

"Four inches. It's a green lizard I snapped beside a twig."

She sank to the sand. "Oh, Quinn!" Even before her outrage exploded again, Hester burst into laughter, explosive, helpless, and cleansing. He joined her.

"The devil take you, Quinn! Sure, you and your evil ways, no one else would!"

She looked at the snapshot again. It was suspiciously creased and dog-eared. "How many people do you bring to your Eye of God to show them that?"

"Those I like. Only one was foolish enough to come on an island picnic with a swimsuit."

She colored, busied herself gathering up picnic things, only to stop and burst into laughter again.

"Good. Very good. Now you're in a proper mood to visit Odella."

"Who's that?"

"I've already told you, girl. Don't you listen? You don't want to see cemeteries or old villages or places to shop. But you must meet Odella. She's a dealer in magic and spells and a test of your character. She's a friend of mine."

The sail filled. Hester sat in stern of the sloop, listening to the flow of his casual talk. The moods in these islands could change, it would seem, as swiftly as the surface of the sea.

The little square house, built of stone and thatch, squatted on a slight slope. The pathway to it was rough with shards of broken coral. They made their way slowly.

"Lends atmosphere," said Quinn. "I hope you haven't any secrets."

"What does that mean?"

"Odella always knows. She's like me. She hates secrets. They make for barriers. And barriers make for trouble. Trouble leads to death or war or any of a number of unpleasantnesses. That's why I got rid of mine. Though the British government took a dim view of it."

Hester was no longer listening. A tall woman stood in front of the house, erect and unsmiling. She was by any judgment the handsomest woman Hester had ever seen. Her features were fine and regular. A deep-purple turban lent a glow to the cream-and-coffee tones of her skin. A captious wind twisted a green-and-purple skirt tight to her limbs. Her carriage, her figure had the fullness of perfection. A Greek statue, thought Hester, who had not seen many.

"*Winged Victory* in sepia," murmured Quinn.

"Quinn. At last. I'm delighted. They've all gone. Come in. The house is cool. So you're Hester?" Her smile had a sudden brilliance, her voice an elegance that might have intimidated Hester had she felt less wary. Odella and Quinn were good friends.

"Hester Brady, madame, with the blood of the ancient Celts in her veins. And no secrets. I warned her that within the waxing and waning of the moon any secret she held would be out after meeting you. But she's one of the innocents."

It was more of Quinn's nonsense. Hester was almost used to it. But not quite. She told herself she only imagined the sudden sharpness in the glance the majestic woman gave her. She followed them uneasily into the little house.

"Hester wants to see everything, Odell. She's going home in two days. She's in love." Quinn lounged in a rattan chair that seemed to have taken his shape.

Hester flushed. "I'll speak for myself on that, thank you, Quinn."

"I think she will," said Odella. It held more command than amusement. "Refreshment, I think, should come first."

She served earthen mugs of a thick creamy milk that tasted warm and sweet. With it small saucers of fine-chopped, raw green stuff that tasted cool and bitter.

"*Berza,*" said Odella. "Very fresh."

"Kale, we call it," said Quinn. He had already downed half the milk in his cup .

"But a very fine kind, dear Quinn."

Odella turned to Hester, in her black eyes a curious intensity. "*Berza* contains all the vitamins, and goat's milk all the protein you need. You could live entirely on what you are now eating and drinking."

"A hideous thought to a man who gave his youth to the glory of intemperance."

Hester was not comfortable. The shadowy little room with its clutter of pillows and books and bird-cages and plants depressed her. The woman dominated it like a great dark-winged bird herself.

Quinn picked the last green crumb from his saucer. "Now let's see your treasures, my queen of the night. The wind's hauling around. I don't want to see this trusting young woman soaked to the skin"—he grinned at Hester—"a third time."

The woman led them on a path around the house to a rough wooden shack. The thick door creaked behind them. Hester found herself in a small room with a dusty skylight and the scent of acrid incense.

"I don't blame you for disliking it, my dear. So do I. One must, however, make a living. My visitors adore it. And they expect it."

Hester found herself wondering uneasily where this stately woman could have come from, with her polished voice, her faint air of amusement, and her uncanny ability to read Hester's thoughts almost as they formed.

"Now come, look around. If there's anything you really like, you may have it. My pleasure."

There assuredly was not. Rough wooden shelves lined the room, bearing an assortment of jars, jugs, glass-fronted boxes, and old-fashioned apothecary glass globes. Hester remembered seeing them as a child, hanging in pharmacy windows and filled with red or blue or green liquid. Odella's globes contained dark, unidentifiable objects. On the wall opposite the door hung a faded purple cloth. It bore a device that Hester could only make out as a circle, and within the circle, a square, and within the square, a very small diamond shape.

"It's called the Eye of God," said Odella. "By those who believe."

Hester flushed and remembered those moments in the pool. She had been foolish and giddy in the spell of that lost place. She regretted every instant of it. More than that she resented her own trusting naiveté. It was all a bag of tricks. She wanted only to escape. She turned to Quinn. He was no longer in the shack.

"He's outside." The woman's ability to read her thoughts was uncanny. "He's seen it all, and there isn't a great deal of room here. I usually take my visitors through one by one."

The shack was windowless. Hester felt stifled. The simplest thing to do was to walk out. Yet the curious pride and power of this tall, intelligent woman kept her from such discourtesy. She moved along past the shelves with what she hoped was disinterest.

"I understand." Odella's melodious voice followed her. "I looked on many of these objects once as you do. But there are some who come here who know more than either of us. They see in my little display some very ancient truths."

She picked up an object. Hester glanced at it with revulsion and turned away. A six-inch lizard, mummified and brown, had been nailed to a cross of twigs. "Unpleasant? I agree with you. A little dark man from the jungles of Honduras brought it to me one day. He said he was one hundred years old and had outlived its spells." Her light laugh dissipated the horror. "I have no wish to live a hundred years."

Odella moved on and held out a four-inch sack of red cloth, tied by its corners. "Spirit soil. My great uncle was an Obeah man in Jamaica. A kind of magician.

He could make a stick dance or a spirit rise. He always carried one of these little bags. They contain earth taken from a new grave. This one comes from a bride's grave. It will bring love to its possessor." She held out the tiny sack. "Would you like it?"

Hester shuddered. This must end soon. "No, thanks, Miss Odella. No. Really. I don't—I never could believe it. I—just wouldn't want it. If you don't mind." She moved along quickly.

"Of course. Of what use is anything one does not believe in?"

Hester darted across the room to the shelves near the door. "What's that?" She pointed to an apothecary globe containing what looked like a lumpish piece of leather. She did not care what it might be but that way lay escape.

"You are sensitive, my dear. That is an object of extraordinary power. The forehead flesh of a stillborn colt. The ancient Egyptians used it in their mummifying vats to assure the dead a safe journey. The witches of Thrace used it to summon power from the winds. Horses have always been a source of mystery to men. You would not find a sorcerer worth his salt who did not have a replica of a horses' head on his premises." She smiled. Again the quick, odd radiance. "It was said that Thomas Aquinas had a brass statue of a horse buried in front of the entrance to his house. For sentiment or safety? Who knows?"

They were at the door. Hester pushed at it. Odella held up her hand. "I would like you to take one little souvenir of this day with you so you won't forget us entirely. It's rather pretty, and I don't think you could possibly mind having it. It would give me pleasure."

She held out a three-inch length of narrow metal, gold in color, that looked like a small penknife. She swung it, and it seemed to pick up whatever light seeped into the place. "The wand of Morpheus. With it you can learn other people's secrets. But I must warn you, it might also cost you your own."

"If I had any," said Hester lightly.

Odella's hand still lay against the door. "No, my dear," she said intensely. "We will part soon. There is no reason to hide the truth from me." She lifted her deep-set, almost expressionless eyes. "The very vibrations in this room tell me. Your secret lies like a stone inside you. Get rid of it, Hester, or it will make you its prisoner to the end of your life."

She thrust the trinket into Hester's hand and opened the thick door. Hester blinked into the sunshine. Quinn stood leaning against the side of the shack. The woman turned her face to the sea.

"The wind has changed. Good-bye, dear friends." She was gone as if the light had swallowed her.

Quinn glanced at Hester but something in her face stopped his question. He did not ask it until they were in the sloop, heeling over to a stiff breeze over ruffled water.

"Did you enjoy yourself?"

"Not very much."

"It's a bit macabre but that's her business."

"She gave me this." She swung the little penknife-like bit of metal in her fingers and found it had a pleasant balance.

Quinn whistled. "Well, she has taken to you. A sleep wand, eh?"

"What's that?"

"Hypnotists use it. See, it's thick on one edge, thin on the other, like a boomerang or an airplane wing. The air flows over and under. So does the light."

"I don't believe it," said Hester. "Any more than I believe any of that stuff in the shack. I think it's a big tourist cheat and I'm surprised that you'd take me there."

"You might also be surprised to know that Odella speaks five languages. She is an authority on Greek and Egyptian mythology. She has been asked to lecture at universities, all over the world."

"Why doesn't she, then? Instead of raising goats and

fooling people?" It was good to get rid of her aggravations for reasons deeper than she could have explained.

"Because she will not go out in the world where she will be discovered. You see, Hester"—his voice softened as if speaking to a child—"Odella is blind."

The sun splashed magenta, flame, and gold across a turquoise sky. The sloop slid alongside the dock. Hester jumped out to the landing before he could help her.

"You haven't forgiven me, have you?"

"I don't carry grudges."

"I don't think you do. I'm sorry about the pool. You were quite beautiful. I saw innocence."

"I can forget it. I've known worse. And I'm sorry about your friend, Odella."

"She wouldn't thank you for that." The salmon light emptied his face of color. He looked yellowed and empty, like a man drained of the last wine of life. She felt a sudden compassion. In another day she would be home, to the harsh, almost welcome reality of snow and rock and challenge. He would have faded—to what?

"Thanks, Quinn. For everything."

"We had one more engagement, if you remember."

"I should spend tomorrow with Julia."

"Should you?" He caught the transparency. "I had hoped to take you to Boar's Head. It's quite remarkable. Especially when there's a party."

She hesitated. Not because she had forgiven him. Not because he had shown her kindness and she had been less than gracious. But because suddenly, inexplicably she had become to herself plain Hester Brady, and the hurt of John Roundtree lay like a living thing inside her.

She shrugged.

"All right. I'll go. Why not? It sounds like fun.

What do I wear? Or is it come as you are?"

If he heard the unsteadiness beneath the bravado, he gave no sign. "Anything you like. Simpler the better," he said gravely. "I'll pick you up at six."

Hester did not watch the sloop tacking out. She walked up the path, pushing the past and the future from her. She would live one more day in this silver suspension, thinking of nothing, letting herself float.

Which left her mind open to a nagging notion. Somewhere, sometime she had seen the little penknife-like souvenir Odella had given her. But where?

The notion slid away at last in broken sleep.

Chapter Seventeen

Boar's Head was one of a string of privately owned islands within the embrace of the Out Islands. Far enough apart for privacy, close enough for reassurance, they stretched spangled and guarded along a channel of seawater known irreverently as Millionaire's Bight.

Boar's Head lay further toward the horizon. Owned and built originally by a shadowy maharaja, it was owned in turn by a shadowy bootlegger, a shadowy Mafia king. Two years ago it had been purchased by another shadowy character, a multimillionaire, a Californian, Simon Gideon. In the transactions the three-mile cay had lost much of its original Oriental magnificence. The sprawling white dwelling rose turreted and minaretted against the sky. Open archways looked out on every mood of mist and light. Long arched corridors, tiled in colors of peacock intensity, opened to the sea. In an endless web of cool, dim rooms, deep divans and ornate chairs surrendered to an Oriental fantasy of silken pillows and sinuous rugs.

Simon had changed nothing. He liked the uniqueness of Boar's Head. He liked its air of mystery. He liked its unreality.

He had bought it for isolation, for tranquility and escape. None of that was in evidence as he stepped from the motor launch that had brought him from the airport, a newspaper folded under his arm. The day's brilliance mocked his mood. So did the scene that greeted him as he climbed the hand-carved steps, passed through an alley of hibiscus bushes and strode through an arch to the pool that hung like a redundant teardrop above the sea. His nephew and adopted heir, Michael, lay beside it. His deeply bronzed body glistened with water, his arm spread across a nymph-like creature, more provocative in three minuscule brown silk triangles than she would have been stark nude.

Michael jumped to his feet, not so much with dismay as with the respect he had learned was useful.

"Hi! Didn't know you were coming down."

"Who's that?"

"She helps Kayda deliver the vegetables."

The nymph had fled.

"This place can be a bloody bore, Simon, without a little action."

Simon had encouraged the informal first name. It veiled the widening years. At this moment he resented it.

"I can end the boredom." He thrust the newspaper at Michael. "Read that."

Michael obeyed without argument. As he had, since the night four years ago when he lifted the lion's-head knocker on the oak doors of Simon Gideon's barnlike mansion in San Francisco, interrupted Simon's solitary dinner, and asked for overnight lodging. The lodging had continued to the present, become his home, and secured his destiny. He had not even been asked to account for the three years since he had left Thatcher, the lost years he called his "black hole," dropped like a burnt-out meteor from his private universe. Life had turned from good to resplendent.

"Read it, Mike. People Who Make News."

Michael read,

"John Roundtree, freshman Congressman from Thatcher, Connecticut, now completely at home in Washington, is spearheading a group of young

congressional tigers in an attack on Felix Twining's nuclear energy bill. Thatcher is one of the
proposed sites. John Roundtree, a lone goer, is apparently willing to stake his newly fledged political career on a win-all, lose-all fight. The nuclear
bill goes to committee this session. Meanwhile the
big power companies around the country are
watching young Roundtree. So are we."

"Your brother's a damn fool, Mike."

Michael slung a towel around his neck. "He always
was. Thought more of a tree than a bank account.
Never even had a woman, that I knew about. I'd bet
even money he's still a virgin."

Normally Simon would have laughed. He did not.
"He's made Washington. And he's getting attention."

"Nothing you can't handle, Simon."

"Nothing *we* can't handle, boy."

"Sure, Uncle Simon. Nothing. The pool's yours."

But Simon was not ready to be dismissed. There
were things about Michael he did not understand.

"You're going to Thatcher with me, Mike. When
the time's ripe."

"I haven't said I wouldn't, have I?"

"You haven't said you would either. This is big,
Mike, maybe the biggest thing I've ever gotten into.
Northern Power is offering me half its shares to—
Christ Almighty, will you listen to me? I've just seen
this man Orlini in New York. He's bought up a lot of
the land in Thatcher, but I think he can be blown
over. He's an odd one. He wants his son in this or no
dice. I've yet to meet the son. Instead he brought in an
associate—he called him Bookman. A phony if I ever
saw one, who's got some kind of hook into Orlini. I
don't trust him. I don't want him in the business. I
want you to fly back to New York with me in the
morning—"

"What can I do?"

"It's an order, Mike."

Michael stopped toweling himself. "Okay. But not tomorrow. Bill Fax is bringing a yachtload from Palm Beach for a party here tomorrow night. Rock group. The works."

"Who's idea was that?"

"Mine." Mike grinned. "Only way I could get Kitty out to this godforsaken heap."

Simon watched the stocky, muscled figure through the archway. He had indulged Mike. He had shown him how to spend and how to live. And Mike had learned. God, how he had learned. Simon had no patience with the notion that every young man had to begin at the bottom. Simon had multiplied his own inherited fortune. Mike would do the same when his time came. That was how power was built, the kind of power that could manage what must be managed in this country.

Simon went into the bathhouse still thinking of his adopted heir. Mike was nearly thirty now, old enough to take the reins himself. Yet here he was, a waster, a playboy, and—he had to admit it—a womanizer. Michael lived with a mask that kept his purposes to himself.

As he emerged in his swim trunks Simon saw it another way. "Waiting for me to die. Is that it? Well, he's got a long wait, and when I do, I'll have the knots tied so tight that boy'll have to get off his butt even to find them!"

Simon dived into the unbroken blue of the pool and swam in long, splashing strokes to the pool's end. He clung to the edge with a sharp intake, shallow breath. A man never knows, he thought. He would have it out with Mike yet. No easy inheritance. He would see to that. And no easy woman to get it away from him. But he would give a lot to know what his heir-designate, Michael Roundtree, really wanted.

The final night of her holiday had come. Hester looked out on the opalescent sea, then around the pale blue silken bedroom in which she would sleep for the last time. It had not been a holiday. It had been an interlude, a transformation, a dropping-out from her own life into an experience that would never come again.

Hester, you're mad, she told her image. *If you were to stay one more day, you'd sicken of all the softness. You're not born to it and sure as milk, you'd stifle on it. If you didn't have a thorn in your foot or a fight in your mind, you'd find one before long. You're going home where you belong. And never mind mooning over the rich that God never cut to your last.*

Yet she had never dressed with more inner excitement.

No, there had been one other time. Just one. As she emerged from the shower, her full breasts tingling, her body lithe and tanned, her senses acutely alive, the memory swept over her.

It was the one party in the Roundtree home to which Michael had taken her. Somebody's birthday. Lowell's, she remembered, which was why he had asked her, no doubt. For everything between them had been kept secret. "More fun," he had told her. For a while she thought so too.

She had used her savings to buy the new dress, the best Bollington could offer. A slither of long green silk to the floor. "It makes emeralds of your eyes, dearie," the saleslady stated. It was the most beautiful dress she had ever owned. "There's not a man on earth good enough for you," Tom had harrumped.

It was a disaster from the moment she had entered the big house. Every girl there wore the most casual of short, clingy dresses above the knee, even showing long, bare legs. She might as well have carried a sandwich board. I AM DIFFERENT.

Later when she came down the gracious staircase with her wrap (they were agonizingly going on to the country club), she caught a glimpse of Michael through a study door. His hand was stroking the thigh of the girl whose black, fringed mini was briefest of all.

Her flushed fury must have showed. At the bottom of the stairs a youngish, brown-haired woman she did not know gave her a sharp knowing glance.

"You're Hester."

"That's right."

The shrewd eyes swept Hester's dress.

"Very lovely."

"Thanks." It was rude. She had to endure humiliation; she would not endure condescension.

The woman smiled, then nodded toward the study door. "He's a Roundtree, you know. Dark side of the escutcheon. So am I."

As Mary would have said, instead of ignoring it, Satan's imp took hold of Hester's tongue.

"Well, I'm not. I'm Hester Brady and that's enough for me!"

The young woman unexpectedly laughed. "I envy you. In this town you're either born a Roundtree woman or, if you love a Roundtree man, you become one. However."—her eyes sparkled, and Hester found she could like her—"if you are pliable and discreet and willing to lie a little, it is not at all a bad life."

Hester never saw the woman again. The next day she and Michael quarreled passionately and even more passionately made up. It was the double edge of their impossible rapture.

"If you are pliable and discreet and willing to lie a little. . . ."

The words came back to her now from the distance. She, Hester, had been all of those things and she had lost. That was past. She was someone tonight she had never been in her life. She would not be fearful of her own excitement.

She dressed carefully. Julia had given her the dress. "Hester, Hester, take your moments when they come. You are young! The joys go. Wear it! I can't!"

It was as if Julia wanted something of herself in the evening ahead.

The sheer white cotton, trimmed in coarse ecru lace, flowed around her body like visible wind. She slipped her bare feet into flat thonged sandals and pinned a yellow hibiscus flower in her loose hair.

Quinn, waiting on the dock, scrutinized her.

"Very good, my girl. Very, very right."

It wasn't so hard after all, Hester thought, to be happy. Like the cabined motor launch Quinn had brought for the trip, she had only to cast off from her old moorings.

In twenty minutes they came within sight of Boar's Head Cay. She stared in amazement. Clusters of white turrets rose above the cay, seeming to float in the gold-and-turquoise evening. Even from the water she could see the countless archways of the vast house, lifting like white fountains above a profusion of green.

"They set five hundred trees on that heap of rock and coral and made them grow."

A gilded light touched the twisting roofline and flowed through the arches.

"It looks as if it would blow away."

"Don't be fooled. That airy fairy palace is built like a fortress. The house alone covers nearly an acre."

"Are there any walls?"

"Oh, yes. Yes indeed. You'd know if you got lost up there."

"I'd love to," Hester said. Mostly to herself. She saw herself suddenly in her white dress drifting through that magic.

The young dock attendant took the mooring rope from Quinn's capable hands.

"Think I can't make fast myself, Roy?"

"Just doing what I'm hired for, Mister Quinn." He was slim and agile, no more than eighteen; his teeth flashed white against the pale mahogany of near-classic features.

"Guests arrived, I see." He nodded to a yacht, moored alongside.

"Yes. But the party hasn't started. Mister Gideon left all of a sudden, about five."

"And the nephew and heir?"

The boy shrugged. "He stayed. He gets his way."

Hester had already jumped on to the dock. She stood staring at the yacht. Dark blue hull, dazzling white superstructure, the gleam of teak decks, the shine of polished brass everywhere. On the afterdeck, among deep-pillowed divans and pots of flowering plants, stood a red-lacquered bar and, most incredible of all, a grand piano, its glistening lid open, sheet music on the rack.

The stern of the boat bore the name CIRCE.

"What does that mean?"

"Circe?" Quinn smiled at her fondly, as he always did, she thought, when she showed her ignorance. "Circe was a siren in Greek mythology, who lured men to their destruction on the rocks of her island. Seducing them, of course."

"Oh."

"Entirely appropriate in this case."

She did not follow that. "Do people live on the yacht?"

"Anywhere from twelve to twenty, depending on how adjustable they are. It can cross the Atlantic."

She was imagining herself among those people, whoever they were, lounging on those divans, listening to that piano. . . .

"Would you like to go on board?"

"Could I?" She stopped. She was sounding like a schoolgirl.

"What about it, Roy?"

"Why not? Everybody's gone up to the house. Only a couple of the crew left."

"Come into my parlor, Hester." She followed Quinn across the narrow, cleated gangway.

A young tousled crewman saluted him, his eyes lingering on Hester.

"Sightseers, Freddie. On your way."

The boy grinned and disappeared.

"You know everybody, Quinn."

"It's my business. Like to see the interior?"

Take every moment you can. "I'd like to see everything. Everything!"

He elbowed her through a corridor and into what looked like a museum of tapestry, marble, overstuffed divans, and a wood-burning fireplace.

"The grand salon, madame. A bit overdone but cozy in a gale. Not that this old war-horse goes very far in one."

"Where does everybody sleep?"

"The cabins are off that corridor. Paneled in oak, if you care. Each with private bath. If you still care."

He led her past the closed doors. Without warning, one was thrown open. A girl stood inside, skeleton thin, with a small heart-shaped face, deeply tanned and lost in a tumble of tawny, frizzed hair. She wore nothing but a pair of briefs. Her eyes were overbright. As she clung unsteadily to the door knob a telltale odor, sweet, cloying escaped from the room.

"Jesus, are we here already? Quinn—lover boy . . . !"

"Pull yourself together, Kitty. The party's starting."

"Who's that?" Her eyes focused with effort on Hester.

"A guest."

"Okay. Okay. You tell that son of a bitch Mike that if he wants me up there, he'll have to come and get me." She eyed Hester again. "Didn't get the name but I'm Lady Kitty Pentweazle, Duchess of Screw. And you?"

"Hester Brady."

"Never heard of you." The door closed.

Hester moved along the corridor. She wanted fresh air. She had long ago given up sitting in judgment on any human being. She had made her own mistake, and it would live with her the rest of her life. In return she had flung herself at fate, indifferent to what people thought or said. Who was she to condemn or even care? Still, at the heart of this most beautiful mirage. . . .

She followed Quinn in embarrassed silence out on deck and across the gangplank.

The evening had turned lavender. Concealed lights glowed beneath the numberless arches. She and Quinn climbed the broad, low steps together. From somewhere came music, soft, languorous, teasing. The house itself spread in every direction and seemed to have a hundred entrances. She was not ready to go in. The evening had somehow, inexplicably, changed direction. Wherever the party was in the distance, she was in no hurry to join it.

She turned for a last look at the placid, darkening sea, the long shadows of trees and archways increasing her sense of isolation.

"A savage place! As holy and enchanted as e'er beneath a waning moon was haunted by woman wailing for her demon lover."

"Quinn, you should have been an actor!"

"In my time, madame, I have played many parts."

"I don't even know what those creepy words mean."

"If you have to understand, my girl, don't listen. You hear them with your soul. Come along. There are sounds of revelry."

Still she lingered. The sky took on the depth of velvet, etched with the thin crescent of a moon. The stars newly brilliant—she closed her eyes to seal this beauty within herself. When she opened them, she was alone. Quinn had gone ahead. She was not surprised. The scene on the yacht lay awkwardly between them. As she had already discovered, his worlds were many, like his secrets.

The music had stopped. When it began again, she would find her way. The long empty room behind her led to others she would explore. She was in no hurry.

She leaned against an archway and breathed the glory of the night.

She was not aware of the broad-shouldered, stocky man entering the far end of the dim room. He paused. The girl in white stood posed like a moth, her back to him. He was angry with the course of the day and the evening. And as always he was curious.

Hester heard the footsteps, hollow and purposeful on the Moorish tiles. She turned. In the dimness she could not see his face. He came toward her. She gave a small gasp.

"Michael!"

"Hester! My God. Hester—Brady!"

Her last name was like a slap, an aid to recall. Yet, why not? How often she had imagined this moment, knowing that whatever she imagined, it would be different.

Now here it was. Instead of the coolness she had promised herself, she felt only a tumult of churning, searing emotions filling the chasm of eight lonely years.

Michael was the first to break the silence. He came toward her with that crooked smile that once could turn her to water.

"So you caught up with me, Hes."

"Caught up . . .?" She stopped. Her heart was pounding, and that must pass.

"I was sure you would. I might say there were times I hoped you would."

The mockery, the easy confidence. And yet, a change. She saw more clearly now in the dim light. The fleshy strength of his features had turned flabby, the eyes that could narrow and chill, were distant. The stamp of something Hester could not define had driven the youth from his face. This was *Michael,* the golden boy of her heady girlhood. Michael, around whom her anger and heartbreak had swirled for eight long years. Michael, to whom she was forever linked.

She steadied her voice. "It was no wish of mine to find you, Michael."

"Oh, come now. None of your pride at this hour of the evening. Let's call it a draw and not bother how you came here or why. You're here. I'm here. Lodestones, Hester. Drawn together. Magnet and steel." The light teasing again. "Did you ever figure out which of us was which? Inevitable, no matter how many years have gone by. Doesn't all this tell you so?"

"It doesn't tell me anything. Except that eight years is a long time."

"Has it been eight?"

"If you've lost track, I haven't."

But he had come closer to her, and she was aware again of his masculinity, even the same scent she remembered, subtle, evocative. A maleness.

He must not touch me, she thought wildly. Even in quarrels, in bitterness, in passionate waiting and shallow excuses, his touch once could dissipate all her resistance. Now as he stood so near, yet so different, she felt fear, fear that the eight walled years might vanish into the shimmering night.

"What are you afraid of, Hester?" She did not answer. "Not us, surely. This is fate. Destiny. Karma. The stars. Or maybe just ourselves."

"No, it isn't. It isn't anything like that. Not anymore. We've changed. You're different. I'm different. What happened is over. It was a long time ago."

"Think so?" His hand went caressingly toward her face. She sprang away.

"Michael, don't try anything like that."

"You have a short memory."

"No, I haven't. I haven't forgotten. Any of it. I couldn't. I would have crawled to you once. I guess I did, now that I look back. High and mighty as you were. Knowing that you might be laughing at me afterwards, but I'd go on for the terrible wanting. But I was proud too, even the night you went off without a look back."

"Not quite right. I stopped at your house. Didn't your mother tell you? To say good-bye. Like a gentleman."

She knew now what lay in his face. Dissipation, weariness. But deeper than either, cruelty. She had caught glimpses of it long ago with a kind of fascination that she had mastered. Now it was fixed.

"I'd like to leave now, Michael. I'm sorry I ever came to this place—Boar's Head. If I had known—"

"Known what? That I own it? Anybody could have told you."

"You—own this?"

"I will someday. A rich uncle, Hester. I told you once old Simon is leaving it to me. That puts a different complexion on things, doesn't it, Hes?"

"No, it doesn't. I don't care."

"I think you do. Or you could learn to. You never had it easy, did you? Stay here with me and I'll show you the rich life. Just the two of us. As long as you like. Better than that kid stuff in the cave, Hes."

She gave a long releasing sigh. He had, without knowing it, set her free. She could hate this man now. Whatever claim he had on her was gone in a fresh wind that blew through her.

"Are you married, Hes? Is that the trouble?"

"No."

"You have a lover." He looked at her closely. "That would account for it. The glow. By God, you're a beauty! Who would have guessed that? But beauty or not, you could always drive a man mad. Tell me the truth, Hester, about this lover. When he makes love to you, you're with me, aren't you? When he kisses you, fondles you, it's me—"

"No! How dare you! That's rotten. He doesn't . . . He—" she stopped, trapped in the face of his laughter.

"You have a lover who doesn't make love to you? And thinks he can hold you? You, Hester!" He gripped her wrist. "Whoever he is, he'll never come between you and me. Let me tell you something I've never told anyone in the world. I killed a man once because he came between me and what I wanted. It was not as difficult as I thought it would be." His voice turned suddenly thin, boylike. "Stay here with me, Hester. For a little while. You've come because you had to. Because I'm the one man you're never going to forget, no matter who you sleep with. Hester, I want you!" It was a cry. His arms caught her.

She broke free. "No, Michael. No! Not ever! I didn't come here to see you. I never want to see you again. You're someone I don't know. You're—you're horrible!"

He leaned back against the doorway, his forehead moist with sweat. For an instant she was terrified, but he made no move to touch her again. Unaccountably her fear watered to pity for this man who had been the horizon of her whole world.

"Michael, try to understand me. I won't see you again. I've found the man I want. I'll never marry him. I—can't. But he's given me all the decency in my life. I love him. Does that answer you?"

Her own words strengthened her.

"Now if you'll please tell me the way down to the dock. . . ." The words trailed. Quinn had materialized from the dark. How much he had heard she could not guess, nor did she care. He was reality. Michael had seen him.

"Looking for her, Quinn?"

"So you two already know each other."

"A long time ago." Michael gave a short laugh. "Just shows, Quinn, my women never forget me. I'll leave her to you and find Kitty. Her charm is that she never remembers me." He turned back into the room, paused once with a grin. "Quite a girl you've picked up, Quinn. I *know.*"

It was cheapening and vicious, but it was over, this nightmare of fantasy and evil. Hester let it drain into the night.

"Let's go," said Quinn abruptly. "Not much of a party anyway."

As Hester followed him down the flagstone path, an odd and fleeting moment returned. Odella's words, accompanying the gift of the little golden talisman. *Wear it carefully. It will open secrets.*

Halcyon Cay blazed with lights as the launch approached. Hester had a small and kind goodnight for Quinn. Wisely, he did not press.

She found Julia on the terrace, awake and distraught.

"I'm going back with you tomorrow, Hester. Nick, my son, is not well. Ben telephoned me. He never telephones me. But he called me, Hester, tonight."

She looked more closely at Hester. "You're home early. Didn't you enjoy yourself?"

"Yes, thank you. It was all right."

"You see? This is what happens down here. At first it's fairyland. You never want to leave. Then you find other things. We all do. And suddenly the sea becomes a prison. And it's time to go. Please keep the dress. You're very lovely in it. Oh, and Hester. . . ."

Hester waited, her thoughts far from Julia.

"I'm going right on to Thatcher with you. Ben's up there now with Nick."

Hester nodded. There would be time enough in the morning to tell Julia that she was not going to Thatcher. But that was all. From the airport she would go into New York City. She would take the long subway ride uptown as she had done so often when her need was great.

She would knock on the plain door of a plain building. She would see the plain face of Sister Agatha, framed in its black and white security of faith.

"Sister, tell me what to do! Tell me everything! Again!"

Part Four

The Cave

Chapter Eighteen

Inevitable as it was, the first March thaw always took the citizens of Thatcher by surprise. Overnight the heavy snow bowed to spreading puddles. The roads gleamed black and bare. The steady drip from eaves and cornices was as welcome as a bird call. On Flagpole Green citizens braved the slush to sit on damp benches and lift winter faces to the sun.

In the woods rivulets shouldered aside the ice to run full and deep. Willard claimed sight of the first bright green of skunk cabbage. But then Willard Roundtree could always see what he wanted to see, in Thatcher's opinion.

In Willard's barn the gray mare moved restlessly. Turned out in the paddock's mud, she no longer kicked up her heels to airy freedom. She moved sedately, knowingly. Her time was near.

Mary Brady let the green curtain stuff she was making up for the pub fall in her lap; even the needle was too heavy.

"Open the window, Hester. I can taste spring."

Hester rose mechanically, obediently, as she did all things these days. The air was sharp, but the sky soft, and the sun's new warmth unsettling. The coming of spring only deepened her sense of isolation. She would like to hold it at bay a while longer.

Nothing had changed. The translucent bubble of Halcyon had burst and vanished. A chain now hung across the driveway to the Orlini house on the Ridge. To her one phone call a brittle voice answered "Not here." There were rumors of odd things about Nick Orlini; both Mr. and Mrs. Orlini had come and gone. But no one knew with any certainty where.

The headlines of the *Thatcher Standard* trumpeted John Roundtree's growing success in his fight against nuclear energy plants. Hester closed her eyes to the stabbing sweetness of his name. Fate had used Halcyon as a decoy, then closed the door to any future. To John, to their brief and fleeting idyll. Firmly and forever, Hester told herself, as she swept and polished, washed bar glasses, and finished Mary's curtains. Firmly and forever she would find her strength in being needed as she watched the frail shell that was Mary's body struggle to contain that restive spirit.

"Don't sit with me, Hester. I can do well enough for myself. Call Mister Willard and see how that mare is doing. She's got spring on her mind about now, I'd say. And mind you," she called as Hester reached the door, "remember to put one-half water in that bottle of Irish Tom keeps for himself under the bar. Might as well not leave all the saving of his soul to God."

The doing was the living, Hester told herself. She flashed a bright, false smile at the customers, tossed her head in the old way, and knew the light glistened enticingly on the little metallic sleep wand she had hung on a chain around her neck. A defiance or a reminder? She did not ask herself. It was the only reality left from her one glimpse of splendor. She liked to say to strangers, "Oh, a souvenir from the islands. I was down there this winter."

And so it might have gone as spring edged nearer, but for two events. The gray mare's colt foal was born, mouse-dark and, Willard reported, perfect, showing every Thoroughbred trait that his unwieldy mother had so long kept secret. Mary rose from her couch, eyes shining, and announced she would go to the barn the next morning if she had to walk.

The second event was no less sudden. That same evening Hester looked up from behind the bar to see the neat, confident figure of Dr. Alexander Bookman. It was months since he last came to the pub. He walked to his regular table, rubbed his soft, well-kept hands, and nodded pleasantly. Hester felt an unexpected chill.

"Well, are you going to wait on the man, m'girl? Or will I invite him to step behind the bar and help himself? No charge. No charge at all."

So she had forgotten to cut the bottle of Irish. She buttoned her smock, took off her apron, and went to the table.

Alec Bookman had never looked more mild-mannered and benign as she stood courteously beside his chair.

"Well, Miss Brady! How are you? You're looking well, very well indeed. I'd say a holiday agrees with you."

"The usual brandy, Doctor Bookman?"

"Come now, Hester, it was Alec before you went away. Will you join me?"

She glanced at the bar and saw an infuriating nod of encouragement from Tom. In this temper he might say anything. She sat down.

"I'm on my work time."

"I won't detain you. You had a pleasant time with Julia, I take it."

She could be as cool as he was. She had not yet caught any direction to this visit.

"I guess she told you. You being up at the house there."

"Mrs. Orlini is not there now. She came home under her usual illusion that her son was ill. The poor chap was indeed miserable while he was in New York. Despite my advice his father took him everywhere. When I managed to get him back here, there was a most unfortunate relapse. An unpleasant little incident over a bird, a myna bird owned by the servants. Nick hated the thing. But that's all over. . . ."

"I took the liberty on myself, Doctor, of bringing you the usual." Tom set down two glasses. "I won't be needing you right away, girl." Tom walked carefully back to the bar.

Hester started to rise and was surprised at the white hand on her wrist.

"Please. Another minute. I came to talk to you, because someone who knows the family, as you apparently do—" *Was the voice sarcastic?* "—should understand. There have been some ugly stories. Utterly malicious. Nick is very well, improving every day, and will as long as I can persuade his rather foolish parents to leave him here in this place he loves, until I say he is ready to leave."

"I don't know why you're telling me."

"Because you can be helpful, Hester. To Nick and to me. To end rumors, to—"

She had a sudden image of Lowell, fallen in the winter woods, of the motionless figure of Dr. Alexander Bookman on the slope above. "It's none of my affair."

"I thought we were better friends than that, Hester. I remember the gray mare. By the way, how is she?"

"She had her foal yesterday."

"Splendid."

Hester rose. "I have to get back to my work."

"Of course. Why don't we talk this over. . . ." But Hester did not hear the rest. As he rose with her, his jacket fell open on a fawn vest. From a gold watch chain dangled a small penknifelike object. Hester stared.

"You notice my little gold penknife? Sold to me by a rogue in Paris who swore that it once belonged to Napoleon the Third and was used to cut the imperial writing quills." He slid the little object into his vest pocket. "We'll talk again, Hester. Good to see you looking so well."

That night Hester lay awake a long time and told herself she was thinking nonsense. What if Alec Bookman's gold trinket was a very replica of the sleep wand Odella had given her? What of it, if he lied to her?

What if he had pocketed it so quickly? What if an educated doctor indulged himself in superstition?

But deeper in her mind, somewhere she could not reach, lay something without a name. When she fell asleep at last, she dreamed of a man on the slope of a hill. He cast a golden shadow that was smothering her.

The spring sunshine lay as warm and sweet on the stable floor as the hay in the loft above it.

Mary Brady, with Willard's help, raised herself on tiptoe to peer into the dim stall. Hester tried to steady her, but it seemed unnecessary. Mary's face was radiant. The new foal was at his mother's side nursing. His small brush of a tail flicked from time to time. The mare's ears were laid flat back.

"Now we're not interfering, mother," murmured Mary gaily. But you're quite right to stand guard over him. Oh, he's a darling you've got there. And a star like your own on his forehead. He'll be a gray, Will!"

"No doubt." Willard Roundtree's eyes were on Mary.

"They're all mouse-color in the beginning but you can see by the sheen—ho, ho, look at the devil in him! Now that's nipping too hard, acushla!"

The mare shook the foal free. His wobbly legs carried him once around the stall, and the elegant little head reached for her small black udder again.

"Name him, Mary."

"Mischief will do for a start."

"Done," said Willard. "Let's hope he won't live up to it."

"Let's hope he will. Did you ever see any young one worth his salt without it?"

They stood outside the box stall for another minute, watching. The foal finished, the mare backed away, moving between the onlookers and her newborn. Beyond her they could just glimpse the awkward yet sturdy little colt sink to his knobby knees, roll over, and lie stretched out in warm contentment. Mary gripped the edge of the stall.

"Would you care to come up to the porch, Mary? The sun's warm on the south side. Maybe you'd test my last elderberry wine."

"I'd like that, Will."

"You too, Hester?"

Hester hesitated. She had dutifully driven Mary out here to the farm. She had been comfortable enough inside the stable. The mare had made it hers. But beyond that. . . .

"I think I'll take a walk, Mister Willard. I'll be back later."

She watched them walk through the dusty sunlight and into the brighter air beyond the barndoor. Mary was leaning on the old man's arm. He bent his head gravely. She heard Mary laugh. It was her own girlish laughter. Willard glanced down at the slight, straight-spined figure with a look of heart-catching tenderness. Then it was gone. A truant notion played in Hester's mind. A long ago portrait in sepia. Not quite faded. Her mother's life had not been easy, often numbing in patience. This strong, kindly, iron-gray man, tough as oak, choosing loneliness as the years passed. Had there been some faraway springtime for them once? Unspoken, unresolved, enduring? She heard Willard's hearty laugh a second time. Mary's steps seemed to lighten. Yet she clung a little closer to his arm.

How little she knew her mother. How little the young wanted to know. As if all loving, all living, all pain, all sacrifice had started the day one was born. She could not imagine anyone doubting the intensity of her own feeling, yet . . . yet. Someday another girl in the heated glow and confidence of her own youth might look on her, Hester, sure that a graying woman could never have known passion.

Hester felt her eyes blur with tears, not in self-pity, not in love for her mother, not in the new awareness of her vision, but a little of all three, in the hopeless swiftness of time. She hardly realized her steps were carrying her across the valley toward the Ridge.

The path was wet with leaf mold, the floor of the woods greening with first trilium leaves, skunk cabbage, and ground cover. She passed a lichen-streaked boulder and knew where she was. It was the path to the cave where she had walked, then run, then raced to Michael that summer now eight years agone. She told herself to turn back. Yet she was drawn on, as if compelled to face the last reminder of her hurt. Turning back would be cowardice. Going on would be a test of her indifference.

The ledge of rock was warm with sunlight. She sat down and looked across to the outer hills. Slowly she opened her Windbreaker, then her sweater, then her blouse. It was the cleansing she wanted, as if the air itself could free her of all memory. She heard a crackle of twigs and quickly buttoned her shirt and sweater. Then she laughed in relief. A ground robin, in gleaming black and cinnamon hopped from the brush and flew to a branch. "Towee," she called. It was happening. The cleanness.

My name is Hester Brady. I am twenty-six. I am me. I can think. I can work. I can even be beautiful. Sometimes. I want things. Lots of things. The good way other people live. The other beautiful things that people have. The places they travel to see. God, You don't punish forever for one mistake? One secret? If You do, I'll show You! I'm strong. I have to be in the world You've given some of us. But I'll have whatever is out there to have. Love again. And a man. And an island of my own. Someday. Maybe You're finished with me, God. But I'm not finished with living! Not me! I've only begun!

Hester flung her arms wide and jumped to her feet. Whether it was prayer or blasphemy or the too long-stifled shout of anger within her, she did not know.

She felt buoyant and free. Tomorrow was nearer than she thought. She could hang her hat on it, as her mother, Mary, used to say.

She had one more mission. She would go into the cave. Just once to complete her self-conquest. She brushed aside the few dead, trailing vines that would leaf again at the entrance. The sun slanted into the cave's mouth, reflecting an eerie light on the rock-solid walls. At the back of the cave the light deepened into darkness. She knew where the rocks slid apart to a drop into eternity. She and Michael had never explored it. She would not now.

For what she saw inside the cave froze her. On a shelflike ridge along one wall, the light caught the random gleam of a glass apothecary globe. Beside it lay a tiny red bag, tied at the top. Beyond that on the wall were scratched lines. Hester did not have to look twice at the circle, the square within it, the small diamond shape. Below it on a thrust of rock lay—Hester stopped the gasp in her throat with her hand—a cross of sticks. Impaled on it was a large headless, dark-feathered bird.

With the clarity of horror, Hester understood. The outward evidence of black arts, she had seen for herself, secreted wherever their practitioners set down their unlikely roots, manifested and shared from time immemorial by those whom fate had cursed and their own nature condemned. She saw in her mind the little gold sleep wand swinging on Dr. Alexander Bookman's gold watch chain.

A shadow fell across the mouth of the cave. She turned with a half scream.

"Who's in there?" The voice was not Alec's.

She slipped from the cave. The man standing outside was tall, lean as a pencil, his black hair touched with gray and his face drawn into gauntness. He leaned on a cane. She had never met Nick Orlini, but her senses, strung to taut-wire acuteness, told her.

"You're not supposed to go in there, you know. Nobody is. Alec says it's private. He doesn't like strangers intruding. I don't either. Who are you?"

"Hester Brady." It was automatic. She regretted it at once.

"I'm Nick. Nick Orlini. I saw you come in here. For a moment I thought it was someone else. But—she doesn't come up to the Ridge anymore. I guess you haven't done any harm. You don't look as if you would. In fact you're quite pretty. I don't have many visitors. I hope I didn't frighten you. You don't have to worry. I won't tell Alec." A little chuckle came, as mild as the voice itself. "In fact there are a lot of things I don't tell Alec. I had an accident, you see. A long time ago. I don't remember now. Alec's helped me. I'm much better. I will be, Alec says, as long as I stay here. And I'm certainly happier here. I never thought I would be. Used to be quite a swinger, you know. City life and all that. Alec is leaving soon. My father wants me in the city. Alec said that would be wrong for me. I'd have another relapse. As he calls it."

Nick held out a hand, dry, tight-boned. "I'm very glad to meet you, Miss Hester. Will you sit down? I can't offer you any refreshment up here. But it's quite pleasant. The rock is warm. It really isn't part of our property. So we're both intruders. Good fun, isn't it? You really are pretty."

Hester found her voice and heard it shake.

"I'm sorry, Mister Orlini. I can't stay. But thank you very much. I was walking and I happened to see the cave and—and—"

She stopped. The little lies would do no good. The man was gentle, distant, and kind. Danger did not lie in his direction. She had only to pass him and reach the path, quietly.

"I've been for a walk too." The compulsive talk continued. "Alec was with me. We went almost to the barn across the fields. There's a newborn colt in there, Alec said. But we didn't go all the way, so I didn't see it. I would like to." He was studying her face.

"You're not like her. The girl who used to come and see me. I don't know why she stopped coming. I get quite lonely sometimes. She used to talk and we'd laugh. Sometimes we'd just sit still. She always made me feel better, stronger. As if I could do a lot more things than Alec lets me do. I don't know why she stopped coming. I miss her." He peered again at Hester's face. "You don't like me, do you?"

"Yes, yes, of course I do." She could easily panic. She must not.

"You haven't smiled. Not once."

"I'm a little late, Mister Orlini."

"Oh. In that case forgive me, Miss—Miss. . . ." He brushed his hand across his forehead. "Would you come and see me someday?"

"Yes. Yes, of course."

"I'll look forward to it. Shall we say Monday? But I mustn't keep you now." He stepped from the path with a slight bow, his cane rustling the dry leaves.

With a half wave she hurried down the path. As it curved away from the ledge she was aware of a sensation she had never known in her life. The clutch of a nameless fear. For, standing beyond in the leafless woods, motionless, she saw the figure of Dr. Alexander Bookman.

Mary Brady lay back against the cushioned rocking chair, her eyes closed. Willard quietly stoppered the wine bottle and moved silently to her side.

Mary's eyes flew open. "For heaven's sake, Will, don't pussyfoot around me! I know where you are!" Her smile teased at him.

They had come indoors from the porch, but the sun through the window warmed her as the wine in its fine cut-crystal warmed her. She sat, half dreaming, through an hour that would never return. "Have you had sight of Hester yet?"

"She'll be back soon. If you're tired, I'll drive you home."

Empty words as they both knew. Time was not to be relinquished yet. But Mary was tired. Her hand dropped like a leaf to the arm of the chair. His, strong-boned and roughened, covered it. Her fingers curled.

"I have your promise then, Will?"

"You have my oath."

She laughed, a faint ripple that broke the spell.

"Oh, Will, throwing hard words into God's face just for the asking of a little kindness."

He looked down at her, his eyes warm. "He's lucky, Mary."

"Who's lucky?"

"Your God. You protect Him from so much."

"Will, Will! There's no dealing with you! You're all in the dark, like a Protestant bishop, and there's no coaxing you out. It won't be God or the angels opening the gates for you. I'll have to do it myself, and it'll be that hard."

Will turned to his wineglass. A call from outside rescued him. Hester stood in the driveway beside her car. He waved.

"She'll not come into the house, Will."

"She doesn't have to." He helped Mary to her feet. She looked very pale and she moved uncertainly. The day had drained her. He held her elbow as far as the car.

"Thank you, Will." It was distant, faint. The blueness of her eyes met his. "I'll not say good-bye."

The car rounded the curve and vanished into the spring mist. Willard knew, as he knew the peepers' first song, that Mary Castle Brady would not come this way again.

He forced his mind, as he had for so long, to the practical remnants of the day. He whistled Clancy from his sluggish spring dozing under the porch. The big dog stretched in joy. Still Willard hesitated, unused to indecision. The lower farm gate needed mend-

ing, the tractor oiling. Then too there was his speech
for the Grange meeting tonight.

He had long known solitude and its peace. He was
not prepared for its pain.

"Let's walk, Clance."

He thought of his promise to Mary and wondered
how he would keep it.

Late that night Hester sat beside her mother's bed.
Mary would have none of doctor, medicine, or hospital.

"I'm just a little tired, Hester. It's my own bed I
want. Maybe some hot milk with a touch of the whiskey. I'm not intending to interfere with God's plan.
And don't you. Or Tom." She had fallen asleep, white
as the pillow case and quiet as the stars.

Hester herself at last slept heavily. She awakened
with a start. Something somewhere had touched, then
eluded her, a sense of danger, a fear, the panic she had
stifled on the Ridge. The air was cold. Dawn was
staining the edge of the sky. She went to her mother's
room. Mary was sleeping, untroubled as a child, a
small smile on her lips, as if she were again watching
the wobbly-legged foal in his mother's box stall.

The foal. Hester's mind was spinning backward like
a reversed tape. The cave. The glass jar that gleamed
emptily. The woman Odella in her shed, explaining,
pointing, describing. In the mind-opening, mysterious
clarity of the first light, Hester saw the pieces fall together, take shape in the pattern that she had sensed
but could not name. Shivering from her own conjec-
tures, she pulled on jeans and a sweater. She stole
down the stairs and into the growing milk-whiteness of
the new day. The car seemed to start with a roar. Actually she slid it quietly onto the road and turned it
toward Willard Roundtree's sleeping farm.

Chapter Nineteen

Bright jets of laughter and high-pitched goodnights filled the chandeliered hall. Washington's most prominent hostess was ending another successful potpourri of the rich, the powerful, and those she saw as potentials.

She laid a light hand on John Roundtree's sleeve.

"Delighted you could come, John. Christina, you must not keep him in hiding."

"I don't keep him anywhere, Cissie. He's devoted to work and doesn't like any of us."

"Now that's not right." John shifted and reddened. "Mrs. Dolan, I've had a great evening. Thank you very much."

Cissie Dolan turned on her expensive charm. "It gave me great pleasure, John. Will you come again?"

"I'd like to, thanks."

Others were pressing behind him. He shook hands awkwardly a second time and moved toward the door. He owed Christina Hall a great deal but not the right to embarrass him. Now she caught up with him.

"You didn't bring me to the party, John, but will you drive me home?"

"Why, yes. Sure. I didn't know you'd be here."

Her laugh was good-natured. "Who did you think got you an invitation?"

He stopped short on the broad stone steps. "You mean you arranged this?"

"I can't believe any man doing as well as you are can be so naive. Come on. We're holding up traffic."

She took his arm. "Oh, John. Don't you see yourself at all? Everybody's talking about you. You've brought this nuclear energy bill to a halt, at least for this session. You're already being considered for the energy committee. The speaker's noticed you and, believe me, he notices few freshmen. You could become a whip in another two years, then the Senate. John, you can go as high as you want if you keep up the momentum. You've got what it takes." She gave a little chuckle, but her voice had become brittle, sure. "Even the Presidency, someday. Don't knock it."

"I don't knock it. I don't want it."

"Standard freshman answer. Very good. Keep them guessing. But you need visibility. You don't think business is done in the House chamber, do you? It's done at Burning Tree and Sans Souci and over Cissie Dolan's champagne. That's where the big moves are made. You need to be seen."

He handed her into the waiting car and saw the streetlight harsh on her makeup. He hated the implications of what she said and once again felt a kind of entrapment. Christina Hall had been everywhere in his first congressional fight. He had hardly realized how she was permeating his career. But doors were opened, pitfalls avoided, contacts made with more ease than he had foreseen. Dorrie, his knowing, straight-backed little secretary, set her mouth in a thin line and remained silent when Christina called, which was increasingly frequently.

He swung the car past the White House, shimmering in the first humid night of spring.

There it stands, he thought, a symbol of public power.

The end and the means. Did the end always justify the means in this city of endless compromise? Was it true of the man behind those white pillars, as well as every office-seeker down to the last congressional page? What about himself? He was already grasping every means he could lay his hands on to stem nuclear proliferation. But where was his integrity? Or didn't it matter?

"That's my building, John."

"Oh. Sure."

She laughed. "Stop worrying, John. Things are going fine. Will you come up for a nightcap? No seduction. I promise. I have to catch the eleven o'clock news. Felix is being quoted, and he gets furious if I don't hear his every word."

That was not all Felix Twining was furious about these days, John knew. But again he owed it to Christina's management that the old lion had not come into open battle. Yet.

Christina poured two drinks, tossed off her shoes, indicated a deep chair in front of the TV, and stretched herself on the long divan. She turned on the picture but not the sound.

"So we'll know when it's on. I told you I mustn't miss a word." She sipped her drink and looked at him across it.

"Who's the girl, John?"

"What girl?"

"The girl who's locking you up."

"Nobody's locked me up." Yet he knew as he denied it that it was true. It was exactly what Hester had done. She had locked up part of his life. Without reason, he told himself in the darkness of his nights. Without any reason. He had forgiven her Michael. Why could she not forgive him his father?

"News is on, John." Christina turned up the sound.

"Good evening, everybody." The familiar face with blow-dried hair and TV ruddiness came alive. "Congressman Felix Twining said last night at a dinner for five hundred major industrialists that. . . ."

John's thoughts wandered. What Felix Twining said or did not say mattered little now. John had taken his stand. Sooner or later Twining and his interests would pick up the gauntlet. Then, abruptly, John came back to the TV.

"A bizarre accident took the life of Nicholas Orlini in Thatcher, Connecticut, last night.

The son of multimillionaire corporate director Benjamin Orlini was found kicked to death by a fractious mare in a horse stall on the property of Willard Roundtree."

"My God, John. . . ."

"The body was discovered early in the morning by one Hester Brady, daughter of a local tavernkeeper, said to have known young Orlini. . . ."

The glass at John's side fell and smashed. He was on his feet, moving toward the door.

"This doesn't involve you, John, does it?"

"I've got to get back to Thatcher right away."

"You mean tonight? But you'll be back Thursday?"

"No. I don't know. No, no." He was at the door.

"John! The White House breakfast!"

"Sorry. Thanks. For everything."

The door closed.

Christina returned to the TV and lit a cigarette. She was curious about the names, but the tragedy left her untouched. In her West Virginia childhood, things happened like that in the mining towns. Earthy, primitive things.

She had spent a lot of time on John Roundtree. Had she wasted it? Her knuckles were white as she twisted out the half-smoked cigarette.

John was special.

". . . The medical examiner has confirmed that Nicholas Orlini had been kicked repeatedly by the vicious mare, kept in the stall with a new colt. A bloodied knife lay near the body, indicating that Orlini may have tried to defend himself. Both mare and foal showed slashes.

"The thirty-three-year-old Orlini had been in the care of a psychotherapist, Doctor Alexander Bookman, following an automobile accident three years ago. Doctor Bookman declared that his patient was almost completely cured and looked forward to joining his father in the management of the senior Orlini's large business interests. 'Nick's concern for wildlife and animals in general had been helpful in his restoration therapy. It was quite impossible' he added, 'that Orlini had entered the stall with any purpose other than kindness.'

"Willard Roundtree, owner of the farm, and his foreman, Charlie Redwing, had been away during the evening, attending a Grange meeting in Bollington.

"The presence of Hester Brady, who found the body in the early morning, was not explained, though it was known she had been seeing Nick Orlini.

"Due to the many unanswered questions, there will be an inquest. Mister Willard Roundtree has asked that no order to destroy the horse be given until the inquest is completed."

The plane droned on. John mechanically refolded the newspaper and looked out the window. They were flying in overcast. There was nothing to be seen.

Nothing. Anywhere.

Chapter Twenty

Three days before the inquest, Mary Castle Brady closed her eyes and did not open them again. Her inner killer had brought growing weakness, though without pain, and Mary had died with the small smile of her last day in the sunlight. She knew nothing of what had happened in Willard Roundtree's barn.

Willard came at once and advised privacy. An early morning Mass, a few loyal friends, and the warming earth scattered on her plain coffin. Hester came down the graveyard walk beside a wizened, aged little man she hardly knew anymore. Walled-in by shock and deprived of the consolation of a rousing wake that would have been only fitting for the loving wife of Bantam Brady, Tom had taken his grief in silence and the last solace left to him. He reeked of uncut Irish whiskey.

Let him! thought Hester. *Let him be.* And longed for a numbness of her own.

She glanced back one last time. Willard Roundtree was standing alone and bare-headed beside the open grave. She saw him thrust his hand inside his coat, bow his head, and drop a small cluster of white flowers into the grave. He turned quickly and came to her.

"Will you come back to the farm, Hester? I'd like you to see how well the mare is recovering."

She shook her head. "Not now." She nodded at Tom. "I want to see him home."

"Will you be alone?"

"No. My mother's friend, Cora, is coming to stay for a few days."

"Good. Good."

"Mister Willard. . . .". She broke the silence passionately. "No matter how many lies they tell at this—this inquest, they won't put the mare down—destroy her—will they?"

"I give you my word, Hester." He was not at all sure how he could prevent it, but having given his word, he knew he would. Somehow.

The pub was closed. Willard saw them to the door of the spiritless little house, and Tom went in, trancelike.

"Thank you, Mister Willard," Hester said tonelessly.

The old man removed his hat again.

"Hester, you know there's nothing to be afraid of tomorrow."

"I suppose not."

"It is not a trial. No one is being accused of anything. It is only an inquest, an asking of questions to find out if there was any"—he tried to choose his words carefully—"wrongdoing. Any suspicion of foul play."

"Who asks the questions?"

"The coroner. You know, Albert Fitch. His family's been around as long as any of us. When he isn't running his feed-and-hardware business, he serves as coroner."

"Who decides who's guilty?"

"There's no question of guilt, Hester. All that is decided is whether a crime has been committed."

"And what do they call a crime?" She was conscious of keeping him there on the stoop but she could not seem to stop the questions. Nor to hold to her own self-pledge of silence.

"Hester, my dear. I don't think there was any crime. A man was kicked by a frightened mare and died. Fitch is doing his duty, I suspect because the Orlinis brought pressure. After tomorrow it will all be over and forgotten."

"And who decides if there's been any crime?"

"Sometimes the coroner himself. In this case there will be a jury."

"Then it is a trial!"

"Hester, aren't you listening? It is not a trial. No one is accused of anything. There are only six people on the jury. You'll probably know them all. Old friends. . . ."

She had heard enough. There was no doubt in her mind who was accused, who was on trial. She, Hester Brady. She had taken satisfaction in defying this tight, respectable town and its tight, respectable first family. If not in acts, then in reputation. Tomorrow they would sit in judgment of her. Willard was still talking.

". . . it may not be pleasant, my dear, but there's nothing to alarm you. I'll call for you at nine thirty tomorrow morning."

"There's no call for that. I can drive myself, thank you."

He smiled. "I'm sure you can. You're a very strong young woman. But you see, I made Mary a promise."

For an instant Hester's eyes showed uncertainty. "What promise would you make her that had anything to do with me?"

"I promised to look after you." He gave her a long look. "If you should ever need it."

Hester looked away. "Well, I don't but—" She hesitated, weights balancing in her mind. "All right. If you want. I'll be ready. Nine thirty."

"Good." He took one more chance. "Hester, John is home. He would like to see you."

He had made a mistake. She turned on him, blazing. "What are you trying to do to me now! Hasn't there been enough? You know what they're saying. That I was seeing Nick Orlini. As if I would! And now you want John to come here with his pity, feeling sorry for me! Well, I don't need that from him or any man alive! I told him once I'd not see him again and I never will. I have my reasons, and they'll not change.

I'll go with you tomorrow, Mister Willard, because my mother asked it of you. And I'll answer their questions. I'll tell them what I've already told them a dozen times over. And if the truth isn't enough, I'll tell them what they don't want to hear, them and the Orlinis! Then I'll wipe the dust of this town off my shoes forever!"

"My dear girl. . . ."

But she had flung from him, tears held too long at bay pouring down her cheeks. The door slammed shut. Willard sighed. The release would be good for her, but he had not been prepared for the wild stubbornness that could make tomorrow so very difficult.

Mary's child, lacking Mary's wisdom.

Upstairs a second door slammed. Hester threw herself on her bed and let long, shaking sobs take possession of her. As if she did not know John Roundtree was back! As if she had not twice hung up on his telephone calls!

Tomorrow. Only tomorrow ahead. Then escape.

The Thatcher Community House, a nearly square, pitched-roof building, was kept proudly in fresh white paint. Over the door ran the legend IN MEMORIAM. Inside, a stranger could read the bronze plaque: IN MEMORIAM, JOSIAH GIDEON ROUNDTREE AND HIS WIFE, ABIGAIL GIBBS ROUNDTREE, WHO GAVE THIS BUILDING OCTOBER 1948. THOUGH THEIR STEPS HAVE TAKEN THEM FAR FROM THATCHER, THEIR HEARTS AND LOYALTY REMAIN WITH US. AND OURS WITH THEM.

Thatcher's citizens had long forgotten them and the legend.

Hester, entering the building beside Willard Roundtree, ignored it. It was another reminder of the web around her. The large buff-walled room was, as Willard had promised, no courtroom. Tall, bright windows filled it with March sunlight. At the end of the room a platform now curtained off, was a reminder of more kindly events—scout meetings, flower shows, ecology drives, protests against river-pollution, concerned citizens for the snowshoe rabbit or the swamp turtle, and, warmest of all, the crepe-paper glitter of the Fireman's Ball and the Lions Benefit. The intensities of Thatcher flowed through this room like lifeblood.

But today only a long narrow table stood starkly in front of the curtained platform, six stark wooden chairs lined up beside it. To Hester's dismay the rows of spectators' seats were already filled.

"There will be no standees. All available seats are now taken. The doors are closed!" It was, of all people, young Billy Haskell, son of librarian Mrs. Haskell. Billy, grown lanky and fuzz-faced, bore the uneasy responsibility of doorman and coroner's aid.

Hester glanced around as she took a front seat. Vivi Vale and Craig Simmons, reporters for the *Thatcher Standard* and at last, to Thatcher's relief, decently man and wife, sat to the side. Hannah Poole, seamstress, sitting upright in the third row, could be depended to beat the *Standard* by twenty-four hours in the winging of gossip. Her wide felt hat successfully screened the Blodgetts, behind her. Miss Wilkes, next to them, had obviously closed her antique shop for the day. Nat Parsons, from the stables behind the fairground, sat with kindness on his face.

No Orlinis were present.

Hester's eyes returned to the curtain behind the table. But not before she had seen John, tall in the last row. He had no right to come, she thought bitterly. Couldn't he see it was a kind of cruelty?

She saw no other Roundtrees.

Dr. Alexander Bookman, immaculate and professional in dark suit and white shirt, sat alone to the far right in the second row.

A rustle stirred the spectators. Billy Haskell signaled them to their feet. Coroner Artie Fitch was entering from a side door, trailed by six citizens, four men and two women, all stiffly self-conscious in their momentary importance. Ed Higgins's shoes squeaked.

"This," murmured Willard, "is all damned silly."

But Hester did not hear. Cold hands tense in her lap, ankles crossed neatly under the chair, she knew she was the target of this coming together, for whatever purpose. She saw it in every pair of eyes.

What Hester did not know was that never in her life had she shown such quiet bearing . . . no, call it elegance, Willard said to himself. Head high, back straight, she sat motionless, her black dress, without ornament or jewelry except for a slim chain that disappeared within the high neckline.

Artie Fitch happily pounded the gavel. There had been no sound, but predictably the gavel sparked a rush of whispers.

"Silence!" yelled Billy Haskell through his voice change.

"The inquest will now open." Coroner Fitch did not drone. He soared nasally as he read the purpose, laws, limits of the inquest.

"We will question first the person who found Mister Orlini's body on the morning of March eleventh. Miss Hester Brady."

Hester drew a tight little breath. She had not expected it so soon.

"Hester—uh, Miss Brady—*Ms.* Brady, I guess you prefer these days. . . ." Smothered ripple of amusement from the younger spectators. The coroner happily gaveled again. "Ms. Brady, would you tell us at what hour and under what circumstances you found Nicholas Orlini in the stall of Willard Roundtree's barn?"

It was going to be endless, Willard told himself. Artie was not going to release center stage easily.

Hester rose and answered as if by rote.

"About six in the morning I went into the barn and saw the latch off the box stall. I looked in and saw Doxy, the mare, at the back of the stall. The colt was on the other side against the wall. I saw she was feeding—"

"Hester, never mind the horses."

"I saw the mare's shoulder was slashed and bleeding. I opened the stall door and saw—Mister Orlini lying there across the entrance."

"You knew he was dead?"

"I didn't know anything. I shut the stall door and ran up to Mister Willard's house."

"To awaken him . . . ?"

"Oh, get on with it, Artie." Willard snapped. "I'm a farmer. By six I'm about ready to start plowin'."

A ripple of laughter. Artie Fitch flushed, lifted his gavel, thought better of it, and waited for silence. Willard Roundtree was a farmer when he wanted to be. He was also the shrewdest trial lawyer in the state. And worse, Fitch's Feed Grain and Hardware's best customer. Artie wrestled for an instant with something that he would not have recognized as conflict of interest.

"Thank you, Ms. Brady. Officer George Shultze."

Officer Shultze, gray and heavy-shouldered, had guided, guarded, and ticketed the frailties of Thatcher for four decades. He had little use for the younger Orlini and his quick way with a twenty-dollar bill.

"I was on duty early that day. Mister Will called headquarters at six twelve. I reached the barn at six thirty-three. Orlini was lying there, like Hester said. He was dead all right. There was an open switchblade knife lying about a foot from him, east, I'd say. It was bloody but I didn't see any cuts on Orlini. The mare and her foal were out of the stall by that time."

"Who did that? That's tampering with evidence."

Willard Roundtree rose. "Coroner Fitch, I take complete responsibility. I might add that there isn't a man in Thatcher County who wouldn't know enough to remove a mare and new foal from the presence of a corpse and spilled blood. Now if you are finished with my client—"

Client. It was the first time the old man had said that. Hester gave him a mechanical, brief smile.

"I am not finished with anybody, Mister Willard. If you don't mind." The coroner settled his rimless glasses, glanced down at the paper in front of him (Rules and Regulations of Inquest), and cleared his throat.

Dr. James Wainwright, acting as medical examiner, deposed the deceased had been dead at least six hours, which set the accident at approximately midnight. He had died of a heavy blow at the heart that could well have been the mare's kick. Dr. Stubbs, the veterinarian, deposed that the foal was unharmed but the mare had been slashed three times, once in the chest, twice on the right shoulder. Possibly by the bloodied knife found near the body.

"She took fright obviously at a stranger coming into her stall and kicked out to protect her foal," Dr. Stubbs added. "Why any fool would enter a horse's stall with an open knife I can't imagine."

"No opinions, Doctor Stubbs."

"She is as gentle a mare as I have ever handled." Dr. Stubbs finished defiantly and sat down. There was a rustle of applause, hushed abruptly as Dr. Alexander Bookman rose to his feet.

"Your honor, Coroner Fitch, I cannot let that inference stand. The late Nicholas Orlini was my patient, my friend, and a potentially brilliant young man. He carried a knife with my knowledge, at my urgency, one might say. He had developed a deep interest in ecology, in plant life. He would bring back cuttings, press them, classify them. He was becoming quite expert in the Tertiary Age flora of this area. It is my belief he would have made a genuine contribution had"—Alec Bookman carefully steadied his voice—"had this dreadful tragedy not occurred."

No one in the room missed his quick, cold glance at Hester Brady.

Coroner Fitch, who felt he had been losing ground, took his cue.

"Miss Hester Brady, please."

Expectancy fanned the room. Hester rose. Willard touched her arm and nodded reassuringly.

"Miss Brady, are you in the habit of visiting Mister Willard's barn before six in the morning?"

"No."

"But on the morning of the eleventh . . . ?"

"My mother was quite ill. I—I wanted to go out and see the mare early before my mother might need me." Lie number one, but Hester felt a growing recklessness. What did she care? What could they do to her beyond what had been done?

"She would have been asleep at midnight also and not needed you, isn't that true?"

"Yes, if I had wanted to go at midnight. But I didn't."

"You knew that Mister Willard and his man, Charlie Redwing, were away all evening?"

"No. Yes. I don't remember."

Coroner Fitch was beginning to feel easier with himself.

"Miss Brady, I believe you spent a holiday with Mrs. Julia Orlini in the Bahama islands a while ago?"

"Yes."

"It is a very luxurious home, I understand."

"Yes."

"After you returned, you began seeing Nick Orlini."

"I did no such thing. Why would I?"

"You met him on the Ridge the afternoon before he was killed?"

"I happened to be—" she stopped. The questions were leading in a direction she could only dimly see. The room was completely still. Every face was looking toward her.

"You also knew that the guard dog, Clancy, was not on the premises that night?"

Clancy! She had not thought of Clancy. Nick never

could have entered the barn if the big dog had been there. He would have scented danger. She turned helplessly to Willard.

Willard's face was as serious as she had yet seen it.

"Coroner Fitch, these are questions beyond the province of this inquest. I have already told the police that I took my dog to the veterinarian's on the way to the Grange meeting. This is springtime, and Clancy often gets into something putrid at this time of year and makes himself sick. Now let's get on with this."

But Coroner Fitch was beginning to enjoy the keenness of the hunt.

"Doctor Stubbs."

"Yes, Coroner."

"Is it possible that the dog may have been given drugs or some kind of poison by someone who wanted him out of the way that night?"

Willard's face went white. "What the devil are you after, Artie? Hester Brady is not on trial!"

"Doctor Stubbs. . . ."

The large, honest-faced man hesitated. "We didn't analyze for that, Coroner."

There was a buzz of talk. The gavel fell sharply.

"Silence!" Artie Fitch congratulated himself. He was managing now, very well indeed. His voice rose scratchingly.

"In answer to Mister Roundtree's question, if anyone in this room doubts the propriety of these questions, let me say bluntly we have some very curious circumstances surrounding a death on our hands, and everyone in this town, the court, the police, the public, and most of all the bereaved parents of that young man have a right to know what happened. What lured Nick Orlini into that barn that night? A tryst with a young woman known to be, let me put it delicately, reasonable about such things?"

Willard was on his feet. There was a shout from the rear. Hester recognized John's voice.

"Hester Brady is not on trial!"

The gavel beat the table. "Order! I will have order!"

John had reached the front of the room. "Fitch, you damned arrogant fool, this is an inquest. Not a court. By implication this girl is being condemned!"

"No such thing! Sit down. The girl is not on trial here, but the honor of this town is. As coroner, appointed by law, it is my duty to uphold that honor. John Roundtree, *sit down!*"

The gavel fell in a series of rifle-sharp cracks. Silence returned. John went back to his seat with a long look at Hester, but she was staring straight ahead over Coroner Fitch's head.

Coroner Fitch, gavel in hand like a club, glared at his spectators. His father, for twenty-years coroner before him, had said often enough, "Artie, when you're sitting at that inquest table, remember everybody in this town likes his say. So let 'em in to fill up the seats, give 'em a little time to let off steam, then get down to business." Artie proceeded to get down to business.

He dropped the gavel once more, laid it beside him, and adjusted his glasses.

"It has been established that Nicholas Orlini was killed by the kick of a vicious horse. Of a horse," he amended, catching Willard's eye. "There are two remaining questions to be answered. I call Doctor Alexander Bookman."

Alec Bookman rose, bowed to Artie, and stood with a confident, understanding little smile. His bearing, like his tailoring, was the epitome of the discreet and sympathetic professional man.

"Doctor Bookman, you are a psychiatrist?"

"And psychotherapist, psychoanalist. I practice in many fields, depending on the needs of a patient."

"Yes, yes. And you had full care of the deceased since his automobile accident?"

"No, no. I was asked by his father to treat Nicholas only after all other sources had failed. I met Mister

Orlini in Zurich, where I had been conducting a very large practice and some very successful experiments."

"So you came here and the deceased showed improvement?"

"Very much so. We were all hopeful."

"What was the deceased's state of mind on the day he met his death?"

"Oh, very good. Very good indeed. He had gone for a walk. A rather long walk. Alone. So long that I went out to see what had detained him. Then, of course, I realized."

"Explain that, Doctor Bookman."

"I met him and a young lady on a path leading up to the Ridge."

"Can you identify the young lady?"

"Yes. She is sitting there." Reluctantly, it seemed, he nodded at Hester Brady.

Artie smiled. His next question, he felt, was masterful.

"Was young Nicholas Orlini fond of horses?"

"No. I'm afraid not. That was a remaining psychosis. He disliked all animals. Horses terrified him."

"Do you know any reason why the victim would go into Willard Roundtree's barn the night of the eleventh?"

"Mister Coroner, Nick Orlini disliked leaving the Ridge at any time. There he found peace, there he was beginning to heal. He had to be persuaded even to take a drive."

"Yet he went down to the barn and into the stall of an animal he feared?"

Dr. Bookman hesitated. Every spectator could read the compassion in his face.

"I do not underestimate the young lady's charms."

Artie Fitch picked up the gavel as if anticipating an outburst. There was none.

"Miss Hester Brady, if you please."

Hester rose, rigid, expressionless, as if encased in wood.

"Miss Brady, were you accustomed to going to Willard Roundtree's barn at any hour?"

"Mister Willard gave me permission. The mare is mine. And when the foal came—"

"Just answer the questions, please. So it was not unusual to go, let's say, at ten or eleven at night?"

"Unusual? It would have been plain madness. Why would anybody in his senses disturb a resting mare and a new foal? I've been listening to him trying to say—"

The gavel pounded. "Stick to the questions, Miss Brady."

"Do what he says, Hester. There's no case," Willard whispered. But Hester had fixed her eyes intently on Alec Bookman. She seemed to hear nothing.

"You deny you were in the barn the night of Nick Orlini's death?"

"I do."

"Yet you felt impelled to return—amended—to go out there at dawn the next morning. Why?"

"I was afraid. For the foal."

"Afraid?" Coroner Fitch leaned forward, his thin nose twitching. "Afraid of what?"

Hester turned her eyes from Alec Bookman.

"Afraid of what might happen to the foal."

"I'll have to ask you to explain that. . . ."

Hester lifted her head and straightened her shoulders as if the weight of a decision had just slid from them. She would leave this room under a cloud or she would tell the truth as she knew it.

"I was afraid the foal might be killed and mutilated."

"Killed? Why?"

She opened the top button of her dress, slid out a narrow, metallic object, unfastened the chain it hung on, and held it swinging in the light.

"By Alec Bookman."

It must be said for Alec that he did not move a muscle. If perspiration appeared on his forehead, no one saw it. His tolerant half-smile deepened.

Chairs were creaking in anticipation.

"Miss Brady," Coroner Fitch rasped. "You've made an insinuation amounting to an accusation!"

"You want to know why?" Hester responded. She swung the chain in her hand before the spectators. "Do you know what this is? It's called a sleep wand. It was given to me in the Caribbean island, where I was Mrs. Ben Orlini's guest. You can hypnotize people with it. Alec Bookman wears one on his watch chain. And I know why."

Hester poured out the words—wild words about a fishing town and a villa on a tropical island, a blind woman who sold charms and spirit soil. One black-magic gimmick, she learned there, was the forelock of a newborn foal. That's what Alec Bookman wanted. He hypnotizes people to do what he wants. And then—then . . . God only knows what he does. Poor Nick told me Bookman had taken him to the barn. Showed him the place, showed him the box stall. I became terrified that he would send Nick to get the forelock of Doxy's new foal. And that's what he did!"

Her voice trailed. *"Don't you see?"*

The wild words fallen on sensible, respectable Thatcher ears left a vacuum. She gazed helplessly from one face to another. Only John was looking at her, and the kindness in his face choked her.

Bookman had risen by his seat.

"When I came here to help the Orlini's son, it was part of my task to discover everything I could about the town from which my patient secluded himself.

"So I learned"—Alec slowly drew a notebook from his pocket, knowing the impact of every gesture— "that on January seven, nineteen sixty-six, Hester Brady left Thatcher to take up residence in the Holy Name Retreat on West Two hundred and fourth Street in New York. There on April twenty-second she gave birth to a boy child."

A gasp came from the spectators, as Willard jumped to his feet.

"I object to these remarks as being irrelevant, immaterial, and prejudicial, Mister Coroner."

Artie Fitch sensed his moment. "I do not think they are. Do you have anything else to tell this inquest, Doctor Bookman?"

Hester was the single focus in the room as she sat, fingers clenched in her lap. She showed no other sign of emotion, not even of breathing itself. In the pause the silence was becoming admission.

Alec smiled, gently, soothingly. "Only a word of professional counsel for this unfortunate young woman. Miss Brady, you must not let guilt embitter you. You must live openly with the facts. That is the way to be healed. In the name of your child—"

Hester was on her feet. "Don't you dare! Whatever kind of devil you are, leave my child alone! He's safe, where no one can touch him. Not you nor anybody else in this place will ever hurt him! I'll see to that!"

She pushed through the spectators and out of the building. John followed as a wave of voices broke after them.

Coroner Fitch lifted his gavel, thought better of it, rose, and led the jury from the room. The verdict would be that the victim met death by accident as he had known from the beginning. But he was satisfied. He had presided over the most sensational inquest in Thatcher's history. That was good. For him. And for business. Very good indeed.

As the spectators milled liked unsettled birds Dr. Alexander Bookman reached under his chair, drew out a folded raincoat and a travel case and quietly slipped through a side door.

Willard Roundtree saw him go but he was not quick enough to reach him. Nor would it have been of any use. Willard knew that the neat little man would not again be seen in Thatcher nor anywhere else, he guessed, as Dr. Alexander Bookman, therapist, charlatan, or devil's disciple. Who would know which?

The valley held the white spring mist like a cup. The three figures moving through it said not a word as they climbed the path through the woods to the top of the Ridge. As they emerged on the stone ledge, the mist fell away and pale sunlight lit the tops of the trees and the mouth of the cave.

Willard took off his cap and wiped his forehead. His face was grim.

"This is my fault, John. I knew. I should have anticipated."

But John either did not hear or his thoughts were too distant to answer. He had no wish to come to the cave. It held only undimmed, lacerating memories for him. Was it all of eight years ago he had followed Michael to this spot, angered by his brother's mockery, and seen Hester fling herself into his arms, laughing, wild-eyed. Seen them go into the cave. . . .

"I might have spared Hester." Willard added.

"Spared her what?" John snapped so sharply that Willard looked at him in surprise. But only for an instant. Now he understood. This was a time of pain for John. It would have to pass like everything else. In time.

Charlie Redwing had already gone into the cave.

"Let's have a look, John."

John nodded. He regretted what he had revealed. He had already made his own peace and knew his future. It was only the damnable tricks of memory that erased time and revived hurt. Leveling his flashlight, he followed Willard into the cave.

It was empty, as Willard expected, of everything except a scattering of leaves on the floor. Something flew from the roof into the light. A nesting bird? A bat? A young blacksnake slithered out into the warmth. At the far rear of the cave Charlie Redwing hunched over like a benign troll in the dimness of his lantern.

Willard played his flashlight over the walls and lingered on a spot above a rock shelf, where the stone had been whitened as if by scraping.

"If what Hester said was true," John began.

It was Willard's turn to show anger. "Everything Hester said was true. Don't ever doubt her, John." In the fragmented light his eyes met the younger man's. "Trust her. Do you hear me? Trust her. That's all she has. Your trust." He gave a twisted smile. "And my insatiable curiosity for the truth."

Charlie Redwing had risen from the rift at the back of the cave and was coming forward, one hand closed. He opened it and handed its content to Willard, a single four-inch black feather, iridescent at the center, darkly stained at the quill.

Willard nodded without surprise.

"Crow?" asked John.

"No. Not crow," Charlie answered unexpectedly. "Crows are birds of the sun. They are honest. They work. That"—he pointed to the feather—"came with death."

"What do you make of this, Charlie?" Willard pointed to the scraped place on the rock wall.

Charlie studied it. Then he picked up some dirt from the cave floor and rubbed it across the scratchings. There emerged faintly the dark lines of a circle, within it a square, within that a fainter diamond shape. Charlie brushed the dirt away. He said nothing. Instead he left the cave, walked to the rim of the stone ledge beyond it, lifted his arms straight above his head, and brought them down slowly. Both men could see the sun between them.

"Let's go now, John," said Willard quietly.

Charlie Redwing, unembarrassed, his eyes distant, turned to meet them.

"Long ago," he said softly, "there was great evil on this Ridge. The gods grew angry. They sent their thunderbolts. When the Ridge would not bow to them, they tore at it with their spears. The wound is still there at the back of the cave. What falls there, never returns. Now the evil has come back. So will the anger of the gods."

Standing in the mild sunlight on Willard's porch, John felt the passing of his own crisis. He longed, with the single-mindedness of long frustration, for Hester's nearness. He faced an uphill battle ahead. He needed her with every fiber of his mind and body. But some-day—he looked out to the awakening land—someday to live on this land, in this house, he and Hester. . . . He caught Willard's eye and flushed.

"Alec Bookman was mad, Will?"

"Not at all."

"I thought for a moment when Hes—" But John would not talk of Hester now if he could avoid it. The question already lived in Willard's eyes.

"Hester knew what she was talking about. As she usually does. We Roundtrees are not always right, John. Though on balance. . . ."

"What I'm getting at is if Bookman wasn't mad, what was he?"

"There's a less complicated word. I suspected it after three minutes of talk I had with him at the fair last fall." Willard chuckled. "Doctor Bookman talked quite learnedly to me about the pH factor in my hybrid corn. He was wrong. All wrong. The pH factor is in the soil. Not in the crops. Such small words to give fraud away."

John concealed a smile at the older man's satisfaction.

"And the Eye of God? Another piece of fraud?"

"Not quite. That's more serious. Since primitive times, men have known the power of the human eye. You saw Charlie today. It is the oldest symbol of higher wisdom, for good and evil. As any book on sorcery will tell you."

"Bookman was no sorcerer."

"Two centuries ago he would have been considered so. He was ruthless, clever, and ravaged by man's most sinister disease. Ambition. He knew the strength of the human mind and its weaknesses. He knew the mind can be governed and manipulated by a man with a purpose. Once that knowledge was called witchcraft. Today it is considered a near-science, a practical tool. Hypnotism.

"Bookman could put young Orlini, already damaged, into such a state of hypnotic trance that he would perform the most bizarre acts. Orlini would never appear well, only more deeply reliant on the man who mastered him. Alexander Bookman—as he called himsef—had a very safe and very lucrative future indeed. Until Hester. . . ."

Willard took his pipe from his pocket. "I've kept you too long, John."

"I've time."

"Well, I haven't. By the way, you know Bantam's pub is being sold?"

"If you're getting around to Hester, she won't see me."

"Didn't think she would. You're not the problem." He walked to the edge of the porch. "Growing time, John. Best time of the year. I've got the richest soil out there in those fields of any man in this state. I'd like to think that someone will keep it living, greening." He returned his cold pipe to his pocket. "Well, an old man's dream doesn't make a young man's life. Never has done, never will. Come see me before you go back to Washington."

To John, as he walked to his car, the waiting land had never looked more beautiful.

"You have no right, John, to come walking in here!" Hester, her hair tied in a knot, her sleeves rolled up, glared at him. The little front room was bare of all evidence of living.

"I'm going with Tom back to Galway, settle him and then—"

"Then what?"

"John, why did you come? You know everything now. You know why—"

"Hester, I don't care! Don't you understand? At least turn your face to me! And listen! I don't care! I only wish to God you had told me the whole truth long ago. And let me help you."

"And what would you have done? What could anyone do? I'm not the first girl and I won't be the last in that kind of trouble. I told my mother. She somehow guessed. Tom would have killed me if he'd known."

"Maybe not, Hester . . . maybe—"

"Maybe what? It's easy for you to say, John. Being who you are. You can arrange things. People are always on your side. But for me. . . ." She shook her head. "Why are you coming here to ask me questions, to make me talk? When I don't want to. When it doesn't help anything anymore. Let me be, John."

"Where is the child, Hester?"

"What difference does it make to you?"

"I'm a man who loves you. And you love me. And no amount of denial will change that! Are we to live our lives out wanting each other and denying each other because of what happened eight years ago? God knows it wasn't easy for me at that inquest. I could have choked the breath out of Bookman, worming his way around this town, all for his own purposes. But I'm grateful for one thing. It's out. No more secrets between us. I love you. I want to marry you. You have a child, Michael's child. I have some right to know where that child is."

She stared out the window. Something was slowly stirring within her, like an ice floe breaking with spring. She wanted to trust. She did not yet know how, even this man whom she loved so deeply, so hopelessly.

She spoke so quietly, he could barely hear her.

"Maybe you have. I don't know why. But anyhow

I'll tell you. There's no reason why not, now. No reason I shouldn't tell the whole town, is there, now?" He knew he had not yet won her. She was deliberately hurting herself.

"When I knew—about the baby. And Michael gone, and I didn't know what to do, I thought first about what most girls around here do. To have an abortion. But I couldn't. Never, never. Lose my baby, destroy it? No! I wanted it. It was part of me. It will always be! I don't expect you to understand that, John."

"Let me do my own thinking, Hester!" He was grim-faced.

"My mother had a friend. Agatha Ryan. From the time we lived in the city. Sister Agatha. My mother said I should go to her in the retreat. I stayed there, and my son was born there. He was—so beautiful. I'd hold him and look at him and tell myself—" She smiled at something so distant John felt himself an intruder. "—tell myself and my son that I would never let anyone take him from me. But of course I couldn't keep him. Not the way things were."

"He was adopted?" John prodded softly.

"Sister Agatha arranged it. She wouldn't tell me where. Of course she was right. But I'd go to see her and she'd tell me he was fine."

"Michael never knew?"

"I saw Michael. By accident. When I was in the Caribbean. He was there. . . ."

John nodded. "I've heard."

"I never want him to know—anything."

He went to her, afraid to take her in his arms, afraid that the wall she still kept between them would not crumble.

"Hester. I must go back to Washington soon. You know that. But I will not go back until you tell me honestly and with all your heart that you have no feeling for me. That you can't love me. That you don't want to marry me or even see me again. Will you tell me that?"

"John, what would it be with Michael's child always between us?"

"Would he be between us?"

She walked to the window. When she turned, her eyes brimmed with tears.

"John I can't—I can't say any more. Let me be!"

He took her in his arms. Her release came.

At last the tears stopped. And at longer last the deep, wrenching sobs.

"Feel better?" With a grin he handed her his handkerchief. "Tom should have told you long ago you can't fight the whole world at one time. Marry me. We'll argue everything else out afterwards."

She clung weakly to a last denial. "And how would it look—his honor, the congressman."

"You don't understand Washington, my darling. I hope you never do."

In the faint smile she managed, John saw all he had wanted.

"Wipe your eyes and brush your hair. We're going out."

"Where?"

Martin Roundtree opened the front door, Edythe beside him.

"Hester. . . ." He held out a frail hand.

Hester hesitated. She was not yet ready for kindness. She had come this far. She glanced at John. John was gazing over her head. She would have to take this last step herself.

She braced and stepped forward. Martin Roundtree took both her hands.

"Come in, Hester. John."

The door closed behind her. The polished hall stretched ahead.

But Martin Roundtree had looked into his own soul. And he knew when to come to a point.

"I understand this calls for champagne."

"It does, Dad."

Martin turned to Hester with all the courtliness that had become his outer life.

"I also understand, my dear, that we are deeply indebted to you." His face was as mellow as John had ever remembered it. "What is the name of this first grandson of ours?"

"Brandon. Brandon Brady."

"Brandon Brady—Roundtree. A fighting name."

She met the older man's eyes. "From a long line, Mister Roundtree."

She heard his quick laugh. Oddly, unexpectedly, it was easy to join him.

"One day at a time." Mary had said long ago. *"Today. Tomorrow will bring its own."*

John's arm went around her. Like the enduring old house, its strength surprised her.

Dell Bestsellers

Claude— The Roundtree Women

BOOK II
OF THIS SPELLBINDING
4-PART SERIES
by Margaret Lewerth

A RADIANT NOVEL OF YOUNG PASSION!

Swept away by the lure of the stage, Claude was an exquisite runaway seeking glamour and fame. From a small New England town to the sophisticated and ruthless film circles of Paris and Rome, she fled the safe but imprisoning bonds of childhood and discovered the thrilling, unexpected gift of love.

A Dell Book $2.50 (11255-9)